# An Iron Fist, Two Harbors

Books in the Two Harbors mystery series:

*Convergence at Two Harbors* (2012)
*Seven Graves, Two Harbors* (2013)
*A River Through Two Harbors* (2014)
*Preying in Two Harbors* (2015)
*An Iron Fist, Two Harbors* (2016)

# An Iron Fist, Two Harbors

Dennis Herschbach

North Star Press of St. Cloud, Inc.
St. Cloud, Minnesota

Cover photo © Diane Hilden

ISBN: 978-1-68201-020-4



This is a work of fiction. Names, characters, places, and incidents are the products of the author's imagination or are used fictitiously. Any resemblance to actual events or persons, living or dead, is entirely coincendental.

First edition: May 2016

Printed in the United States of America.

Published by
North Star Press of St. Cloud, Inc.
P.O. Box 451
St. Cloud, MN 56302

www.northstarpress.com

## *Dedication*

*An Iron Fist, Two Harbors* is dedicated to all those who give of their time and effort to help women escape abusive situations, and to those who work at North Shore Horizons, the women's shelter in Two Harbors. It is also dedicated to the memory of a friend, Pastor Ira Livingston, who died several years ago while serving a congregation in Two Harbors. His life helped shape my theology to what it is today.

## *Acknowledgements*

Special thanks go out to all those who have helped make this mystery series possible: the folks at North Star Press who have given me the opportunity to have my work published, my friends who have encouraged me with their kind words, the readers who have given me so much positive feedback, and those of you who have attended by book release parties.

I am continually grateful to my wife, Vicky. Without her continued support and encouragement, I doubt this series would have been written. She is my sounding board, my gentle critic, and most importantly, my preliminary editor. Vicky was involved with the establishment of the Central Minnesota Task Force on Battered Women in the late 1970s.

# Chapter One

TWO MEN HUNCHED OVER their beers and glared at nothing in particular. Both looked rough, each sporting a five-day growth of whiskers on their sullen faces. One wore a camouflage cap with the word BROWNING and a stag's head embroidered above the bill. The other's head was bare, his greasy hair falling to his shoulders.

A man across from them sat at the end of an L-shaped expanse of polished mahogany and stared blankly at a glass of local brew. Other than a female bartender, they were the only people in the place. There were no sounds except for the clinking of glasses being washed and the drone of an ESPN talking head going on about the prospect of the Yankees acquiring a young pitcher to buoy up their aging staff.

"You know who that is?" the guy with the cap asked, tilting his head toward the patron sitting alone.

"No, should I?" his companion answered.

"Ya dumb shit. Why don't ya climb out from under your rock once in awhile and take a look at the world?" He paused and took a sip of beer from his glass. "He's that prevert who just moved into town." He hadn't mispronounced the word on purpose. "His picture was in the paper. You'd have recognized him if you could read." He continued his verbal assault on his partner's ignorance. "He's a registered sex offender. Served ten years for rape, and now he's out. Livin" right here in our town."

Jake Burns heard the comments and didn't look up. He was used to being ostracized and knew there was no use acknowledging the slurs being directed at him. Besides, he couldn't issue any sort of disclaimer. What they said was true, and no matter how hard he wished it wasn't, his sin would follow him wherever he went. Since he was released from prison two years ago, he had lived in three different communities. The first had been in a remote area of Minnesota, a town named Bigfork. Things had gone pretty well for him there. He worked for a logger who didn't ask questions and was only concerned with how many truckloads of pulpwood went out every day. At night Jake stayed in a shack in the woods, near the logging site. It was a lonely existence, but his employer appreciated having someone to keep watch over the expensive machinery when the crew was gone. Then the bottom dropped out of the timber market, and Jake was let go.

He moved to Duluth, a port city at the tip of Lake Superior, and tried to get work on the docks. Each day he would show up at union headquarters and wait for the call that extra help was needed. Most days he went home empty-handed, but when he did manage to get work, he would put in a sixteen-hour shift. After the union took their dues, the government their taxes, and the port their cut, he had enough to pay his rent and have a few beers. The good thing was no one asked questions about his past, or his future for that matter. But the shipping season came to a close a few days after Christmas, and he was out of a job again.

By February, Jake was also out of money, so when he landed a janitorial job in a steel fabrication plant in Two Harbors, he moved. Unfortunately, in that small town he wasn't able to hide. Whenever he walked down the street or sat in a bar, as he was doing today, he could feel eyes following him. He wished that somehow he could become invisible.

The two men finished their beers and made a point of walking out side by side, and as they passed Jake one went out of his way to amble closer. He thumped Jake in the back with his fist, and said loud enough for Jake to hear, "Damn prevert! Get out of town."

Jake didn't look up. He downed his beer and motioned for the barkeep to fill his glass. Other people came and went, some singly, some in small groups, but no one paid attention to him except to steal a glance once in a while, and then whisper to whoever they were with. At ten o'clock. Jake picked up his change, left two dollars on the bar as a tip, and wandered out the door.

He walked down to the breakwater and sat on a bench, watching the lights from the ore docks reflect on the water of the harbor. Gentle swells rolled in and rhythmically splashed on the concrete wall of the breakwater. Jake was alone with his thoughts, totally alone. As he walked the road back from the harbor, he was illuminated by the headlights of a pickup truck, a large 4x4 decked out with chrome trim and sporting a spotlight on top of the cab. Shielding his eyes as it was turned on, he tried to make out who was in the truck. The driver stopped beside him, and the passenger window rolled down.

"Need a lift?" someone asked, and Jake made out two forms lit by the green reflection off the dashboard lights.

# Chapter Two

JAKE SHOWED UP FOR his night shift on Monday. Working nights was okay with him. The welders and draftsmen, the foremen and machinists didn't work that shift, only he and another janitor. The expansive shop was empty, quiet, except for Bert Fielder, another social outcast. Everybody called him Junior; most didn't even know him by any other name.

Like Jake, Junior didn't fit the mold. When he was a child, Junior had been swimming with other kids near the park in town where a twelve-foot cliff offered a challenge for anyone who dared jump from its edge into the icy waters of Lake Superior. Junior took the dare and survived the plunge, but another boy, impatient for his turn, leaped into space before Junior could get to shore. The other boy struck Junior on the head with his knee, knocking Junior unconscious. By the time he was hauled out of the water and 911 was called, Junior had stopped breathing. He was revived, but not before his brain had been deprived of oxygen for too long. Junior's speech was affected, as were his fine motor skills, and one side of his face drooped from paralysis, giving the impression that he was mentally impaired. Those who took the time to know him realized he wasn't, but not many took that time. Junior compensated by losing himself in the bottle. He and Jake made a good team, and they worked at cleaning the shop without much conversation between them.

At two in the morning, break time, they sat down together on a bench outside the shop. The cool night air felt good, and Jake inhaled as deeply as he could.

"What happened to you?" Junior asked, his speech slurred because of his injury.

"Nothin' I want to talk about," Jake answered, and he took a bite of the sandwich he had packed in his lunch pail. He took a slurp of lukewarm coffee from his thermos cup.

"Well, you look like hell," Junior continued. "Somebody work you over?"

"I said I don't want to talk about it, so drop it." Jake stared at the sky as if he wanted to escape to someplace far away.

"I know all about you," Junior persisted. "I know you were in prison, and I know that people in town don't want you around." He paused and Jake tried to ignore him. "You're like me. No one wants me around, either. I make them uncomfortable." He stumbled over the enunciation of the multi-syllabic word.

Jake's hand went to his face, and he gingerly fingered his split lip. His left eye had turned a deep purple, and a raised welt covered his cheekbone. He considered himself lucky that those were his only injuries. Other beatings he had received since being released from prison had been more severe.

"Did you report this to the police?" Junior slurred.

"What for? They know who I am, and they're not going to do anything. Their hope is that I'll move on, but it isn't that easy. No, I'll just lay low and stay out of people's way. I made my bed, now I have to sleep in it. But, Junior, it gets pretty damn lonely."

"I hear you, man," Junior commiserated.

The two men had to return to work if they were going to finish cleaning before the day shift came on, and the conversation abruptly ended. Three weeks later, they were still following the same routine. Junior never brought up the subject of Jake's past or of his beating again. The bruises on Jake's face healed and for Junior, the incident was forgotten. That is, until the night when Jake failed to show up for work and Junior was left with the job of cleaning the shop alone.

# Chapter Three

DEIDRE JOHNSON SAT ON the porch swing watching her eight-year-old twin boys wrestle on the lawn, and she couldn't help but smile at how they each struggled to gain the advantage over their brother. Jack was the oldest by four and a half minutes and was an inch taller, but Steve was slightly heavier. The boys grunted and laughed, strained and twisted until both were exhausted and the match ended in a draw. They flopped on their backs and rested, their chests heaving as they tried to catch their breath.

"Hey, guys," Deidre called out. "Come up on the deck. I've got lemonade and cookies. You look like you could use some." Her sons loped across the lawn and settled into chairs, then helped themselves to treats.

As Deidre admired her boys, she couldn't help but wonder how time had passed so quickly. Here she was, forty-seven years old. Her twin step-daughters were going to be twenty-two on their next birthday. She and Ben had been married seventeen years, and he was already eligible for his twenty-year pension from the FBI, if he chose to take it. Deidre doubted he would, but still, the option was there.

Her memory wandered back to the day she had started working for the Lake County Sheriff's Department. She was twenty-one, roughly the same age as her daughters. Over the years, she had experienced more than her share of excitement as a law enforcement officer, and after the twin boys were born, she decided to hang up her badge for good. Taking care of infant twins, and later toddlers, was a full-time job, and the years had sped by. Now she was content to watch her family grow.

Megan and Maren, the twin girls, had graduated from high school with honors. Next fall, Megan would be beginning her junior year at the University of Minnesota, Duluth. She was a biology major and hoped, someday, to become a researcher. During the summer she worked on campus in a lab, trying to jumpstart her career. This would be her second year as an assistant to a professor who had a grant for something or other. Deidre really wasn't sure what, and she made a mental note to try to be more interested in what Megan was doing.

Maren had started college, but during her freshman year met a young man, Dave Mason, with whom she fell deeply in love. He was athletic, competed in road races and marathons, was good looking, and was charming—so much so that at the end of her first year of college, Maren announced that she and Dave would be moving in together and she would be taking a hiatus from school.

Over both Deidre's and Ben's objections, she and Dave had worked out an agreement, they said. Dave would be a senior studying accounting at the university and was on schedule to graduate in the spring. Maren had a job as a waitress in the restaurant of an upscale hotel near Two Harbors. She would support them for a year. Then, when Dave graduated and had a job, she would return to school and finish her degree in elementary education.

And that's what happened. Dave finished school at the end of the winter semester and within a month had secured a job with a large accounting firm in Duluth. Maren was registered to resume class beginning in the fall. Even better, she had confided in Megan that she thought Dave was going to propose they get married next winter.

Just as Deidre was getting ready to go inside, her cell phone buzzed. She saw on the caller ID that it was Dave.

"Hi, Deidre? This is Dave. Is Maren at your place?" Dave spoke without waiting for a reply. "I took the afternoon off from work, because we planned to go on a hike in Gooseberry Park. She said she was going to pack a picnic for us. I'm home, but she isn't around. I thought maybe she had come out to your place to pick up something she needed."

"No, she hasn't been here today," Deidre said. "In fact, it's been at least two weeks since I've talked to her. I'm sure she didn't go far. Maybe she went to the grocery store to pick up things for your picnic. Or maybe she's visiting with a friend and lost track of time. She'll probably be home soon. By the way, how's the job going? Everybody's been so busy we haven't had time to talk lately."

"I know, and I feel badly about that," Dave answered immediately. "The job's great. I couldn't be happier with the way things are going. The pay is good and conditions are even better. When Megan finishes school and gets a job, we'll be able to really sock away money for retirement. I know we're young, but one thing I've learned, save while you're young and you'll have a good life when you're old." He laughed. "Well, that's a way off, and we've got a lot of living to do between now and then. Have Maren call me if she shows up, will you?"

Deidre assured Dave that she would and heard the call disconnect. She went in the house and busied herself fixing supper for her family. The boys had recuperated from their wrestling match and were playing catch with a baseball in the yard.

Ben arrived home at five o'clock. Over the years he had worked diligently as an FBI agent out of the office in Duluth, and his work had not gone unnoticed. A half-dozen years ago he had been promoted to supervisor of the division that handled interstate kidnapping cases. Like Deidre, Ben had seen his share of traumatic events—murders, kidnappings, even terrorism—and he was weary of the inhumanity he was sometimes forced to witness. He entered the kitchen where Deidre was watching a pot on the stove.

"Don't you know a watched pot never boils?" he said as he kissed her on the nape of her neck. Deidre started at his touch, and Ben chuckled. "Hey, I didn't mean to startle you. What's for supper?"

"Your favorite, you big goofball," she shot back without looking over her shoulder. "Corned beef and cabbage." Deidre turned and put her arms around Ben's neck and kissed him. "That should be good for something later on, don't you think?"

Ben played dumb. "Oh, yeah. And what would that be?" He gave her a hug and lifted her off the floor. Just then the boys came storming into the kitchen, interrupting their playfulness.

"Come on outside with us, Dad," Steve said as he pulled on Ben's sleeve. "We need you to hit some fly balls for us to shag. We've got a half hour before supper." Jack turned to Deidre. "Can Dad go out and play?" He laughed at his own joke.

Dinner was a carefree affair, as it so often was. The brothers were remarkable in the way they got along, and the rivalry that occurred so often between siblings hardly existed between them. It was a joy for Ben and Deidre to understand the bond that existed between the two. It was the same bond that existed between Maren and Megan, only without their competitiveness.

Supper over, Ben and Deidre took their normal evening stroll up the road, holding hands and talking over the day's happenings. Nothing too exciting had gone on, and soon they were walking in silence, content to be in the presence of each other. They returned home about eight thirty, just as the sun was setting. Jeff and Steve were still outside, throwing a baseball back and forth. The four of them sat on deck chairs and listened to the world go silent. In the background a whip-poor-will began calling, and overhead, chimney swifts cartwheeled through the deepening blue sky. Their chirping calls added to the feeling that all was well.

When the mosquitoes began to hum around their heads, the family headed indoors, and Deidre reminded the boys to shower before getting into bed. "I put clean sheets on the today, and you don't have to grubby them up the first night," she hollered as they reached the top of the stairs. She heard the bathroom door close just as the phone rang. Ben answered and Deidre listened in on the one-sided conversation.

"Oh, hi, Dave. . . . No. Why do you ask?" Ben glanced Deidre's way. ". . . No, we haven't seen her this evening. . . . Dave, calm down.

There's probably a simple explanation. . . . Dave. Dave! Have you called Megan to see if she's been there?" Deidre was becoming alarmed, getting the gist of the conversation. Maren hadn't been home.

"Dave. Take it easy. I want you to come out here right away, and we'll try to figure out where she could be. While you're driving here, Deidre and I will call the police and the sheriff. Chances are it's nothing to worry about, at least not yet. Anyway, don't speed getting here. It won't do any good for you to get a ticket. . . . Okay. See you in fifteen minutes."

Ben hung up the phone. "That was Dave," he said, not realizing he was stating the obvious. "Maren didn't come home today, and he hasn't been able to track her down. He's frantic, and I said we'd help him locate her."

Deidre was nearly in shock. "My God, Dave called earlier today, looking for her. I kind of blew it off and haven't even thought of it again until now. What do we do?"

"Call Megan and see if she knows anything. If she doesn't, why don't you suggest she drive here tonight? I'm a little worried about this, and we might need help trying to find where Maren has been today. While you do that, I'll make some calls."

Deidre hit Megan's name on her cell phone's favorites list, and her daughter picked up on the second ring. "Megan, it's Mom. Listen, honey, have you seen Maren today?"

"Mom, what's going on? Dave called three times today, looking for her. The last time was only a few minutes ago, and he sounded terribly upset. You sound really worried, too. What's wrong?"

Deidre tried to sound casual. "Probably nothing, but it isn't like Maren not to check in if she's going to be late. Dad thinks you should come home, in case we have to go looking for her."

"Have you called the women's shelter in town?" Megan blurted out.

Deidre saw a red flag coming. "Why do you ask that? Has Maren told you something?"

There was a pause on Megan's end. "No. She hasn't said a word to me. In fact, we haven't even talked on the phone for at least three weeks, but I know that she visited there a while ago when Dave was at work. Why don't you give them a call, just in case?"

As Deidre was looking up the shelter's number, she heard Ben on the phone to the police dispatcher. "I know she's only been missing a few hours, but this isn't like her at all. . . . I know she'll probably show up before long. . . . Well, I'd like this to go on the record, and I'd like to have a bulletin go out with her license plate number."

Before Deidre could make her call to the shelter, Ben was hanging up after talking to the sheriff's dispatcher. A car swung into their driveway, and both of them had an instant of hope that it was Maren, stopping to tell them everything was okay.

# Chapter Four

DAVE BURST THROUGH the door, not bothering to knock, and immediately looked around the room to see if Maren was there. Deidre could see the panic in his eyes, and he rushed over to her and threw his arms around her in a tight embrace.

"Have you heard anything?" he managed to get out between sobs. Deidre had to tell him no, but they were working on finding Maren. She led him to the living room, and Ben put his arm around the distraught man's shoulder. Together they guided him to the sofa and eased him down. Deidre couldn't help but notice how his hands were shaking, and she tried to calm him.

"Megan will be here soon. She may have some insight into where Maren might be. In the meantime, let's try to figure out where she could be. Did you know she had visited the women's shelter a while back?"

Dave's face lost a little of its color, and he responded, "Who, Megan?"

Deidre could see that Dave was too flustered to follow a conversation. "No, Maren."

A momentary look of panic swept over his face and Dave blurted out. "Why would she do that?" He regained his composure. "No. I didn't know. I suppose she might have mentioned it to me, but you know how we men are. Sometimes I'm not as attentive as I should be." He covered his face with his hands, and the three of them sat in silence until they heard footsteps coming down the stairs.

Jack and Steve plopped down in chairs, their hair still wet from the showers they had taken. "What's going on? We heard you guys talking and wondered who was here." They looked around the room. "Where's Maren?" Steve wanted to know.

Deidre tried to sound unconcerned, but the strain in her voice gave her away. "Dave's looking for Maren. She hasn't been home today."

Jack was blunt as only an eight-year-old boy can be. "Did she leave you?"

Dave looked up with a start, but before he could say anything, Ben interrupted. "Jack, that wasn't a good thing to say. Of course she didn't leave Dave. There's just been some kind of mix up. I'm sure she'll be calling any time now. Tell you what, why don't you two hun-yucks head up to bed. We'll call you as soon as we find out where Maren is. Scoot now."

The boys made their way upstairs, but Deidre could tell by their gait that they knew something was amiss.

"Who's her closest friend?" Deidre thought to ask Dave.

He considered the question for several seconds. "You know, I really can't say. Maren stays home a lot. In fact, she almost never goes out in the evening. Always is home when I get home from work, and never talks about her friends to me." He looked at Deidre and Ben and held out his hands as if to say, "I don't know any more."

Ben asked him if Maren's car was at home, and Deidre wondered why she hadn't thought of that when Dave had called in the afternoon.

His answer was immediate. "No, that's what makes me think she may be in trouble somewhere. She could be having car trouble and is stranded. I've tried to think where she might have driven, if she ran off the road into a gully and is trapped in her car." He buried his face in his hands, and when he looked up, his eyes were red-rimmed. "Oh, God, if something's happened to her, I don't know what I'll do." He put his face in his hands again, and his shoulders convulsed.

Deidre moved so she was sitting closer to him and rubbed his back with one hand while she grasped his hand with her other. "Dave, don't think of the worst-case scenario. From experience, I know the worst seldom happens. I think your first thought is most likely. Her car is probably stalled someplace, and she's waiting for help. Maren likes to hike the logging roads up the Drummond Trail. If she drove into the woods a ways, and after a hike her car wouldn't start, she might have had to walk out. Some of those roads go into the forest five or ten miles. That would be quite a jaunt, even for her."

Dave looked at her through teary eyes. "I hope so, Deidre. I hope so." He sat staring blankly at the floor.

"Mom, Dad," Steve called down from the top of the stairs. "Somebody just drove into the yard."

Deidre rushed to the door and stepped out on the deck. She could see someone coming up the walk, and her heart skipped a beat.

"Maren," she called out, starting down the steps to greet her wayward daughter.

"It's me, Megan," her other daughter called out, and Deidre's heart sank.

"Oh, Megan. I'm so sorry. I think I so wanted you to be Maren that I saw what I wanted to see."

Megan hugged her mother. "We are identical twins, you know," she said, trying to lighten the mood, but her effort fell flat. Together they went into the house.

Dave stood up and tried to hug Megan, but after a cursory brush of his cheek, she pushed away and went to Ben. She said nothing, wrapped her arms around his waist, and wouldn't let go. Ben rocked her back and forth for several seconds before he stepped back. Both of them had tears running down their cheeks.

"Do you have any idea where we should begin searching?" he asked his daughter. "What friend might she be visiting? Is their anybody who might have needed her help?"

Maren looked at Dave, and said. "Maybe Dave would know. I haven't talked to Maren for quite some time, other than a few minutes here or there on the phone. I think it's been two months since we've seen each other, so I feel kind of out of her circle."

Deidre sensed hostility in Megan's attitude toward Dave, and she attributed it to the fact that Maren had fallen in love and had developed different interests. She thought that must have been hard for Megan to accept, because the girls had been so close when they were growing up. Perhaps it was the old competitiveness rearing its head. Maren had met the love of her life and Megan was still looking.

"Both of you have been so busy these past few months that I don't wonder you haven't had time to see each other. Do you have any idea where she might have gone?"

Megan looked dejected and said no more. Morosely, she shook her head and went to the kitchen. Deidre heard water running and assumed she was getting a drink. When she returned to the living room, Megan was holding a wet washcloth to her face. No one had an idea of where to turn, and shortly before midnight, Deidre punched in a series of numbers on her cell phone.

"Jeff," the others heard her say. "Ben and I need you to come out to our place as soon as you can. We've got a problem."

# Chapter Five

DAVE WAS INCONSOLABLE, and while they waited for Jeff to arrive, he paced the floor like a wild animal in a cage. He would sit down and immediately stand up, go to the window and part the curtains as though he were expecting Maren to materialize at any moment. He was the first to spot a set of headlights approaching the driveway and was on the outside deck before the car turned in. Dave rushed to meet the car, and Deidre's heart was broken when she saw his shoulders droop after realizing the car wasn't Maren's.

Jeff and Dave walked to the house together, and for some reason, Deidre was surprised that Jeff was out of uniform. Then it dawned on her it was after midnight and she had probably gotten him out of bed with her frantic call.

Jeff was one of her oldest friends. They had been hired the same summer by the Lake County Sheriff's Department, and they had experienced too many good times together to count. During their friendship, there had been some tough times as well. He was Deidre's second in command during her tenure as sheriff, had cared for her when she was shot by a terrorist, had talked her down when she was on the verge of executing a drug dealer who had killed her fiancé, and had replaced her as sheriff when she was forced from office.

Eight years ago, Jeff had been ambushed, shot in the back by a militia member, and Deidre had helped bring his assailant to justice. Other than her husband, Ben, Jeff was her best friend, the one person she felt she could call on for anything. She noticed he still had a limp from having been shot, but the slight drag of his right leg wasn't enough to keep him from performing his job as sheriff of the county.

Deidre thought he must have been about retirement age, but he had never given an inkling that it was something in his near future.

Ben rose to greet Jeff and gave him a hug. Jeff went to Deidre and hugged her, too. "It sounds like this is urgent," he said to her. "What can I help you with?"

"It's Maren," Deidre said as she looked at him with fearful eyes. "She's been missing for about," she looked at the clock on the wall, "for about eight hours now. We know that's not all that long, but it's so unlike her. No one has any idea where she is."

Jeff thought a moment, not wanting to increase everyone's alarm by overreacting. "Have you tried calling her friends? Her boss at work? How about the city police? Chances are somebody will know something."

Deidre was quick to answer. "We've contacted all of them, and have gotten no answers." Then it dawned on her that after talking to Megan, they hadn't called the women's shelter after all. She found the number of their hotline and in seconds was speaking to the person manning the line.

"Hello, this is Deidre Johnson calling. I believe you know my daughter, Maren VanGotten. . . . Yes, I was sheriff several years ago. I wonder if you could tell me if she has been to the shelter today. . . . Yes, I understand you can't give out the names of your clients, but I'm not sure she was a client. . . . Yes, I understand. Thank you for your time. Oh, and if you do see her or hear from her, please tell her to call her mom and dad. . . . Thank you."

Ben could fill in the words of the person who was taking the hotline calls, and before Deidre could relay the conversation, he spoke up.

"They haven't seen her, have they? But it seemed they knew who you were talking about." He looked at Megan. "You said Maren had visited the shelter. Did she tell you that?"

"I kind of blew it off," Magan recalled. "But I know the last time we talked on the phone she said she had an appointment there. I just assumed she was visiting a friend."

Ben turned his attention to Dave. "What do you know about this? Was Maren going to the shelter for some reason?"

Dave looked shocked. "I, I have no idea. Like I said, I don't remember her mentioning it to me." Deidre thought Dave became even more agitated.

"I've got some calls I want to make," Jeff said. "Would it be okay if I went in the kitchen?" Ben motioned him to go. Before leaving the room, Jeff asked for a description of Maren's car and its license plate number. Deidre stood and caught Megan's eye.

"I'm going up to check on the boys. Why don't you come with me? If they're still awake they'll want to see you." Megan followed her up the stairs, but once in the hallway, Deidre turned to her daughter.

"I couldn't help but notice that you were pretty cold toward Dave when you came in. Any special reason? Do you know something you're not telling us?"

Megan lowered her voice. "I really don't know anything. It's just a feeling I have, as if Maren has been avoiding me for several weeks. I miss being her close friend so much, and everything changed after she moved in with Dave."

Deidre took Megan's hand and led her into the guest bedroom, the one that had been Maren's and Megan's room before they left home. They sat on one of the twin beds.

"Did Maren ever say anything against Dave?"

"That's what's so strange, Mom. Maren adored him. I never heard her say anything bad about him. It was always, 'He's so thoughtful,' or, 'he wants to spend all his time with me.' She was always telling me how he wanted to do everything with her: grocery shopping, clothes shopping, even just going for walks around town. She said she was lucky to have somebody who wanted to be with her all the time."

Deidre had other questions. "Do you think she was really happy?" Megan nodded. "Could it be that you resent Dave, because subconsciously you think he took your sister away from you? The bond between twins can be very strong." Megan shrugged and a single tear trickled down her cheek. She tried to smile.

" I suppose you're right. Maybe I am jealous of Dave." She dried her eyes. "Let's get back downstairs and hear what Jeff has to say."

Jeff was coming back to the living room as they came down the stairs, and they heard him announce, "I put a call through to the State Patrol and gave them the info on Maren's car. They'll keep their eyes open. Also, all of my deputies who are on patrol will check the out-of-way places like gravel pits and rest stops, places where a parked car might go unnoticed. The city police promised to make a sweep of the parking area by the boat landing, the city park, and the parking lot for the hiking trail. I'm sure something will turn up soon," he said reassuringly.

Dave was becoming more fidgety by the minute, and Deidre thought he would explode. She was right.

"Oh, God, what's going on?" he cried out. "Can't somebody do something?" Deidre went to his side and knelt on the floor. She placed her hands on top of his and spoke quietly.

"Dave. Dave, look at me." He raised his eyes to meet hers, and for the first time it occurred to her that Dave had beautiful eyes. She realized that her thoughts were far from what should have been on her mind, but she could only think that his eyes were beautiful. In that instant, as she took in the soft brown of his irises, the long, dark lashes, and his dense brows, the thought entered her mind, *I can see why Maren fell for him.*

Deidre cleared her throat. "We're doing all that we can right now. It's going to take a little time, but all the departments have been alerted, and once it's daylight, they'll be able to make a better search for her car. In the meantime, all we can do is wait and pray." She really wondered why she said that. She wasn't particularly spiritual and always wondered just how much power prayer held.

Once, after a race riot in a southern city, a minister had said during an interview on TV, "The only hope we have now is prayer." Deidre had answered the TV, "And how is that working out for you so far?"

Now she wondered if the results of any prayer she might say would be the same as the minister's.

# Chapter
## Six

JEFF STAYED WITH THEM until one o'clock. "Sorry folks, but I have to get a little sleep," he said apologetically. "Got a busy day tomorrow. If Maren hasn't shown up by morning, we'll get out a statewide notice of her disappearance." Ben and Deidre were standing side by side, and Jeff put his hands on their backs. "This has to be really tough on you guys, but you have to remember that most missing persons show up the next day with one excuse or another. I'll call you in the morning, and we'll go from there."

Jeff patted Dave on the back as he passed him. "Hang in there, Dave. We'll hope for the best, and pray that by tomorrow night you two will be home together."

*There's that word again. Pray. For God's sake, Jeff,* do *something,* Deidre thought.

Megan curled up on the couch and seemed to fall asleep. Deidre reached over and stroked her daughter's hair, remembering how she was always the one who used sleep as an escape when anything traumatic was going on. But never before had the tension reached tonight's level.

"Get you a cup of coffee, Dave?" she asked. He looked at her with dead eyes and nodded. Deidre busied herself in the kitchen trying to channel her nervous energy. "I don't remember," she called. "Black or with cream? Sugar?"

From the other room she heard, "Huh?"

"Black or with cream? Sugar?" Deidre repeated herself.

"Oh, ah," Dave responded, his mind having been far away. "Black. I take it black."

Deidre brought him a cup of freshly brewed coffee and a couple of cookies she had managed to scrounge up. Dave looked up at her, and she thought of a wounded deer she had once seen alongside the road. They had the same look in their brown eyes, as if asking, "Why?"

"Thanks, Deidre," he managed to say.

All the while, Ben sat and stared at the empty fireplace. He didn't move from that spot for over an hour. Twice Deidre sat down beside him and tried to take his hand. Both times she felt as though she was holding an inanimate object. There was no response, and she knew Ben had drifted into another world. She wanted him to hold her and tell her everything was going to be all right, but in her heart she knew that wasn't going to be the case.

When the sun began to rise, the four were still awake, because each had slept so restlessly, if at all. Deidre asked if they wanted breakfast, but there were no takers.

"Why don't we go out on the deck and watch the sunrise," Ben suggested, and without discussion, everyone shuffled through the doorway. They sat in silence, listening to the birds claiming their territories with song, and Deidre wondered at how the mood had changed since last evening, when the night hawks and whip-poor-wills had soothed her spirit. This morning her world was a jumble, and the bird calls only a background cacophony.

"Let's pray." It was Ben's voice that broke their silence. Deidre saw Ben and Dave and Megan bow their heads, but she couldn't, or wondered if she just wouldn't. Ben's voice was clear and strong. "Lord God. Our Maren is missing, Lord, and we are at our wits' end. Where is she, Lord?" Ben paused and Deidre wondered if he was going to continue, but he swallowed hard, and did. "Be with Jeff, and help him find her. Protect her while we wait." Deidre could tell he was struggling to hold it together. "If something has happened to her, give us strength to accept the truth. We trust that your will is for no harm to come to our Maren. Please bring her safely back to us." There was a long pause before he said, "Amen."

Deidre wasn't sure how she felt about God's ability to undo what may have already been done, but she took comfort in her husband's faith. She reached over and placed her hand on his, and they sat in silence.

# Chapter Seven

DEIDRE OFFERED AGAIN, but no one wanted breakfast. Ben took a shower. She splashed cold water on her face in an attempt to stay alert. Megan had slept curled up on the couch, and her clothes were a wrinkled mess. She used the downstairs bathroom to freshen up as best she could. Dave was still walking around in a daze, his eyes glazed and his hands shaking whenever he wasn't holding onto something for support.

Steve and Jack were the only ones who ate anything, each wolfing down a bowl of Cheerios. Deidre announced that Grandma and Grandpa, Ben's parents, were coming to take them for the day. She promised they'd be doing something fun. The boys knew they were being shuttled out of the way, and they grumbled, wanting to know what was going on. Deidre told them that Maren hadn't come home last night and they were trying to locate her. Her last words to the boys as the pair headed out the door were, "Don't worry. She's going to be all right."

At seven thirty, the landline phone rang and Ben was the first to reach it. The others listened expectantly, straining to hear any glimmer of hope in his voice. After a brief conversation, he hung up.

"Jeff says a deputy found Maren's car. She isn't in it, and it appears as though something bad has happened." He slumped onto a chair and clutched his head as though to quell a massive headache. Deidre placed her hand on his back and felt the convulsions heaving through his body.

"Did Jeff say where they found the car?" Deidre asked.

"It's about ten miles from here, at the end of the Spooner Road. He's on his way there now. Wondered if we are able to meet him there to identify any belongings in the car. He said he'd understand if we can't do it." Ben looked expectantly at the others.

"I think we have to," Megan gave her opinion, and Deidre agreed. Dave said nothing.

"Okay, we go," Ben said, settling the issue, and together they prodded themselves to get in Ben's SUV.

Ben knew the area well, because it was an area favored for grouse hunting. He turned right on the paved surface of a county road and then left onto the gravel surface of the Drummond Road. The four rode in silence until they came to a green street sign that read SPOONER ROAD. Deidre had always thought the sign looked absurd, a street sign to mark a logging road, and today it looked even more out of place to her. Ben turned onto the little-used road that was hardly more than a trail. Grass grew in the center between two dirt ruts, and Deidre heard a rock scrape the undercarriage of the SUV every so often. They bounced along at a crawl.

They were further into the forest than she had ever traveled on this trail, and it became rougher and more narrow with each passing minute. Soon, brush hanging from the sides of the road was scraping on the finish of the vehicle, and Deidre wondered if they were getting lost. Eventually, they reached a small clearing at the end of the road. It had been a staging area for whoever had last logged there, and Deidre could just barely make out skid trails that led even deeper into the woods. At the back edge of the clearing sat Megan's car. Two deputies' cars were also parked in the clearing, and she recognized Jeff's sheriff vehicle, as well. The officers were standing by Megan's car, but when Jeff saw Deidre and Ben, he came over to meet them.

He hugged Deidre and clapped Ben on the back, nodded to Dave and squeezed Megan's arm.

"We got a call early this morning from the County Forestry Unit. One of their workers was supposed to do a timber assessment of this area and lay out the route for a new haul road to a tract of trees a half mile further into the woods. He was going to begin from this clearing, and became suspicious when he saw Megan's abandoned car. He called it in right away."

Jeff noticed Dave beginning to shiver. "You look awfully chilled. The morning dew can be pretty uncomfortable, even if it is the beginning of May. Do you have a jacket in the car?"

Dave looked startled, as if he just realized he wasn't wearing one. "Uh, no. I guess I forgot it when we left." He wrapped his arms around himself, and Ben offered Dave his own jacket. Dave shook his head and looked away.

Jeff looked across the clearing at Maren's car. "I'm sure that's it," he began, "but I need you to verify that's her's."

Ben nodded, and Jeff wasn't quite sure whether that meant he understood the situation or if it meant that, yes, this was his daughter's car.

"It's a 2008 Ford Focus. You can see the color. It's got a small dent near the gas cap cover. Do you think it's her car?" Again, Ben nodded.

From where they stood, everyone could see grass and weeds hanging from the front bumper, and the tail pipe appeared to be hanging loose.

"I'm surprised that little car made it back this far. It doesn't have much clearance. My SUV bottomed out a couple of times on the way in. Any other damage to the car?" Ben wondered why he asked that question. It was totally irrelevant if her car had been damaged.

Jeff didn't answer, but said, "Okay, I'd like to have you come look at the interior. You don't have to if you think it will be too difficult, but I'd appreciate whatever help you can give us right now. I'll warn you, there 's a little blood on the headrest of the front seat. I'll have a deputy cover it with an evidence bag so you won't have to see it."

Deidre stopped him. "How much blood?"

Jeff looked at her sympathetically. "I know what you're thinking. It's only a small smear, not enough to have caused death by any means. Basically, I need you to identify items in the car to verify they are your daughter's belongings and not things left by her assailant."

*Assailant?* That word brought Deidre up short, because until now, she hadn't pictured an actual violent act being leveled at Maren. For a moment she lost her resolve to look in the car but then steadied herself. "I'll look," she heard herself say.

"I'll come with you," Ben volunteered. Megan took her dad's arm and the three followed Jeff, each lost in their own thoughts. Dave hung back, turned his back on them, and leaned over the hood of Ben's vehicle. He rested his head on his forearms, hiding his face.

Deidre was the first to look in the abandoned car, and she gasped when she saw Maren's favorite lap robe balled up on the backseat. The image of her teenage daughter curled up in front of the fireplace with that blanket wrapped around her flashed through her memories. She took Ben's other arm and put her cheek on his shoulder. Megan began to sob.

Jeff and a deputy wore rubber gloves and had several evidence bags handy. He reached into the car and carefully removed the lap robe. "I assume you recognize this?" he asked, and Deidre verified it was Maren's. One by one they sorted through odds and ends. By the time they were done, they had collected several loose pieces, none of which seemed to be of any significance. The items would be sent to a forensics lab in the hope the abductor had left microscopic clues.

"We've dusted the surfaces for fingerprints, but everything has been wiped clean," Jeff gave them the bad news. "Whoever did this took a lot of time. Even Maren's prints can't be found."

Ben stood stoically beside Megan and Deidre, but he couldn't help glancing from time to time at the covered headrest. "It doesn't look like Maren was hit hard enough on the head to have killed her," Jeff said, wanting to reassure Ben. "There were no hairs stuck to the blood, no tissue of any kind. It seems that her head wound, if that's what it was, is superficial." He intentionally used the present tense, indicating she was still alive.

"That's about it for now, folks. I've got a lead or two that I want to follow up on, and I'll try to get back to you later this afternoon."

Dave hadn't joined them and when they came back to him, he finally looked up, obviously not looking back toward Maren's car. "What did Jeff say?" he wanted to know.

"They're going to tow her car back to the impoundment lot in town. The deputies will make a more thorough search of the area, and Jeff has a couple of leads he wants to explore. Other than that, we're going home and try to deal with this. He said he'd call later today."

"What kind of leads does he have?" Dave blurted out, and then gathered himself. "Does he know anything about where Maren might be?" Ben shook his head.

The ride back was made in silence, and when they got out of the SUV in the driveway, Dave announced that he wanted to go home. He said he was exhausted and would sleep better in his own bed. Everyone exchanged hugs with him, and Deidre told him to come back for supper that night. He said he would.

As Deidre walked through the living room she spotted Dave's jacket slung over the arm of a chair and picked it up, making a mental note to give it to him when he came for dinner. She found a hanger in their crowded closet and hung it at the end of the rack.

# Chapter Eight

DEIDRE WAS LOOKING in the refrigerator, wondering if she could make anything for lunch that would interest Megan and Ben. She had just given up and closed the door when her cell phone rang, and she noticed on the caller ID that it was from a Two Harbors number. She groaned inwardly but answered. "This is Deidre."

"Hello, Deidre," a male voice greeted her. "This is Pastor Ike. Jeff stopped by my office and told me the news about Megan. I'd like to come out and talk to you and Ben if you don't have any objection. I know you probably don't know where to turn right now. You don't have but a sketchy idea of what has happened, and I thought I might be a sympathetic ear you can talk to. I have an appointment in a few minutes but could be at your place by one thirty. If you'd rather be alone, just say so, but I think you can use all the support that can be mustered right now."

Deidre hesitated, but then, the thought of rambling around the house waiting for Jeff's call didn't sound good either. "Sure, Pastor, I think that will be fine. We'll be waiting for you."

Before she could hang up, Pastor Ike had another thought. "You probably don't have much desire to eat, and I doubt if you feel like cooking meals. May I have your permission to set up a meal delivery service for your family? There'll be many people wanting to do something for you, and from past experience, there'll be several volunteers who would like to bring meals to you for the next many days."

Deidre found herself saying yes without his request really registering in her brain. She hung up, sat down at the table, and stared out the window, seeing nothing, but feeling an empty hole begin to gnaw at her insides. She stepped out on the deck, where Ben was sitting in his favorite chair, just staring. He didn't bother to look up when Deidre placed her hand on his shoulder. Megan joined them and plunked down in the porch swing. Neither reacted one way or the other when Deidre told them Pastor Ike was coming to see them.

They sat that way for the better part of an hour, each absorbed by their own thoughts. It wasn't until Pastor Ike swung into their drive and got out of his car that they stirred. Megan sat up, and Ben and Deidre went down the steps to greet him. Deidre noticed he carried a small green book with him, but it didn't mean anything to her.

They escorted the pastor up the steps and offered him a chair on the deck. "Can I get you anything to drink, Pastor? A soda, coffee?" She found herself relieved when he asked if she had a Diet Coke, and as she made her way to the kitchen to retrieve the drink, she realized it was a moment of normalcy, something she craved. Returning with the full glass, she took a seat beside Ben, and he responded by taking her hand,

"I thought maybe you needed someone to be with you this afternoon," Ike began. "Have you heard any more from Jeff?"

Deidre shook her head, and Ben mumbled, "No."

"Not knowing is probably the most difficult part of what's going on," the pastor continued. "I've had a number of calls from people in the congregation wanting to know what they can do to help. News travels fast in a small town. A few have been the usual busybodies trying to pump me for information, but most just want to help. My wife is arranging for meals to be delivered to you. She'll bring supper for you tonight, and others will take turns each evening afterward. If you have any questions, contact her."

"What if we're gone for a day or two? Can we cancel the delivery?" Deidre realized it was a foolish question, but she was at a loss for what to say. She had never been good at accepting help. Pastor Ike nodded.

"Just call my wife, and she'll take care of it."

After several minutes of small talk, the pastor opened the green book he had been carrying. Deidre noticed the gold embossing on the cover, *The Lutheran Book of Occasional Services*, and she wondered how many occasions like theirs came up.

"I'd like to read to you from the book of Isaiah, the forty-third chapter." As he began to read, Deidre's mind drifted to other thoughts, and she was barely cognizant of his words. But somehow one phrase punctured her fog. "When you pass through the waters I will be with you; and through the rivers, they shall not overwhelm you; when you walk through the fire you shall not be burned, and the flame shall not consume you."

The remainder of his reading went unheard. Deidre pictured herself being plucked from a raging tumult, pictured herself in the middle of a forest raging with fire, and she pictured herself wrapped in a shield. She was brought back to reality when she heard Ike ask if he could say a prayer. *Why can't he just talk to me like a friend?* Deidre wondered. *All I want is for him to tell me how sorry he is, and to admit the situation is out of anybody's control. All I want are some answers.*

No one answered, and the pastor shuffled the pages of his green book. She saw him look down at the pages.

"Almighty and merciful God, our only source of calmness and peace: Grant to us, your children, a consciousness of your presence. In our pain, our weariness, and our anxiety, surround us with your care." He paused before saying "Amen."

This was the first time in her life that Deidre had actually heard someone pray specifically for her, not a prayer for a miracle, not a prayer for something out of her control, but for her. She wondered what peace and calm would feel like. She wondered if she had ever really been calm and at peace.

Pastor Ike took a small leather-bound case from his pocket and opened it. Inside were four small communion glasses, a canister of wafers, and a vial of wine. "I'd like to serve you communion, if it's all right." Ben nodded.

Deidre was taken by the sincerity with which the pastor approached the ritual, and as he distributed the elements he looked directly into each person's eyes. He placed his hand on each one's head, and Deidre saw his lips move in silent prayer. For one moment, she felt a wave of peace, and then it vanished as she thought of what had happened.

Pastor Ike stayed a few minutes longer, and then excused himself. Megan decided to take a walk to the family's picnic spot by the river. Ben said he was going to lie down and close his eyes, and Deidre went out back. The mid-spring flowers in her garden were beginning to bloom. The tulips were almost done, and the peonies were unopened buds, but the irises were in full bloom. She sat in a strategically placed chair and felt totally enveloped by the garden, bowed her head, and wept until tears came no more.

# Chapter
# Nine

SOMETIME AFTER FIVE O'CLOCK, Pastor Ike's wife, Estelle, knocked on the door. She was carrying a large basket, and when Deidre answered the knock, she could see it was full and heavy. She invited the woman in, feeling awkward because she hardly knew Estelle's name.

"It's a simple meal, but easy to reheat what's left over," Estelle stated. "I know this is a difficult time for you, and I'll not stay, but rest assured, you and the others are in my prayers. I'll specifically pray that your family be given strength to withstand this ordeal." She gave Deidre a hug and left without saying more.

As Deidre unpacked the basket, Estelle's words kept going through her mind, and she realized her pastor's wife hadn't said she'd be praying for a miracle. Instead, Deidre realized, she said she'd pray for strength and perseverance. That sat well with Deidre. She believed she was going to need all the strength she could muster in the days to come. As she was pondering that thought, Dave tapped on the door and walked in without invitation. He went over to Deidre and kissed her on her cheek.

"Has Jeff called?" was the first thing he wanted to know. Deidre said no, but they were expecting his call at any time.

Dave wandered into the living room, and Deidre heard him ask, "Is Ben around?" Deidre didn't want to shout, so she left what she was doing and stood in the living room doorway.

"Ben's upstairs. He laid down after Pastor Ike left and is resting. I hope he slept some. He was looking pretty frazzled."

Just then they heard movement upstairs, and Ben started down to them. He looked worse than when he had laid down to rest.

Megan came behind him. The two were near the bottom step when the phone rang, and Ben sprang across the floor to answer it.

"Hi, Jeff. We've been waiting for you to call. Have you discovered anything? . . . Oh. . . . Yeah, I've heard of him. . . . No, don't really know anything about him. . . . Well, do they have any idea where he is? . . . I understand. . . . Tomorrow morning. Eight? Sure, that would be okay, I guess. . . . Yeah, see you then."

The others couldn't piece anything together from Ben's side of the conversation.

"That was Jeff?" Deidre asked, and then realized her question was redundant to what she had heard. "What did he have to say? Does he have any idea where Maren is, or who she might be with?"

"Why don't we sit down? I'm still a little groggy, but I'll tell you what Jeff told me. They haven't found Maren, but he thinks they might have a lead." He happened to look at Dave and couldn't help but notice he was distressed. He was perspiring and his hands shook worse than ever. When Dave saw Ben looking at him, he wrapped his arms around himself to steady his hands. Ben didn't think much of it. They were all trembling.

"There was a notice in the paper a few months ago about a sex offender moving to Two Harbors," Ben said. "I don't know if you remember. His name is Jacob Burns, goes by Jake. Jeff checked on him to make sure he was still at the listed address, and he couldn't get anyone to answer the door. He checked at his workplace, and his boss told him that Jake hasn't shown up for work for three nights in a row. He said that Jake doesn't have a telephone, so there's no way to contact him. Jeff's going to get in touch with the proper authorities to report him missing. They'll put out a bulletin asking other agencies to be on the lookout for him. That's about it. Oh, and Deidre, Jeff wants to see us in his office at eight tomorrow morning."

Dave looked startled. "Did he say what he wants to talk about?"

"No. He just said he wanted to include us in the investigation. Said outside help will be valuable." Ben covered his eyes, and again, Deidre could see his chest heaving.

"I'm setting the table for supper," she said. "We have to eat something, and Estelle Johnson brought us a hot dish and the rest of a meal. Come, Megan, give me a hand."

Deidre heard the crunch of tires on the gravel in their driveway and then a commotion as Steve and Jack leaped up the steps and ran across the deck. The kitchen door was thrown open, and before Deidre could say, "Take it easy," Steve asked expectantly, "Did Maren come home?"

Deidre knelt down to be at their eye level. "We don't know where Maren is yet. Go upstairs and wash your hands for supper, please. We'll talk about it then."

The four adults managed to choke down a few mouthfuls of food and drink a sip or two of water. No one, except for the boys, had much of an appetite. Ben took his plate to the garbage and scraped most of his meal into the plastic bag. He went outside and sat staring into space, lost in his thoughts.

"Dave, come outside and play catch," Jack urged. "We've got an extra glove, and we can play three-way."

Dave looked at Deidre and Ben and half smiled. He followed Jack and Steve outside, and Deidre wondered where he found the energy to accommodate two eight-year-olds. After a half hour he begged off the game and came into the living room where Megan, Deidre, and Ben were seated. Deidre thought he looked refreshed from the physical activity.

Soon he was wandering around the room and then announced he was going back to town. Before he left, he hugged Deidre and whispered in her ear, "It will be okay." He shook Ben's hand and said, "I'm sorry." His eyes held such pain that Ben wrapped his arms around Dave and patted him on the back.

"We'll see you tomorrow. The only way we're going to get through this is if we lean on each other."

As Deidre saw Dave's car pull out of the driveway she thought, *Damn, I forgot to give him his jacket. Oh well, tomorrow.*

# Chapter Ten

DEIDRE AND BEN CLIMBED the stairs to the sheriff's office on the top floor of the Law Enforcement Center, feeling as if their feet were cast in concrete, neither of them wanting to face what Jeff might have to say. They were buzzed in, and Jeff invited them into his office.

"Well, first of all, we haven't found Maren. I'm afraid that's the best news I have for you. Have you talked to Dave since I saw you last?"

"He was at our house when you called yesterday," Ben said.

"How did he seem to you?"

Ben and Deidre looked at each other, and Deidre answered. "Dave's pretty broken up. He seemed really dejected to hear that this Jake Burns has disappeared. He didn't say anything, but I know he was thinking the same thing we were, that Jake had abducted Maren and might be holding her. We had supper together, and he left for home quite early in the evening."

Jeff paused, deep in thought. "Did he tell you that I spoke with him yesterday?"

Deidre flared. "Now wait a minute, Jeff. We've known Dave for two years, and he has become a part of our family. I know he seems very agitated, but we all are. He doesn't know which way to turn. You saw how upset he was when we were at Maren's car in the woods. He couldn't even go over and look in it."

Ben cleared his throat, and put his hand on Deidre's. "It's okay, Jeff is just doing his job. In most cases, a disappearance is related to a family member or close acquaintance. Jeff has to keep an open mind. Let him do his job." He turned to Jeff. "Did Dave reveal anything?"

"Nothing. He said he was at work until one o'clock on the day Maren went missing. I checked with his employer, and he confirmed that fact. The day before that, he worked all day. In fact, he worked late that night. Didn't leave the office until six, and was back to work at eight the next morning, the morning of the day he reported Maren missing. He could account for almost all of his time, except for the hours he would have been alone with Maren. But that would be expected. They were living together."

"How did he seem to you?" Ben questioned.

"Same as you said, really upset. I don't think he's responsible for Maren's disappearance, or he's one heck of an actor."

Ben fiddled with his wedding ring.

"Then how about Jake Burns. What do you know about him?" Deidre wanted to know.

"Jake spent ten years in prison for a crime he committed when he was nineteen. According to state guidelines, he was sentenced to fifteen years by a hard-nosed judge. Jake served ten of those fifteen with no incident. He was deemed not a risk to repeat his crime and was released under supervision. This is the third community in which he has stayed with no incidents."

"Do you know the specifics of his crime?" Ben asked.

"His record is public. When he was nineteen, he and some buddies had been drinking heavily in a lake cabin. They left and he stayed behind. Two eighteen-year-old girls were boating that night, and their motor conked out in front of Jake's cabin. They paddled the boat to shore seeking help, and Jake invited them in. He offered them alcohol, which they consumed, and while they were impaired, he raped both girls. The next morning they all woke up, and the girls left to find a ride into town. They went to the police and filed a complaint, were tested for rape evidence, and the rest is history for Jake. After reading his record, both of his time in prison and while he's been out, I doubt if he had anything to do with Maren."

"But you will follow up on him, won't you?" Deidre demanded.

"Oh, we will. I'm interviewing one of his co-workers this afternoon. The guy might have been Jake's only friend in town. And, also, I notified the state corrections office, and they're using their connections to locate him. Just don't set your sights on him quite yet. We've still got a lot of work to do."

*****

"ANY IDEA WHAT YOU'RE going to do today?" Deidre asked Ben on the way home.

He shrugged. "Hadn't given it any thought. I called the office yesterday, and they said to take as much time as I need. I don't know, maybe work would be good for me. Take my mind off the pain."

Deidre reached across the armrest and patted his hand. "Don't rush it. Give yourself time to absorb what has happened." She began to sob. "I think we have to begin to face the possibility that Maren will never come back to us." This time it was Ben who tried to comfort her with his touch. Neither felt like talking anymore.

When they were getting out of the car at home, Deidre asked Ben if she could borrow his SUV. He asked where she was going.

"I need to be alone for a while. I think I'll take a ride up the Drummond and walk one of the trails. Maybe I can clear my head." Ben nodded and asked her to not get off the trail.

"Be home by five?" he asked, and he looked at her in a way that told her he knew where she was headed.

Deidre turned off the Drummond Road onto the Spooner Road. She didn't intend to drive all the way back to where Maren's car had been found, but she knew she wanted to walk the trail where Maren might have been. It wasn't logical, she knew, but not knowing what had happened was eating at her insides.

She parked the SUV partway in and began walking, not paying attention to time or distance. She came to a long, low spot in the road that had been underwater until recently. The standing water was gone, but the clay mud lingered, a plastic kind of mud that held its shape. Several vehicles had been driven through the mud, each driver following the track of the previous. She remembered riding through it yesterday when they had come to examine Maren's car. She tried to walk the edge but even that was muddy, and her feet sunk into the goop. The brush and other vegetation came to the very edge of the trail, and Deidre could see patches of standing water in the shallow ditches. She decided the only way to get past the low spot was to put up with the wet clay.

She happened to look at the other side of the road. A set of foot-tracks was preserved in the mire, heading toward the main road. She began to pay closer attention and realized there were no tracks going in. If she kept walking, which she intended to do, she would have to come out the same way. She would leave tracks going in and out. Whoever left the other set had not walked in. She walked another fifteen minutes, and the nagging realization that she had possibly discovered a vital clue forced her to turn back. By the time she got home, the mud on her shoes had dried and made a mess of Ben's SUV, but she ignored it.

"Hello, is Jeff in? . . . Jeff, I think I may have discovered something of value." She was in the process of explaining what she had found when Ben came into the kitchen. Deidre was alarmed to see the deep purple bags under his eyes, and she put one arm around his waist while she finished her conversation. Ben heard her say, "Okay, I'll meet you at the entrance to the Spooner Road in twenty minutes."

"What's up?" Ben asked, a puzzled look on his face.

"I think I found the footprints of whoever has taken Maren. Come on. I'm meeting Jeff there in a few minutes."

Ben looked dazed. "No. No, you go ahead. I don't think I can do it, and besides, I want to be with Steve and Jack. Megan's had them all day, and I think she deserves a break."

Deidre kissed him. "Would you sweep up the dirt I tracked in? And call Dave. Tell him we want him to come for supper again. Tell him we need him and he needs us." She rushed from the house to the SUV and sped away.

Jeff brought a kit used for making casts of footprints, and before dark he had three very clear molds of someone's shoe prints.

# Chapter
## Eleven

NOTHING WAS NORMAL at Ben's and Deidre's home. Megan had moved back home for the time being so she could be with her parents, and so she could be there to receive the latest news. Dave surprised everyone and returned to work only a couple days after he discovered that Maren was missing. He said he'd go crazy if he had to sit around and wait for something to happen. Everyone grieved in their own way. Ben pretty much sat on the deck and looked out over the neighbor's hayfield, and Deidre tried to stay busy. The only ones who seemed oblivious to Maren's situation were the boys.

On the sixth day of their ordeal, Pastor Ike called and asked if he could pay them a visit. Receiving the family's consent, he arrived at mid-morning. They met on the deck, where they could smell the grass, hear the birds, and feel the slight breeze that wafted across the field. Deidre brought out a tray holding several cookies and four glasses of iced tea. They sat for a few minutes, nibbling at the cookies and sipping the tea.

"I won't ask how you're doing. You're probably sick of people asking that question. Instead, I'll ask, is anything you'd like to talk about?" Pastor Ike sat quietly, not rushing an answer.

"How will I get through this?" Ben asked in a voice so quiet it could hardly be heard. Ike waited to see if he had more to say, but Ben sat still, staring into the empty sky.

"I don't know, Ben. Everyone handles stress in their own way. I do know this: you're walking a terrible journey right now. But if you look around, you'll see that you're not alone. First you have Deidre by your side, because both of you are on the path, together. And I am convinced that you have God walking with you. There's a well-known scripture from the book of Ecclesiastes, 'Though one may be overpowered, two can defend themselves, but a cord of three strands is not easily broken.' You have that core of three strands: you, Deidre, and God. But you have so much more, Ben. Every day someone has delivered a meal to you. Law enforcement is working to find answers, and although you might not feel it right now, there are countless people praying for you, people you don't even know. Lean on these people, Ben. Let them be a part of the cord that will sustain you."

Deidre was totally taken by the pastor's words, and she could almost picture herself being woven into a many-stranded rope. For an instant, she believed she would make it, but that belief disappeared as soon as it came. She, Ben, and Megan said nothing for a long time, trying to digest what Pastor Ike had said. "I wish I had an answer for you, but only time and work will bring you the closure you need," he continued. "My prayer for you is that you be given a patient spirit and eyes to see those who are by your side."

No one said a word, and after a few minutes, Ike stood and offered his hand to each of them. "God bless you," were his parting words.

Again, Deidre was struck by the pastor's words, or rather by what he didn't say. All he had said was that God was with them, and she became aware that she had given up hope of ever seeing her daughter alive.

Jeff called in the afternoon to ask if he could swing by. He said he wanted to bring them up to date on what was happening with the case. Deidre repeated the same motions she had when Pastor Ike had visited in the morning, iced tea and a few cookies. Jeff passed on both, but Deidre, existing in her own world, brought them anyway.

"We've gone over Maren's car as thoroughly as possible. Whoever is involved did a lot of planning and wasn't panicked. Every possible place where there could have been fingerprints left was wiped clean, the lab said probably with something like Lysol and paper toweling. That made it easy for the abductor to burn any evidence. I told you there looked to be blood on the headrest of the driver's seat. It was tested and wasn't blood after all. Lab people think it was a stain caused by some sort of dye quite some time ago. So we drew a blank with her car."

He decided to take a sip from the glass of iced tea Deidre had left on the stand next to his chair. Then he continued.

"Jake Burns, the convicted felon, hasn't been seen for over a week. I spoke with his fellow employee. He said about two weeks ago, Jake showed up for work looking like he had been beat up pretty badly. Jake wouldn't talk about it, and his co-worker said they never spoke of it again. We got a search warrant, and Jake's landlady let us into his apartment. Kind of sad, actually. It was only three small rooms and a bath. Pretty neat and clean for a bachelor pad, but Spartan I guess is the only word for it. He left clothes in the closet and personal belongings in the bathroom. We thought we'd find some porn magazines or stuff on a computer. Heck, he didn't even own a computer. The books and magazines we found were mostly history or news related. All in all, I think he was just a loner. There's a nationwide alert for him, though. It would be nice to know where he is."

Jeff took a gulp of the tea while the others waited for him to continue.

"Then there's Dave." He paused and examined the facial expressions of the others. "Has he been in touch with you?"

"Dave eats supper with us every night. He went back to work shortly after Maren went missing. Said it gave him something to do besides moping around. Why do you ask?" Deidre wanted to know.

"Just wondering if he said anything about our questioning him."

Deidre answered, "He hasn't said a word about that. Poor guy. I suppose he's too embarrassed to tell us he's being treated as a suspect. But I'm telling you, Jeff, he's really hurting. When I look in his eyes, all I see is pain."

"Sometimes there's a fine line between pain and guilt," Jeff said, as if thinking out loud. "Or fear. Anyway, we asked Dave if we could look at his car and in their apartment. He never hesitated. Said any time, that he had nothing to hide. We went through everything in the apartment, in the car, and didn't come up with one speck of evidence that Dave is involved, other than being a grieving partner. They weren't married, were they?"

Megan came to her sister's defense. "No, but Maren said they would be in the near future."

"One last thing. Did Maren usually carry a purse with her, credit cards?" Jeff asked, as though it was hardly worth a second thought.

Megan was the one who spoke up. "She had a favorite. It was brown leather with a short shoulder strap. I don't think I ever saw her without it, because she always said most of her worldly possessions were in that bag. I know she had both a debit card and a credit card. Other than that, she usually carried a few bucks and her makeup. Oh, of course her driver's license and her social security card. I always warned her not to have it in her purse. I told her she was smart enough to memorize nine digits, but she just brushed me off. Said if anybody wanted to steal her identity, they were welcome to it." Then Megan choked up.

After assuring the family that his department was doing all it could, Jeff excused himself. The three continued to sit on the deck, absorbing the smells and sounds of late spring. The blank look in Ben's eyes worried Deidre.

They sat in nearly a catatonic state until a parishioner from their church drove up. Another meal was on its way, and Deidre wondered if she could have managed to fix meals for the family up to this point. The man who was delivering was a complete stranger to her, and as he greeted them, Deidre sensed a the deep compassion he felt for them. After a few words of instruction about the meal, he turned away with the words, "I'll pray that you have strength to make it through another day."

*And I'll take strength from wherever it comes,* Deidre thought.

# Chapter
## Twelve

NONE OF THE FAMILY could muster the energy to attend church. They knew it would be awkward, with too many well-meaning comments. "How are you doing?" "Are you okay?" "She's in God's hands." "We're praying for a miracle." "God works in mysterious ways." "Remember, God has a plan." Deidre wanted none of those platitudes. She drove into town and bought copies of the Duluth and Minneapolis papers. She and Ben sat on the deck again, paging through them. When she was done, she couldn't remember a thing she had read. Ben folded his section of the paper and, staring into space, said nothing.

Megan walked to the place by the river where she and her family had spent so much time together. There, she sat looking wistfully at the rock she and her sister had sat on so often when they were teens, and she remembered the times they shared secrets with each other. Today, she wondered what she would do without her sister in her life.

Sunday passed with no word, and the members of the family attempted to find things to do. Ben tried watching a baseball game on TV, the Twins playing the White Sox, but he couldn't concentrate. After a few minutes, he found the announcer's voice to be grating, and turned the set off. Megan was reading a book and found herself scanning the same page over and over. She eventually gave up. Deidre went upstairs to check on her sons and found them engrossed in a video game. *Thank God for those games,* she thought, and then felt a pang of regret that they had been left alone so much the past days.

"Why don't we go for a walk," she asked, hoping to get the boys outside and away from the handheld screen. "Let's go down by the river. You can fish and maybe catch a trout."

"Naw, I don't feel like fishing," Steve said.

"Me neither," Jack chimed in. "But I'd like to just go sit by the river with you. Okay?"

"That would be great," Deidre affirmed. "Just the three of us."

Together they walked the familiar path to the family's gathering spot. The trail was well worn. Deidre thought about when she and Ben and their two little girls had first started to follow the same route through the woods and how eventually a path had formed. She remembered the time they had spent clearing the way, pulling up brush by the roots and grubbing out the larger rocks until an easily discernable trail was formed. She remembered the laughter they shared when they splashed in the crystal water of the Knife River.

Then the boys were born, and she carried one of them in a pack strapped to her back while Ben carried the other. It seemed her family had grown up following the river and playing in the picnic spot they had cleared and improved over the years. Her thoughts were interrupted when they reached that area.

"Let's sit over there," Steve suggested, pointing to a shady spot beneath a cluster of cedars. They had been decent size when she and Ben bought the property. Now they were majestic. She leaned her back against one of them after she sat down. Each of her sons did the same, and for a few moments they sat within touching distance of each other, listening to the gurgle of water as it spilled over partially submerged rocks. A belted kingfisher dived from a branch into a pool and came up with a minnow in its bill.

"Maren's in trouble, isn't she?" Jack said out of the blue. His question caught Deidre by surprise.

She looked at the river for a moment before answering. "Yes, I'm afraid she is."

"Tell us what you know." This time it was Steve who spoke.

"Your sister has been missing for a week, but you know that," Deidre began. "Sheriff Jeff has been doing all he can to find her. We found her car up the Spooner Road. You know where that is. Dad's taken you there when he's been grouse hunting. We don't know much more."

After several seconds passed, Steve asked, "Who called to tell you she was missing?"

"Dave and Maren were supposed to go on a picnic last Monday. He left work early, but she wasn't home when he got there. He called me, but I didn't think anything of it. Not until he called later that night. You remember when I got his call?" The boys nodded.

"Do you think Dave took her away?"

Deidre looked shocked. "Of course not. Whatever made you say that?" It had been Steve who asked, and he looked chastised for having uttered the words.

Deidre reached over and patted his leg. "I'm sorry I was so sharp. It's just that we're all on edge. You've seen how upset Dave is. He's worried sick about Maren. He loves her very much. She's said that, and he's said that. No, Dave's part of our family, and family doesn't do things like that."

Jack turned so he could look directly at his mother. "I heard you and Dad talking about a sex offender in town. What's a sex offender?"

Deidre felt herself being pulled into a place she didn't want to be. "A sex offender is a person who does really bad things to other people. You know how we've talked about people's private parts? Well, a sex offender does bad things to people's private parts. Offenders are almost always men, and they overpower women and girls and force themselves on them." She knew that wasn't the whole truth, but she didn't want to get into the pedophile issue right now. The boys had enough on their plate without bringing up that horrid issue.

"Do they kill the women?" Steve asked, his brow furrowed.

"Many times," Deidre answered honestly.

"Do you think the sex offender killed Maren?" Deidre was shocked by where this conversation had led.

"Jeff doesn't think he's involved for several reasons. But he doesn't know where the man is. He disappeared a little while after Maren did."

"That sounds suspicious to me," Jack said, sounding more grown up than he was. Then he asked Deidre, "Do you think Maren's dead?"

Deidre was speechless, but eventually she squeaked out, "Perhaps. But we have to keep hoping for the best."

First Steve began to cry, and then Jack.

"Come over by me," Deidre said, her voice so quiet it was hardly audible. The boys scrunched over, and she put an arm around each one. She sat with them until she felt them stop shaking, and then she hugged them closer.

"Let's go home. Dave's coming for supper and Dad will be wondering what's happened to us." She helped dry their tears, and hand-in-hand, they walked back to the house.

# Chapter Thirteen

THE DAYS OF NOT KNOWING what happened to Maren stretched to two weeks, three weeks, and then a month. At first, Jeff visited them quite frequently, but as time passed, the visits became fewer and fewer. Nothing was the same for the family.

Megan returned to Duluth. Her summer job at the lab required her attention, and she needed the money for fall tuition. She had friends to be with and things to do that took her mind off her loss. But when she was alone, she would sit and brood, imagining what her sister had endured, imagining where she might be, hoping that Maren would someday walk in the door as if nothing were wrong. And sometimes she would weep.

Ben returned to work with the FBI. He was irritable, and on a few occasions he blew up at his co-workers, especially those who reported to him. Everyone walked on eggshells when he was present. There were times that he was needed and would be found in his office with the blinds closed and the lights out, just sitting in the dark. His superiors were beginning to wonder if he should be placed on medical leave. More than once they spoke to him about seeking counseling, but he always rejected the idea.

Dave's visits to the house became fewer and fewer, and even though Deidre tried to maintain contact, he gradually left their lives. Sometime toward early July, Megan called Deidre to tell her that she had seen Dave at a nightclub with a woman. She said it looked like they were more than friends. Deidre remembered someone telling her to count on one year of grieving for every five years of togetherness after her fiancé, John, had been killed. At that rate, Dave's grieving period would be only months. She knew that wasn't logical, and he might be pushing it, but then, everyone grieves at their own rate, she thought. She told herself that Dave was a young man who was lonely and had needs. But still, she wished he would stay in touch with her and Ben.

Jack and Steve acted as though nothing was out of the ordinary. They played ball, went swimming, and fished in the river once in a while. But Deidre recognized signs that all was not well. Several times since Maren's disappearance they had thrown tantrums over insignificant requests, refusing to tidy up their rooms or take the garbage out when they were asked. Once they got into a terrible row with each other that ended in a knock-down-drag-out fistfight. Deidre knew they needed more than she was able to provide, but she didn't know what.

She was lonely, spending most of her day in the garden, turning the soil over time and again, pulling weeds out by their roots and leaving them to wither in the sun, potting and repotting some of the annuals. More than once she picked up a stone and hurled it with vengeance into the woods. She got no enjoyment from her toil, but it helped pass the time. She had long since stopped the delivery of meals by her church, and each day she went through the motions of preparing food for the family. It was repetitious and without creativity. One day she decided she needed to talk to Pastor Ike.

He was waiting for her at the church entry when she arrived and escorted her up the stairs to his office. He offered her a chair and a cup of coffee. She declined the coffee.

"Things are difficult," he stated rather than asked. Deidre nodded, and before she could say anything, she burst into tears.

"Damn, I told myself I wasn't going to cry, and here I am bawling my head off before we even have a chance to talk." She grabbed a tissue from the box that had been conveniently placed on the chair next to where she sat, blew her nose, and wiped her eyes.

Ike looked at her. "Do whatever you have to, Deidre. This isn't a race you have to finish in a few minutes. I have nothing on my calendar for the remainder of the afternoon, so get out what you have to get out."

Deidre took a deep breath. "You know, Pastor, that I'm not very religious, at least not like some people. To tell you the truth, I don't know what I believe." She paused. "Or even if I do believe. Right now, I'm so damn mad at God—if there is a God—that I'm having a hard time thinking he's the God I hear you preach about on Sundays. Speaking of which, we haven't been able to get up the gumption to come to church once since Maren has been gone."

"I've noticed, but I haven't wanted to pressure you to attend. You've got a lot to work out, and I had faith that sooner or later you'd want to talk. I wouldn't have waited much longer to contact you, but I wanted to give you a chance to decide when the time was right. It seems that might be now. You say you're angry with God. Can you tell me why?"

"People say that God controls everything. If that's true, why didn't he save my daughter?"

Ike put the fingertips of each hand together and contemplated them for a few seconds. "Deidre, I've struggled with that kind of question for most of my adult life, especially since becoming a pastor, and I have no answers. I wish I did, but I've seen parishioners die who were fervently prayed for, and I've seen non-believers recover. It seems that people get sick, some die, some get well." He paused again as though he was afraid to continue, but he did.

"I've come to the belief that God doesn't control everything that happens on earth." Deidre looked at Ike with disbelief in her eyes, but before she could respond, he went on. "I've looked at all the pain and suffering in this world and have come to the conclusion there are just some things God can't control, like an abductor's actions."

Deidre took minutes to digest what the reverend said. Finally she voiced her question. "Then what good is God?"

"God walks with us every step of our lives, but not to take away every ill that might befall us. There will be wars and there will be abductions. There will be accidents and there will be murders. But, and I'm talking of the survivors now, God walks with us every step of the journey."

Ike smiled. "Let me tell you about an experience I had that changed my thinking. Do you know where the Pines Picnic Area is? Up Highway 2?" Deidre nodded, wondering where this was going.

"One time my family was there with another pastor and his family. There's a nature trail in the park that winds its way through a patch of old-growth white pine. They're massive, two hundred feet tall and eight feet in circumference. At one point the trail passes between two giants that grow only four feet apart. A sign says to close your eyes, walk between them, and you will be able to feel their presence. We all tried it and every one of us could stop exactly between the two trees. My friend's wife said, 'Isn't that just like God? We can feel his presence when he is with us.' My friend said, 'No, just the opposite. God is with us always. We only sense Him when we choose to pull away, and then we sense His absence.' Perhaps part of your emptiness is because you've wanted to pull away, when what happened wasn't God's fault at all."

Deidre didn't feel much better, but she was beginning to mull over what Ike said when they parted with a handshake and a promise to meet again in a few days. On the way home, she wondered if she could pray. She never had.

# Chapter
## Fourteen

THE FAMILY GATHERED for supper, including Dave, whom Deidre had invited, and excluding Megan, who already had plans in Duluth. The talk was stilted, no one quite sure what should be said. Finally, Deidre asked the question she hated the most when asked of her.

"How are you doing, Dave?" she asked. He toyed with his food before answering.

"It's been really tough. I don't sleep well at all, and it's difficult to concentrate. That's not good for an accountant. On the brighter side, though, I've gone out a few times with friends and have been able to have a good time. But then I think of Maren, and I sink back into the pit."

Deidre looked at the sad expression on his face. "Megan said she saw you one night in Duluth, but you didn't see her. We're glad you're getting out."

Dave looked shocked, but went back to eating. Ben studied his face for several seconds, and excused himself from the table. In a few minutes he came back and ate a few more mouthfuls of food before pushing his plate away.

"Has Jeff talked to you any more?" he wanted to know.

Dave's face flushed. "No. Why do you ask?"

"Just wondering," was Ben's answer. "The Twins play ball tonight. Do you want to stay and watch the game with us? We've got snacks."

Dave begged off, saying that he had to be at work early the next day, and excused himself.

"Why did you ask him if Jeff had talked to him? I think you know that makes him nervous," Deidre said as she cleared the table.

"Just wanted to see his reaction. I got an e-mail from Jeff today, asking if we could meet with him in the morning. I told them at work I'd be a couple of hours late. I don't know what he wants, just assumed it might have something more to do with Dave."

Deidre stopped what she was doing. "Do you know something I don't?" she asked as she put her hands on her hips. Ben looked a little defensive.

"I don't know anything, but I've got a feeling Jeff has some important news for us." He went in the living room and turned on the TV. The boys had gone outside, and Deidre finished cleaning up.

*****

DEIDRE THOUGHT THE WORD "strained" didn't exactly define her and Ben's relationship. As they rode into town the next morning, she decided that "empty" was a better word. They didn't joke with each other the way they had before Maren disappeared. They didn't touch each other the way they had. Too often they were in their own worlds, separated by their own thoughts. When Ben parked the car, he looked at Deidre with a crooked smile.

"Well, let's find out what's so important." They held hands as they walked to the Law Enforcement Center, and Deidre realized this was the first time they had touched in at least two days.

They were ushered into Jeff's office by the receptionist, where they waited nervously for him. A few minutes later he came in and closed the door behind himself.

"I think we might have a lead. It's a long shot, but it's something," he began. Before he continued he asked, "Can I get you a cup of coffee? We've got a few cookies left out there." Ben and Deidre shook their heads, and Deidre muttered a "no, thank you." Both were sitting on the edge of their chairs looking intently at Jeff.

"Here's what we have. After putting out information about Maren's disappearance, the story has been picked up by other agencies around the country. Computers have really changed this job," he added, and Deidre wanted to scream at him, "Get to the point."

"There've been a string of abductions of women across the country, and they seem to fit a regular pattern," he continued. "They might be connected, and have been occurring about every two weeks." Jeff placed a map of the United States on an easel so they could see. A string of red dots, starting in Boston and ending in Oklahoma City, was easy to follow.

He pointed at Boston. "A twenty-year-old waitress disappeared on February twenty-eighth. Her body was found two days later under a bridge. She had been sexually assaulted before she was killed."

Ben moved the pointer to the next red dot. "On March fifteenth, a nineteen-year-old college freshman went missing in Syracuse, New York. Her body was found by two joggers as they followed a trail through a nature preserve on campus. She, too, had been sexually abused." Deidre and Ben shifted uneasily in their chairs.

The next dot was placed near Cleveland. "On April first, a young lady who had been serving as a nanny didn't show up for work. She was found the next day by a police officer when he investigated a report of a body found in an alley. She had met the same fate as the previous victims." He pointed to Toledo, Ohio.

"I'm sure you see the pattern. Each city in which an abduction and murder took place is along the I-90 corridor. It seems the perpetrator is moving east to west. In Toledo, a first-year kindergarten teacher didn't come to work on a Monday. That was April twentieth. The next victim was discovered in Rockford, Illinois, on April twenty-fourth. That was followed by a similar incident a little over a week later in Madison, Wisconsin."

Jeff cleared his throat. "You first missed Maren on May fifth. Can you see it might fit the timeline? Then, on June second, a woman's body was found in a gravel pit in Sioux Falls, South Dakota, and on June twelfth, another victim was discovered floating in the Cheyenne River near Rapid City."

"Do you have evidence that the same person is involved?" Jeff nodded.

"We're certain. He makes no attempt to disguise the evidence. He doesn't use a condom and has left plenty of DNA in each victim. Strands of his hair have been found on nearly everyone of the victims, along with fibers from his clothing. It seems he wears the same heavy shirt or jacket each time."

Ben had been studying the map and the notated dates. "He's about ready to strike again, if he follows the same pattern, isn't he?"

Jeff looked a little surprised, but then realized he shouldn't have been. Ben had worked as an FBI agent for over twenty years. "Unfortunately, yes. But the good news is, if he does select another victim and follows the same MO, we have a pretty good idea of where it will be." He pointed to Billings, Montana. "And to go along with that good news, Billings isn't a huge metropolis, which means the job of enforcement will be a little easier. If not Billings, then Butte is the next city on I-90."

"Do you think this is the person who took Maren?"

Jeff collapsed his pointer, stretched it out, and collapsed it again. "Personally, I see some problems with that. True, the time frame fits. This suspect has struck roughly every two weeks or less. That would about fit the time difference between the Madison murder and the Sioux Falls murder. Here's the problem: Two Harbors is a long way from I-90. If we're talking about the same person, he would had to have gotten on I-35, driven over two hundred miles north, committed the crime, and then driven two hundred miles south. It just doesn't fit the pattern. That said, you know as well as I do that this kind of criminal is irrational, and we don't know what is going through his mind."

The three sat for several moments waiting for someone else to say something. Jeff decided he had to be the one.

"We tried to find a match to the casts we made of the footprints left in the mud on the Spooner Road, but we drew a blank. When we searched Dave's place, there were no shoes in the apartment that matched. We have microscopically examined the mud, and feel certain we can match it to samples on clothing or shoes if we find any. So far, that hasn't happened. I know this isn't much for you, but I felt you deserved to know we're doing all we can to find out what happened to Maren. If anything more develops, I'll let you know right away." He stood and offered his hand to each of them in turn. "Take care, friends."

Deidre felt like a scab had been torn off a festering wound. Nothing had changed except there were more questions that had to be answered.

# Chapter Fifteen

BEN CAME HOME from work at his usual time and immediately buried his face in the day's edition of the Duluth newspaper. He had kissed Deidre on her cheek but said little. She worried about the hollow look in his eyes, but before she could initiate a conversation, she heard a ruckus outside and rushed to break up a scuffle between Steve and Jack. This was more serious than their usual roughhousing, and she was sure if she hadn't intervened, punches would have been thrown.

"What's gotten into you two?" she demanded. "Look me in the eye. Steve. Look at me!" Steve toed the ground and finally looked up. "Now tell me what this is about." Neither boy answered. "If you don't talk to me, you're going straight to your room until supper." Deidre folded her arms across her chest and waited.

"Steve said Maren is dead, and we should quit pretending she isn't." Jack began to tear up.

Deidre's heart took a leap. No one in the family had ever voiced those taboo words until now. She placed her arm around Jack and glanced at Steve. He looked like a puppy that had made a huge mistake, and knew it.

"Come here, boys," she said as gently as she could. "Come on up on the deck so we can talk." She led them up the steps and hollered through the screen door.

"Ben, come out here, please. We've got to talk." She heard the paper rustle, and in a few seconds Ben was at the door, holding the sports section between the fingers of his right hand.

"What's the matter?" he wanted to know.

"Come out here and sit with us." Ben knew this was not the time to ask his wife why or to object. He folded the newspaper and tossed it on the kitchen table, then emerged from the house, a puzzled look on his face. He sat on the porch swing next to Deidre. It faced two chairs in which the boys sat, both of them looking as if they expected an anvil to fall on them.

"I think it's time we talk to each other, and I mean really talk to each other," Deidre began. "We've been pussyfooting around, never really saying what we mean, avoiding the obvious for too long."

"Steve, what made you say what you did to Jack?" Deidre asked. Ben looked from Jack to Deidre, wondering what had happened, but kept his mouth shut, hoping to pick up the gist of the impromptu meeting.

Steve swung one leg and kept his head down. "After ball practice today, Jimmy Johnson was walking with me and a couple of other guys who had been with us in the outfield." He paused.

"Go on," Deidre prodded.

"He said everybody knows that Maren is dead," and Steve burst into tears. He tried to dry his eyes with the back of his dirty hand, which only left a mud smear on his face.

"And why did that cause a fight between you and your brother?" She looked at Ben and noticed that his lips were so pursed that they were white.

"I thought about what he said all afternoon, and I think he's right. I said so to Jack, and he said, 'don't ever say that again.' Then he tackled me and tried to hit me."

Deidre let a burst of air escape from her lungs. "Okay, guys, I think we have to talk about this right now and get it over with. Don't you agree, Ben?"

Ben knew how he wanted to answer, and he knew how he'd better not. At that moment he wanted to rush into the house, bury his head in the sports page, and let the world go by. Instead he heard himself say, "Your mother is right. It's time we talk."

Deidre sensed she was going to be the leader in this conversation. "All right, Jack, have you ever thought about what Steve said? Before today, I mean?"

Jack shrugged, then muttered, "S'pose so."

"Ben, what about you?"

He looked surprised to be confronted so forcefully. He opened his mouth but no words came out. He forced himself to say "yes."

"Well, I think about that every day," Deidre continued. "It's the first thing I think in the morning, and it's the last thing I think at night, and it's what I think about all day long. It seems Steve has been the only one brave enough to say the words."

The other three looked at her with amazement and apprehension. They had never seen their mother and wife act this way.

"Steve is right. Maren is probably dead. If she weren't, we should have heard from her by now."

Jack spoke so softly the others had to strain to hear his words. "But I just heard on the news about a girl who had been kidnapped ten years ago, and then she was found and rescued. What if that's what happened to Maren?"

Deidre was careful how she responded. "Things like that happen, but not often. If we go around moping until she's found or walks through that door," she pointed at the kitchen door, "we're going to ruin the rest of our lives. We're going to allow this to destroy our family." She stomped her foot on the deck.

"I'm going to be honest with you about what I think. And when I'm done, I want each of you to tell the rest of us what you think. And then I'm going to tell you about the meeting Dad and I had with Jeff this morning." She saw Ben's head snap up and his eyes widen.

"I think, I believe something very bad has happened to Maren. I think someone abducted her and killed her. I don't know how. I don't know why. She may have suffered, or she may not have. We don't know that right now. But I do believe in my heart that she is dead. You don't know how badly I want to pick up the phone and hear her voice, or to be able to hold her in my arms, or to get a message saying she's okay. If that happens, I'll rejoice like you can't believe. But, honestly, I don't think that's going to happen."

She turned to Ben. "What do you think? And don't tell us you don't know, because you've got to be thinking something." Moments passed.

"I think, I believe that Maren is dead," he said, and buried his face in his hands. When he looked up, his eyes were red-rimmed and his lip quivered. "I hope I'm wrong, but inside, I doubt that I am. Someone will find her body, and then we'll know for sure." He took a deep breath and leaned back in the swing, eyes fixed on the sky.

"What about you, Jack?" Deidre asked in a hushed tone.

Jack shrugged and drug his toe across the floor. "I think Maren is in heaven and is safe." He couldn't say more for a long time, and Deidre waited for him to continue. "I don't want that to be right, but I don't want her to be afraid or to be suffering. I think she's dead."

Deidre looked at Steve. She wasn't going to make him repeat what he had said to Jack. "You've already told us what you think. Now here's what I want to say to my family. We have to begin sharing our hurt and our thoughts with each other. If we don't, we're each going to drift away into our separate worlds. If we stick together, we're going to be like a rope made of four strands woven together, and that will be a rope that cannot be broken." She hesitated, realizing she had just paraphrased what Pastor Ike had said to her, and suddenly she believed what she said. She was on a roll.

"Every day after Dad gets home from work, we're going to sit out here and talk, talk about how we feel that day, talk about what we did to take care of ourselves that day, talk about what is bothering us that day." She turned to Ben. "You can read the paper after supper, but every day we are going to talk to each other. Understand?" Wisely, no one objected.

Steve shifted his weight, causing the chair in which he was sitting to creak. During her tirade, Deidre had forgotten she had more to say.

"Well, we've more or less laid our cards on the table, so I think we can face what Jeff said." She saw everyone become more attentive. "There has been someone, a man, traveling across the United States, abducting young women and killing them. He has left a trail of bodies along I-90, killing someone about every two weeks. He's making no effort to conceal clues about his identity. Jeff says it is as though he wants to be caught. His path would have taken him through Minnesota about the time that Maren disappeared."

"Does that mean he's the one who took Maren?" Jack wanted to know, not quite being able to utter the words "killed Maren."

Deidre shook her head. "Jeff doesn't think so, because Two Harbors is quite a way north of I-90, but on the other hand, he won't rule it out."

"Will they catch the man?" Steve asked hopefully.

"Jeff thinks they will, soon."

"Has anyone told Dave?" Ben gave the swing a push with his leg, and it moved back and forth like a metronome counting time.

"I don't think so. Speaking of Dave, he hasn't been around lately. I suppose he's busy at work. You remember how he threw himself into it right after Maren was gone. I think he's one of those people who finds solace in his work. I suppose that's okay. Whatever works." Deidre tried to remember when they had last seen him. "I suppose one of us should call and let him know." The swing kept moving and Deidre closed her eyes, letting herself feel the rhythm. She wondered when and if their lives would find a rhythm again.

"Let's go inside. I've got brats and potato salad made, and fresh raspberry pie for dessert. A perfect summer meal." She moved through the door and everyone followed, Jack with his arm around Steve's shoulder.

# Chapter Sixteen

DEIDRE CALLED DAVE'S cell phone. It was a little after noon, and she hoped he was on his lunch break.

"Hello, Deidre," Dave answered. His voice sounded strong, and Deidre was pleased to hear him sounding normal. "How are you and Ben doing? It seems like forever since we saw each other. I'm really sorry, but I've been slammed at work. Usually don't get home until nine or so."

Deidre said they were getting by, and wondered if he could come to supper that night. Dave began to say he couldn't make it, but Deidre told him that Jeff had given her some news he might be interested in hearing. There was a long pause on the other end of the line, and Dave came back on.

"You know, I was looking at the wrong day. Yeah, I'm free tonight. What time should I be there, six-ish as usual?"

Deidre told him that would be fine.

*****

DAVE PULLED INTO THEIR driveway at exactly six, and Deidre was glad he didn't have to work late. Her family had had their ritual meeting, and both boys said they were happy to learn that Dave was coming to dinner. Deidre thought their daily sessions were helping. At least Ben didn't bury his face in the newspaper as soon as he got home.

Deidre met Dave on the deck, and she gave him a warm hug. "How you doin'?" she asked as she stepped back to look at him. "You look a lot more relaxed. You're so tan. You must be spending time on the golf course."

Dave laughed the half laugh Deidre so liked. "Not as much as I'd like. I told you work has been wild, but it takes my mind off things." They walked arm in arm into the house.

Ben greeted him with a two-handed handshake. "Dave, it's sure good to see you. Only a few minutes ago, we were saying how long its been since we got together. We miss you. I suppose part of it is you make us feel connected to Maren. Anyway, come on in. We're ready to sit down to eat." He clapped Dave on the shoulder. "Glad you're here."

The conversation during the meal was relaxed, and Deidre was thankful everyone was able to take part. The boys wanted to know if Dave would play catch after supper, and he said just for a few minutes, as he would have to get back to town soon. To her relief, there actually was some laughter. But the most poignant part of the get together was just before they began to dish up the food. Ben asked if he could say grace. Everyone held hands, forming a circle at the table. Deidre was holding Dave's hand.

When Ben thanked God for Dave and for the joy he had brought into Maren's life, Dave's grip became so intense she thought she would cry out. And then he relaxed. Deidre was happy that the mention of Maren's name brought such a response. He hadn't forgotten.

After dinner, Dave and the boys went outside to play ball. They wanted him to hit grounders to them, and Deidre watched from the windows as they stumbled over their own feet, trying to scoop up the bouncing hardball. She just hoped one of them wouldn't end up with a split lip.

Dave had warned them he needed to be back to town early, and as he was heading toward his car, Deidre walked with him. "So, you said Jeff had given you some news?" he reminded her. Deidre thought she detected a hint of anxiety in Dave's voice but wasn't surprised. After all, she was sure Dave needed answers as badly as they did.

"I must be losing it. Totally spaced out why you came." She went through the litany of what Jeff had told her about the I-90 murders.

"Does that mean they'll be going after him for Maren's murder when they find him?" There was such a note of hopefulness in Dave's voice that Deidre hated to tell him this probably wasn't the man. She did anyway.

"But they're pretty sure they can find him, right?" Dave was perspiring more than usual. Chasing errant throws and batting the ball wasn't easy for someone who held a sedentary job, Deidre thought.

"They're pretty confident they'll have him in custody in a few days, at least if they get a break or two. Jeff said he would stay in touch."

"What will happen if they catch him?"

Deidre was beginning to be a little exasperated with questions for which she didn't have answers. "I don't know for sure. Depends on a lot of things. I just know things will play out. They always do." She looked at her watch. "You'd better get going or you're not going to be home early like you wanted. It was great having you with us. Don't be a stranger."

They had been talking beside Dave's car, and as he got in he asked, "Will you call me as soon as you find out anything, about that guy, I mean? I have to know what happens."

# Chapter Seventeen

LESS THAN A WEEK PASSED before Jeff called. He asked if he could come out and speak with them when Ben got home, said he wanted them together when he told them the news. Deidre wanted to blurt out the question, "Did they catch him?" but she didn't, and Jeff didn't volunteer.

They were waiting for him when he arrived. Ben and she had talked it over, and they decided to include the boys in all conversations from now on. They had as much right as anyone to know the facts.

"Can I get you anything to drink, Jeff?" Deidre asked. He said ice water would be fine. Didn't want to spoil his appetite for supper, said they were having his favorite, pot roast.

Deidre placed the water glass on the table next to his chair, and Jeff began to fill them in on what he knew.

"I told you about the serial murders that were happening along I-90. They caught the guy who was committing them in Billings, Montana. That's more than good. He's one messed-up person who wasn't going to stop his rampage until he was stopped. Funny thing, he didn't put up any resistance when he was captured. Kind of gave in without a whimper." He took a drink of the water while the family waited expectantly.

"Unfortunately, we're certain he isn't the one who took Maren." Jeff could see everyone deflate, as though someone had pulled a stopper out and let all of their energy escape. "He's a very messed-up guy. He waived his right to remain silent or to have an attorney present while he made a statement. He immediately began to confess, beginning with the crime in Boston and following the I-90 corridor west. But he had nothing to say about stopping in Minnesota."

Deidre broke into Jeff's monologue. "Was he asked specifically about Maren?"

"The interrogators let him talk, and he led them along the murder trail case by case, giving details about each abduction that only the police and he would have known. He said nothing about Maren. When asked, he said he had driven straight through Minnesota, stopping once for gas. Inexplicably, he kept all of the receipts of his journey—every restaurant, every gas station, every motel. In the pile of receipts, one from a gas station in a little burg, Beaver Creek, was the only record of his being in Minnesota. They asked about Two Harbors, and he said he never left I-90. Had he driven to the North Shore, he would have had to buy gas up here."

Ben wanted to know what the murderer's motive was for going on a killing spree.

"He said he was bored and wanted to see how far he could get before he was caught. If he had made it to Seattle, he intended to leave a suicide note and kill himself. Like I said, he's a real crazy. As to what makes him tick, some psychiatrist will have a field day with that. Probably will get rich by writing a book about what he thinks he discovers."

Jeff drained the glass. The ice cubes stuck to the bottom, then came loose, causing water to splash down his front.

"Damn, that always happens," he complained as he tried to dry himself off with a napkin. "Well, folks, I gotta get going. Sorry the news isn't better, but there will be other leads along the way, be sure of that. Take care."

Deidre, Ben, and the boys watched him walk to his SUV, its door stenciled LAKE COUNTY SHERIFF.

"I thought for sure this was going to be the end of everything, that he'd tell us where to find Maren," Deidre sighed. "Well, supper's ready. Let's eat." Deidre led the way to the kitchen.

# Chapter Eighteen

THE SAME EVENING JEFF brought them news of the serial rapist and murderer being apprehended, Deidre called Dave, but he didn't answer. She left a message on his answering machine simply stating that Jeff had been to visit with news of the I-90 killer. She and Ben had been in bed for a half hour, reading, as was their custom, when her phone rang. She glanced at the red digital numbers of the clock radio, which read 11:32 p.m.

Her heart leaped to her throat, and her first thought was that something had happened to Megan. Deidre sprang out of bed, beating Ben to the phone.

"Hello," she answered anxiously, not taking time to look at the caller ID. Ben heard her say, "Oh, hi, Dave," with a mixture of relief and exasperation in her tone. "Yeah. Yeah he was here. . . . Yes, they did. . . . He more or less gave himself up. . . . No, they're quite sure he's not the one. . . . Well, he confessed to all the murders along I-90, but denied any involvement with Maren. . . . Yes, they do. . . . The puzzle pieces just don't fit together. . . . I suppose so. . . . Good night, Dave."

"What did he want?" Ben asked, trying to calm himself after the dash out of bed.

"I called him earlier and left a message saying that Jeff had been here with news. I didn't expect Dave to react with such urgency. He wondered if they were sure the killer hadn't had anything to do with Maren's disappearance. He sounded pretty bummed that enforcement believed him when he said he hadn't been to Two Harbors. I think Dave wanted him to be the killer and put an end to all this wondering." She looked at herself in the wall mirror before coming back to bed. "I suppose we all want some answers. It would make it a lot easier."

It was too late to read any more, and they turned out the light. Deidre realized she was too wide awake to fall asleep and contemplated getting up. She rolled on her side and curled into a semi-fetal position. Ben spooned behind her and put his arm around her chest, pulling her close to him. She decided not to get up.

*****

THE DAYS PASSED, and Deidre was adjusting to the new normal. Dave came for supper once every other week or so, usually on Wednesday or Thursday. The first time after his late-night call, he seemed agitated and questioned if the law enforcement units involved in the I-90 case were doing a thorough job. Deidre and Ben pointed out the discrepancies between the abductions of the other women and Maren's disappearance.

First, all of the women's bodies, except for Maren's, had been found a short time after their disappearance. The killer made no effort to conceal evidence such as DNA. Besides hair and fiber samples, he had even left teeth marks on their necks. Near several of the victims, he had left wads of chewing gum containing his saliva. Whoever had driven Maren's car into the woods had wiped it clean. There wasn't a speck of evidence left, an indication that her abduction was carefully planned and covered up.

Then, too, each of the known murders had taken place no more than a couple of miles off I-90. Two Harbors was at least a three-hour drive from the freeway. That didn't fit the pattern at all.

Finally, the killer made no effort to hide the victims' cars. Jeff suspected that if Maren hadn't been killed in her vehicle, at the very least her body was transported in it to wherever it had been disposed of. After that evening, Dave didn't bring up the topic of the I-90 killer again.

Deidre and Ben got together with Megan at least twice a week, and their visits began to form a pattern. During the week, Deidre would drive into Duluth and let the boys go to the Sports Arena, where they could take turns in a batting cage, shoot baskets, even get involved in a pick-up game. While they were occupied, she'd visit the antique shops nearby.

They'd go to Megan's for supper, usually take-out that she supplied, and Ben would meet them there. Most Saturdays, Megan came home, staying until late the next day, when she returned to Duluth and her job. They attended church together on Sunday, and had brunch at the resort where Maren worked before she disappeared. It was good to visit with a couple of waitresses who had been her friends. The rhythm was comforting to Deidre—no surprises.

There were days she almost forgot what the family was facing, days when the joy of her flower garden returned, days when she was happy.

All that changed on the morning Jeff called. She could tell by the strain in his voice that something had happened.

# Chapter Nineteen

"DEIDRE, THIS IS JEFF." Deidre almost made a wisecrack, asking him if he thought she couldn't read her caller ID, but something in his voice, a quaver or a hitch, something made her swallow the words.

"Deidre, we might have a break in Maren's case." Her guts immediately twisted and she felt her knees go weak.

"What is it, Jeff? Tell me." She was sure he was going to say that Maren's body had been found.

"A guy who owns a hunting shack up the Clark Road found a body this morning. I haven't been out there yet. He just left my office. I've got a deputy on his way to secure the area. From what the shack owner told me, I think he might have found Jake Burns, the registered sex offender who is missing. You and I have been friends for a long time, Deidre, and I have the utmost respect for your abilities as an investigator. I'm asking if you'd come with me to the scene. For one thing, I'd like you there to be able to identify anything that might belong to Maren. I sure will understand if you don't want to go, though."

By that time Deidre had regained her sense of balance, and her heart rate had settled down to near normal. "No, I'd like to come with. Okay if it takes me twenty minutes or so to make arrangement for the boys? I can meet you in the parking lot of the Center."

"From what I've been told, this guy isn't going anywhere. The shack owner was pretty shook up by what he found. See you when you get to town."

Deidre quickly called her in-laws. It was decided they would bring the twins home before suppertime, and would also prepare a meal for the evening. On the way into town she dialed Ben's number and let him in on what Jeff had said, and where she was going. His only response was to thank her for having the courage to face the new evidence.

After Deidre dropped the boys off at their grandparents' house, she headed straight for the Law Enforcement Center's parking lot. Jeff was waiting, leaning on his sheriff's vehicle. In seconds they were on the road.

"Deidre, you've been a good friend for a long time," Jeff said. "Maybe my best friend, and you've been a lot of help to me with your advice and insight. I think I have to level with you on one thing."

Deidre looked at her friend, a little anxious about what he would say next.

"I know you are really fond of Dave. I picked up on how you were sure he wasn't responsible, and that's why I didn't tell you that we were looking closely at him. In fact, Dave was our primary suspect."

Deidre squirmed in her seat, not knowing how to respond and wondering where the conversation was leading. Fortunately, Jeff didn't wait for her to say anything.

"We checked at her workplace, the resort where she was waitressing. The first co-worker we talked to told us that Maren had shown up for work one day about three weeks before she disappeared with a swollen jaw, as if she had been hit in the face. I was ready to go after Dave then. Do you remember her having any injuries or bruises about that time?"

Deidre shook her head, trying to remember. "You know, we hadn't been together much leading up to the day Dave called, wondering if I had seen her. I guess with the boys finishing up the school year, Megan finishing her semester at UMD, and all the things going on in our lives, we just didn't get together as often as we used to. Do you really believe Dave would have hit Maren?"

"I was certain of it," Jeff confessed. "But then I interviewed another employee. The day before Maren showed up with the swollen jaw, she and this other lady had been carrying some boxes down the stairs of the restaurant to the lobby of the hotel. Maren tripped and fell down three steps to the landing midway between floors. She hurt her elbow and wrist when she landed. The next day when she showed up for work, her jaw was swollen. Maren said her face had hit the wall when she fell and that her cheek swelled up overnight. I checked with the complex manager, and he pulled out an accident report from the day she fell. He was afraid she had broken a bone in her arm and wanted her to go to the hospital to have it checked out. Maren declined, told him she would be fine."

"Do you think Dave beat her?"

"That's why I'm telling you this. I checked with various medical people, and they all told me the same thing. If one part of the body is injured more severely, in this case Maren's wrist, than another injury, the lesser, often doesn't register. I asked about the delayed swelling, and they told me that happens quite frequently, especially in fleshy areas where blood has room to pool before the tissue expands. They said that can be true of the cheek area. Believe me, I checked out the story as closely as I could, and nothing traced back to Dave. I'd be surprised if Dave had anything to do with Maren's disappearance. Some evidence would have turned up by now if he was involved."

Deidre felt a wave of relief flood over her. She had thoughts about Dave's involvement from the beginning, nagging thoughts she didn't want, and now she could lay them to rest, at least as much as possible.

Because of their deep conversation, the ride went much faster than Deidre had expected. When she began to pay attention to where they were, Jeff was turning onto a haul road that led to one of the many county gravel pits. The road ran along the Gooseberry River, and from time to time, through the balsam and birch trees, she caught glimpses of sunlight on water. Jeff parked his SUV near a small mountain of class-five gravel the county had stockpiled, and Deidre could see the tracks of all-terrain vehicles that had driven up its steep slopes. A deputy's squad was parked nearby, along with a car she didn't recognize.

"We have to walk from here. The guy who built the shack wanted it to be secluded. He told me he hauled all the timbers in during a summer dry spell. Too bad this happened. It's a pretty nice place, as far as hunting shacks go."

They followed a path through the woods that twisted and turned around stumps and boulders, crossed a makeshift bridge made from two railroad ties bridging a rivulet, and came upon a snowmobile trail.

"Only another hundred yards from here," Jeff said. Deidre was puffing. She wasn't a young chick any longer.

As they approached the building, Deidre could see what Jeff meant about its construction. The shack was built of six-by-six timbers, each eight feet long. They were laid one layer on top of another, Lincoln-Log style, the corners alternating so the upper level overlapped the one below. Some of the logs were not quite as large, so when they had been slabbed, a few rounded edges remained, giving the cabin the appearance of having been built with a broadaxe.

The shack was small, probably big enough for a couple sets of bunk beds, a small barrel stove, and a table. A deck nearly the size of the building projected toward a small steam that ran in front of it. It looked to Deidre that the whole structure was built of peeled timbers and rough-sawed logs. It fit perfectly with its surroundings.

The deputy and another man were standing away from the shack, and as she and Jeff approached, Deidre recognized only the deputy.

"Hi, Jeff," the coroner called out. "Good to see you again. How's it goin'?" The informal atmosphere struck Deidre as being rather unusual, but she figured the coroner had seen about everything during his career and couldn't be shocked easily.

"Oh, pretty good," Jeff answered. The coroner was new in town, replacing the previous person to hold that office. Deidre didn't recognize him.

"Jim," Jeff said to him, "This is Deidre Johnson. She was sheriff before I got elected. She's one heck of a law enforcement officer. Hope you don't mind that I invited her to come along." Jim extended his hand and assured them that Deidre was welcome. "What do you have here?" Jeff asked.

The coroner tilted his head toward the shack. "Not pretty, that's for sure. I don't think we're looking at foul play, though. Take a look for yourself." Deidre trailed the pair as they trudged up to the deck. The door was open, and Deidre was revolted by the stench before she came close enough to look inside. By Jeff's reaction, she wasn't sure she wanted to look.

Deidre looked inside from the porch. The shack had an open ceiling with two five-inch peeled-log stringers tying the walls together. The walls were hardly seven feet high, so the stringers weren't much more than that. Deidre covered her mouth and nose with a scented tissue.

"Looks like a suicide to me," the coroner opined from just inside the doorway. "Course, we'll know more after an autopsy, but it looks like he hung himself. I think he stood on that stool and cinched the rope tight to the support, then kicked the stool away. If he'd been a little taller, his feet would have touched the floor. No, I think he was determined to kill himself, for whatever reason." He shook his head.

Jeff turned to Deidre. "See anything that might be a link to Maren?" Deidre shook her head. "Well, if you're up to it, let's go inside and look around. Doubt if we'll find anything, but it would be best if we take a look."

Deidre followed him inside. By that time she was becoming immune to the smell. *Funny,* she thought, *how our senses adjust to unpleasant surroundings so quickly.* She tried not to look directly at the corpse hanging from the stringer, but she couldn't avoid it in such close quarters.

She didn't have medical training, but even so, she could tell he had been dead for quite some time. His skin was dark, almost black, and his tissue was shriveled. He reminded Deidre of pictures of mummies she had seen in science magazines. One thing immediately caught her attention and made her question the coroner's judgment. The dead man's hands were bound together behind him, and she was about to say to Jeff that the coroner must be a total idiot to think this was a suicide. She heard a sound and turned to see the "idiot" standing behind her.

"I know what you're thinking," he said. "How could he have hung himself with his hands bound behind his back? I think what he did was fasten a plastic tie around each wrist. Then he got up on the stool and placed the noose around his neck. By feel, he connected the two ties that were already on his wrists with a third, and cinched it tight. The way they're made, once you tighten them down, they lock, and the only way to get them off is to cut the tie. Then he kicked the stool away. He wanted to make sure that at the last minute he couldn't undo what he started. Like I said, he was determined to kill himself."

Deidre still wasn't convinced. "But that would take some pretty nimble fingers. He wasn't Houdini, you know." The coroner didn't take offense.

"No, he wasn't, but he did leave a note on the table." He pointed to a piece of paper that had already been placed in an evidence bag on the table. Deidre had been so trying not to look at the corpse that she hadn't noticed it. "You can read it through the plastic." Deidre picked it up and silently read the man's last words.

> *I've decided I can't go through life this way. I know I've caused a lot of harm to others, and for that I'm sorry. I got what I had coming to me, and maybe I deserve this, too. It's better for everyone this way. My hands will be bound behind my back. I will have done that myself. You can figure out how. I don't want to chicken out at the end. Tell Junior I'm thankful for his friendship.*
> *Jake Burns*

Deidre could barely read the last line through the moisture clouding her vision. "How sad," she said, handing the bag to Jeff. He scanned the writing and said nothing.

It took only a few minutes to look around the one-room shack. Deidre saw nothing that would have been a link to Maren, and she and Jeff walked out to where his vehicle was parked. Not one word was exchanged between them until they were on their way back to town. No matter how hard Deidre tried to get the smell of death out of her nose, it was still there. She pictured her sinuses filled with fumes from the shack.

"I left instructions with the coroner to make sure scrapings are taken from under the nails of the victim, just in case," Jeff said. "But I don't think we're going to find anything related to Maren." They rode again in silence until Jeff said, almost as a thought to himself. "When we get back to town, I'm going to check up on a few loose ends about this guy. I want to be sure to touch all the bases."

# Chapter Twenty

ON THE WAY HOME, Deidre made a mental note to call Dave and tell him about the sex offender's death. She appreciated Jeff letting her ride along, and she more than appreciated his honesty about Dave. For the first time, Deidre had no nagging doubts in the back of her mind.

Jeff had a few more hours to put in, and he stopped at The Pub. The bartender looked at him with a mixture of apprehension and disapproval, but she asked if she could help him. She knew he hadn't stopped in for a beer.

"I'm looking for information about a man, Jake Burns. Do you recognize the name?"

"Nope," she said, not seeming particularly interested.

"How about this. Ever see him?" Jeff slid a picture of Jake across the bar to her.

"Oh, him. Yeah, I've seen him. Used to come in here three, four times a week. Always sat there." She pointed at a chair around the L of the bar. Haven't seen him for quite a while. Want me to give you a call if he comes in?"

Jeff could tell she thought there might be something in it for her, like a reward. "No, that's okay. I doubt if he'll be back." Then he stopped. "Did he ever have friends with him when he was here?"

"Him? Never. He was always alone. The only time I ever saw anybody give him the time of day was when two rednecks gave him a rough time. Called him something, and one gave him a jab in the ribs when they left."

"When was that?"

"Man, must have been one, maybe two months ago. He quit coming in after that."

"Do you remember who the two men were, their names?"

"Sure, everybody knows them. A couple of troublemakers. One is Josh Philips, the other is . . . oh, man, what's his name? Brad . . . Brad . . . Brad . . . Brad Blaten. That's it, Brad Blaten."

Jeff thanked her and was leaving when she called out, "Is there a reward if you find them?"

"We'll be in touch," he said over his shoulder.

Two Harbors is a small town, and it was easy to locate the men. They rented a couple of rooms in a rundown boarding house. When Jeff arrived at their address and walked around back, he spotted two men sitting on a sagging porch. The steps leading up to it looked as if they were ready to collapse from their own weight, and everywhere he looked, paint was peeling from decaying wood surfaces.

Do you know where I can find either Josh Philips or Brad Blaten?" he called up to them.

"That'd be us," one of them said, and he snickered as if something was funny.

"I'm Sheriff Jeff DeAngelo. Would you mind talking to me for a few minutes?"

"That'd be okay with us, Sheriff. Ain't that okay, Brad?" he asked the other.

"Yeah, that'd be okay. Come on up, if you trust them steps." Both men snuffed out what they had been smoking and sat up straighter in their chairs. Jeff sat down in a rickety deck chair that almost tipped over from his weight.

"What can we do for you, Sheriff?" the one who Jeff assumed to be Josh asked. He had an insolent smirk on his face.

"Do either of you know a Jake Burns?" The two men glanced at each other and the smirk disappeared from Josh's face.

"That prevert? What's he done now? Been playing with some little girls?" He snickered, and Jeff's dislike for the man intensified.

"No he's dead. Possibly murdered," he added, thinking that would shake up the two dickheads.

"I have a witness who says you two were giving him a hard time in The Pub. That was shortly before he dropped out of sight. Is that true?"

Brad spit over the railing. "Could be. We don't like those preverts hanging around where we drink. When was this supposed to have happened?"

"A little less than two months ago. Is it true?"

"That damned Sally. She was the only person in there, other than me and Josh, and that prevert. She's the one that told you, ain't it?"

Jeff looked Brad square in the eye and neither man flinched. "It doesn't matter who told me. So it's true you gave him a hard time?"

Josh butted in. "Ain't no crime in that. Just a little foolin' around is all. So what's all the fuss about a dead prevert, anyway? Just saves you some trouble down the line, Sheriff." He emphasized the word "sheriff."

Jeff had about enough of the two. "Can you account for your time between the dates of May fourth to May ninth?"

Josh chuckled, picked out a cigarette from a pack, and lit it. After he had inhaled, he said, "That's a long time ago. And it's quite a bit of time to account for. What about you, Brad? Do you remember what you were doing those days?"

Brad took a drink of amber-colored liquid from the glass he was holding. "Let me think. May what to what?" he asked Jeff.

Jeff was having a difficult time remaining civil, but he had no reason to haul these two sorry specimens in. "May fourth to May ninth," he repeated.

Both men rocked back in their chairs, and Jeff wished one of them would go over backwards. After pretending to try to remember something, Brad spoke up.

"Now I remember. We were down in the Cities. You remember that, Josh. The gun show."

Josh answered. "You know, you're right. We were at a gun show. Lasted three days, and then we did some sightseeing, at night, on Hennepin Avenue." He laughed. "If you know what I mean."

Jeff was revolted by the pair "Is there any way you can prove that?" He knew there had to be, and that they had been ridiculing him and his position.

"Yeah. We stayed with a friend and his girl," Josh said as he dug a cell phone from his pocket. Jeff saw him push a couple of buttons and then say, "Here it is. Call Dick Jackson, 651-555-3274." Jeff had to ask him to repeat it, because he hadn't been ready to write the number down.

"Now get the hell out off our butts," Brad ordered. Both men stared at Jeff, sneers on their faces.

As he made his way down the creaky steps he heard them laughing, and he wished he could go back and bust their heads.

Back at his office, Jeff immediately dialed the number he had been given, expecting no answer, or perhaps an answering machine to pick up."

"Hello," a woman said after the second ring.

Jeff was startled to be talking to a person. "Uh, hello. This is Jeff DeAngelo, sheriff of Lake County, calling." He heard a sharp intake of breath, as though the woman were used to such calls and wondered what this one would be about.

"What do you want?" Jeff almost expected her to finish the question with "this time."

"I understand there was a gun show in the Cities about two months ago. Do you have any recollection of that?"

After a hesitation the woman answered. "Yes. Yes, I do remember that. Why do you ask? I didn't go, and neither did my boyfriend."

"Is your boyfriend's name Dick Jackson?" Jeff asked.

"It is, but like I said, he didn't go."

Jeff felt sorry for the anxiety he was causing. "Please relax. This isn't about you or Dick. Just bear with my questions a bit longer.

You've been very helpful already," he said reassuringly. "Did you have any visitors during that time?"

He could sense by her answer that the woman was not as tense. "We did. That's why I remembered there was a gun show. Two of Dick's high school classmates stayed with us and went to the show." She went on the offensive. "What kind of trouble are they in? I told Dick I'd never let them back in my house again. They gave me the creeps. Dick said they were from his past and that he didn't want them around, either. Did they kill somebody with one of the guns they bought?"

The thought went through Jeff's mind that those two were the kinds who should never be able to get their hands on a gun, but he didn't voice his opinion. "No. If you give me their names, and they match what I've got, the two of them are in the clear."

"One's name was Josh and the other Brad. I never heard their last names and don't care if I ever do. Do you want me to have Dick call you when he gets home from work?"

"I don't think that will be necessary. Do you know where these two guys are from?"

"Two Harbors."

Jeff thanked the woman for her help and said it cleared up an issue for him. He hung up thinking she was a good judge of character.

*****

DEIDRE TRIED TO DO some work in her garden, but she couldn't get the vision of Jake Burns hanging from a rope out of her mind. As she dug weeds from the dirt, she thought of his wizened form hanging like a piece of dried meat. He had looked so small, but then, she thought, his corpse was desiccated, had lost a significant percentage of weight. The image in her mind was so sharp that she could picture the shoes he wore, dirty jogging shoes with the laces untied.

Deidre dug her cell phone out of her pocket, and as she dialed Jeff's number, she looked at her watch. It was 4:49, almost quitting time, and she hoped he was still there.

"Jeff," she said, more abruptly than she had intended. "Do you know what size shoes Jake Burns was wearing when he was found?"

"Well, hi to you, too, Deidre." He was laughing.

"Sorry," she said. "I guess I'm still a little wound up after what we saw today. Anyway, I've been trying to kill some time and had a thought about what he was wearing. Do you know?"

She heard paper being moved near Jeff's phone. "I've got his folder right here. Haven't had time to look at it yet. Just a sec." Deidre waited a few moments while Jeff looked over a one-page report. "He had on Nike running shoes, white-leather uppers," he reported." Here it is, size eight. Not big for a guy. Course, he didn't look to be a large person when we saw him."

Deidre shot her next question at him. "You have casts of the footprints left in the mud by Maren's car, remember? Have you checked to see if they match Jake's shoes?"

"To be honest with you, Deidre, I hadn't given it a thought. Probably should have," he rationalized. "But it's something that has to be done. If I remember, though, the footprints in the mud seemed to be good size. Tell you what, I'm getting ready to pull the pin for the day, and I'll swing down to the evidence room and take a look. Get back to you in a few minutes."

Deidre gave up trying to beautify her garden, stomped the dirt off her feet, and was pouring herself a glass of ice water when her phone rang.

"Hi, Jeff here again. No one has checked out the size of the prints yet, but I've got it right here in front of me. I wear a size eleven and I checked my shoe's sole against the cast. It's at least as large as mine, so I guess that pretty much rules out Jake. His shoes didn't have any red clay on them, and we didn't find any in his place when we searched it. He was probably wearing the only pair of shoes he owned, except for his work boots. We'll keep at it, Deidre. I promise."

She sat on the deck, waiting for Ben to get home and the twins to be delivered from ball practice. A familiar hollow feeling crept over her.

# Chapter Twenty-One

DEIDRE LEFT A MESSAGE on Dave's voicemail, asking if he could come for coffee and dessert that evening. She told him that Jake's body had been found, and if he wanted to talk, she and Ben would be home. Twenty minutes later her phone rang. It was Dave.

"Deidre, thanks for your message," he began, and she thought he sounded out of breath, as if he had been jogging or something. "I called as soon as I checked my voicemail. What did they find out? Do they think Jake had anything to do with Maren?"

Deidre wished she could say yes, the case had been cracked, and now they could have some closure. "No, nothing like that. Ben and I are missing you, so are the boys. We'd like to visit, if you have time. There are a couple of things I'd like you to know about what was found, and we can catch up on what you've been doing."

Dave hemmed and hawed for a second or two, then said he'd change his schedule to make it work. For an instant, Deidre felt like he was doing them a favor, making room to talk to them. She thanked him and went back to nursing her hollowness.

******

IT WAS LATER THAN DEIDRE had planned when she heard Dave pull into their driveway. She heard a car door slam and heard the thump of his footsteps as he crossed the deck. He knocked on the door and waited to be let in. This jarred Deidre a little, and then she realized Dave had always rapped once or twice and walked right in. It was as though she were inviting a stranger into her home.

Dave gave Deidre a cursory hug, barely a light squeeze of her shoulder, and stepped back. "Been a long time," he said. "Is Ben home?" Deidre pointed to the living room and watched him leave the kitchen. She felt she had just been mildly rebuffed.

"Ben, how's it going?" Dave asked as he strode across the floor to where Ben was reclining in his favorite chair. "Don't get up." Deidre entered the room in time to see Dave and Ben shaking hands, Ben still in his chair. She heard Jack and Steve running in the upstairs hallway.

"Dave," they called out as they rumbled down the stairs and threw their arms around him.

"Man, I think you guys have grown since I saw you last. How's baseball going?" After a couple of minutes of small talk, Deidre told the boys it was time for them to begin getting ready for bed. They climbed the stairs, mumbling to each other.

Deidre asked if Dave wanted coffee or iced tea with dessert, and he opted for coffee. She remembered how he drank it. When she returned with their drinks and generous slices of cake on a platter, Dave had made himself at home and was sitting in the chair he usually claimed. Deidre looked at him and was glad Jeff had shared with her what he thought about Dave's involvement—or lack thereof.

"So, you said you had some information to share. Anything significant?" He looked expectant.

"I don't want to go into detail, especially while were eating," said Deidre. She wished he had waited until they had finished with the food.

They ate in silence. When they finished, Deidre began, "Jake's body was found yesterday. Apparently, he committed suicide." She was happy Dave didn't ask about the circumstances. In fact, he didn't act surprised or remorseful, or show any other emotion. Instead, he asked only one question.

"Did he leave a suicide note?"

"He did. It didn't say much. Only that he was sorry for what he had done, and that he couldn't take it anymore, whatever it was."

After a moment of looking at the floor, Dave said rather pensively. "Do you think the thing he was sorry for was Maren's murder?

Maybe guilt was the thing he couldn't take anymore. He did have a history of sexual predation. Wasn't he a registered sex offender?"

For a second Deidre wanted to believe his theory. It would be a comfort to stuff everything about Maren's disappearance into one small box, lock it away where it wouldn't haunt her, and go on living. But she knew the facts.

"The coroner, Jeff, and quite frankly, I, too, don't think there is much doubt of what happened. Jake's crime was committed years ago when he was a kid. Since then he's been a model of decency. He had to live with a lot of guff since his release from prison, and I think his life was so empty he simply couldn't cope any longer. I'm sorry, but that's about all I know. Mostly, I, we, just wanted to get together with you. By the way, Jeff shared with me things pertaining to you." It was like a wave of fear passed over Dave's face, and Deidre kicked herself for having opened her mouth.

"Like, what did he tell you?" Dave blurted out.

Deidre was in too deep to back out now. "He said after Maren disappeared, you were his primary suspect."

"I really expected that." Dave interjected. He laughed self-consciously. "I've watched enough TV mysteries to know it's always the husband or boyfriend." Then he quickly wanted to know what Jeff had said.

"He said he had made a thorough investigation of you, even searched your car and your apartment. He also said that he thought your panic and grief was genuine, and that there is no doubt in his mind that you had no part in Maren's being missing."

Deidre saw Dave's shoulders visibly relax. "How about you, Deidre, or Ben? Does that change how you feel about me?"

She hadn't seen that question coming and was relieved when Ben came to the rescue. "I have to admit, and I'm guessing Deidre does too, that we had a sliver of doubt. We haven't talked about it, and this is the first time it's come up." Deidre nodded. "But I think I can speak for the both of us," he continued. "We didn't want you to be the one.

We really love you and want to remain friends. It's like you're a connection to Maren. Hearing what Jeff told Deidre this morning only reinforces what we wanted to believe, *do* believe."

Dave rested back in his chair. It seemed as if his body drained of pent-up tension, and his eyes misted. "Thank you," was all he said. There was a period when the three of them sat silently, and Deidre could hear the ticking of the wall clock. Dave looked at his watch.

"Gosh, I hate to say this, but I've got to be at work early tomorrow. Thanks so much for everything, but I'd better be going." This time he hugged Deidre like it meant something.

After he left, Deidre noticed that Dave had hardly touched his cake and drank only a few sips of coffee. "I feel sorry for him," she said to Ben. "I think he's lost a lot of weight since we saw him last. Look at this. It's his favorite cake, and he hardly touched it. I hope he's okay."

Together, they straightened up the living room and made their way upstairs.

# Chapter
## Twenty-Two

In a way, Deidre envied the other members of her family. Ben had the routine of work. True, when he left the house each morning, his step lacked enthusiasm and his shoulders sagged, but at least he had something to do to keep his hands and his mind busy.

The boys were, well, boys, and although Deidre knew kids had a knack for burying their troubles and pretending nothing was wrong, she knew they, too, had a piece of their lives missing. But they had each other in their own make-believe world. She watched them play by the river, capturing minnows in a homemade trap, chasing down a hapless frog and kissing it to see if it would turn into a princess, exploring a world that to them was new every day.

Megan had her routine in Duluth. As she gained experience, she had moved up from chief test tube and beaker washer and now was actually working with a researcher. She put in long hours, but at least she was busy—and with other people.

Dave had gained status with the accounting firm, partly because of his ability, mostly because of his work ethic. It seemed every time Deidre called to invite him to dinner or a family occasion, he was going to be working late, had just gotten home from work, or had a similar excuse for not joining them.

But—and Deidre knew it was her own fault for withdrawing—she had too much time to brood. After Ben left for work and the neighbor picked up Jack and Steve for ball practice, she wandered down to the river. She tended to avoid their favorite picnic spot, but found a new clump of cedars to sit under. They were so close to the river that at one location the swirling water washed a few roots clean. Sometimes she sat in the coolness for an hour or more.

It had been a long time since she spoke to Pastor Ike and he had shared his theology with her. She grappled with the idea of a God who wasn't all-knowing, who couldn't cause good things to happen, who couldn't prevent bad things from happening. All this made her wonder who, or what, God really was. Did God even exist? If God could have prevented what happened to Maren and didn't, what was the reason? *If there is a reason, it better be a damn good one,* she thought.

Eventually, she would get tired of trying to find answers and return to the house. Perhaps she would work in her garden a little, fix a sandwich for lunch, watch the mid-day news on TV while she ate, and begin to think about what to fix for supper. Maren was never far from her mind.

Deidre knew she should be getting out more than she was, that she was rapidly becoming a recluse, and that wasn't healthy. But she had never been a tea-time person. She had tried to be a part of a group of women from church who met at Louise's Café once a week, but their conversations about hemlines and heel height bored her to distraction. She didn't particularly like the idea of getting a job that required her to be on a schedule, and the idea of volunteering didn't appeal to her, either. She couldn't picture herself visiting residents in a nursing home, and even that made her feel guilty.

Today, she followed her lonely routine. It was time to start supper, and she was going to make one of Ben's favorites, pasties. She had already rolled out the dough for the crust and was in the process of chopping the vegetables for the filling. The two halves of a rutabaga lay on her cutting board, and Deidre was getting ready to quarter it and then reduce it to half-inch cubes when an idea struck her. She put down the knife she was wielding and sat down at the table.

She began to doodle on a pad of paper. Deidre had always been a doodler—did her best thinking with a pencil in her hand. She absentmindedly began marking the paper while she thought, then realized she was drawing a crude map of the Drummond Road. As the pencil moved, a latent idea from somewhere in her mind came to the forefront.

"Whoever left those tracks in the mud on the Spooner Road must have had a way back to town. That means whoever drove Maren's car back there and left it either had an accomplice or hitched a ride." Deidre realized she was talking out loud to herself and half smiled.

"What if whoever did this walked out to the main road? That'd be about an hour-and-a-half hike. Maybe he intended to follow the Drummond to the paved road and hitch a ride from there." *Or maybe he's a runner, someone who could cover ten miles in a couple of hours,* she thought.

Deidre returned to chopping the rutabaga, carrots, and potatoes. It was a miracle she didn't slice a finger off. She was busy formulating a plan.

# Chapter
## Twenty-Three

BEN DOVE INTO HIS pasty as if he hadn't eaten for a week, and Deidre almost laughed. It was good to see his appetite returning. He had lost so much weight after Maren disappeared that she had begun to be concerned. But then, when she looked in the mirror, she could see the same hollow eyes and sunken cheeks in her reflection. Ben finished one pasty and helped himself to half of another. Steve and Jack never needed an excuse to gorge themselves, and they ate with an intensity possessed only by growing boys. Deidre had invited Dave, but he said he was at the office and wouldn't be home until after nine. She was beginning to wonder why he didn't move to Duluth so he didn't have to do so much driving.

After supper, she and Ben took a walk, as they so often did. They enjoyed the physical contact of holding hands, but the best part of it was they could talk without being interrupted. Deidre couldn't begin to count the number of problems they had worked out while wandering up the road.

The late July sounds were comforting and ominous at the same time—comforting because they fit the rhythm of nature, ominous because they foretold the coming of fall. Deidre moved closer to Ben and threaded her arm through the crook of his.

"I thought a lot about Maren today," she said. "Wondered if they'll ever catch the . . . murderer." They walked several more steps. Ben didn't answer. "Had an idea I might follow up on. Somebody abandoned her car in the woods, then walked out to the Drummond, remember? Of course you remember," she said, realizing she had asked a rhetorical question. "Anyway, whoever came out needed a ride into town. It's at least ten miles. I got to thinking, what if we put up some posters along the Drummond Road asking if anyone might have seen a man hitchhiking during the week Maren was taken? What do you think?"

"It will be a long shot. First of all, it's been over two months since it happened. Most people don't remember what happened yesterday. Second, he probably would have been out on the road at night, or at least late evening. It's so desolate nobody drives out there then."

Deidre's heart began to sink, and she anticipated him saying it was probably a far fetched idea. Ben continued.

"But I say go for it. We're going to catch a break sometime, and we don't know from where its going to come. Maybe we'll get lucky. You gonna to tell Jeff?"

Deidre said she thought he had enough to worry about without her going vigilante, but she would. Before they arrived home, she had designed the poster in her mind. All she had to do was transfer the design to her computer.

*****

AS SOON AS BEN LEFT for work the next morning, she woke up her computer and typed out the format for a poster. When she finished, she realized that it wasn't very catchy, but thought it would have to do. She wanted to get rolling on her project. As her printer was spitting out the copies, she pulled one out of the stack so she could examine it.

WANTED

Information Relating to a Missing Person

Did you or anyone you know see a man walking on the
Drummond Road at night during the first week of May?
This person may have been involved in an abduction.
If you have any information, call Deidre Johnson.
Phone: (218) 555-6120

In minutes she had a stack of twenty-five, all she thought would be needed.

"Boys," she called. "We're going to take a ride. Jump in the car. Let's go."

"What's up?" Jack wanted to know. This was an unexpected event.

"We're going to take a ride to Stewart Lake. Maybe a little farther. I've got some notices I want to put up this morning. Should be fun. You guys can wade around by the boat landing for a little while if you'd like." She thought it wouldn't hurt to use a carrot.

Deidre counted how many places she'd put up the posters, and by the time they reached the turnoff to the lake, she had mentally reached her quota. Four miles in, they came to a hill and as they crested it, she could see blue water ahead. The wheels of the car had hardly stopped rolling before Steve and Jack spilled out of the backseat and were heading to the reeds along the shore.

She took a couple of posters from the folder lying on the front seat and picked up the stapler she brought with. To the side of the boat ramp was a sign on which had been tacked warnings by the DNR to clean off boats and trailers. Another said to not dump minnows in the lake. Still another asked anglers to refrain from using lead weights. Deidre moved one of them to make room for her poster and drove staples into its corners to hold it in place. Then she stapled another to a large tree near by.

She watched her sons lying on their bellies on the dock, and Jack fished a branch out of the water. "Mom, look at this," he called.

Deidre went over to see what they had. Jack held the branch in front of her face, too close for her eyes to focus on it. She pushed it away so she could see.

"See that green stuff? Our science teacher brought a sample like this to school last spring. Feel it."

Deidre gently squeezed the mass, expecting it to be slimy, but instead she felt it crunch between her fingers.

"Our teacher said this is a freshwater sponge, and what you felt crunching between your fingers was its skeleton that's made out of tiny glass spikes. Pretty neat, huh?"

"Pretty neat," Deidre agreed. She roughed up Jack's hair, and he looked up at her, a smile creasing his summer-tanned face. She thought this was the most beautiful moment of the summer.

"Okay, guys, we've got more of these to put up. Let's get going." Before they got in the car, she saw the boys go over and read what her poster said. The magic was broken, and everyone was quiet as Deidre started the car.

She tacked another poster to a wooden post beside the road near the stop sign, hoping that if anyone looked for oncoming traffic they'd see it. She put up posters near every intersection, anywhere that traffic was forced to slow down. An hour later, they were home. The boys decided to dig worms and try catching creek chubs in the river. Deidre walked to her favorite spot under the cedar trees.

*God, if you do anything, let the right person see my signs.* She sat for another twenty minutes and decided to catch up with her sons. They wouldn't be boys forever, and she was missing some of the best times of their lives at home.

# Chapter
## Twenty-Four

TWO DAYS AFTER SHE and the boys put up the posters, she began to wonder what response she might get, if any. At times during the day, the thought didn't cross her mind as she went about her daily routine. She attended a ball game the boys played and cheered along with the other moms and dads. Jack was more of a natural, but Steve seemed to have more of a competitive edge about him. Deidre was glad things evened out, and on the way home she was able to find enough good things to say about their games that each boy was validated.

Her afternoon was spent cleaning berries they had picked the day before, and then it was time to make supper, something she hadn't planned ahead for. She scrambled to throw together a meal of some leftovers and fresh food. They had almost finished with dinner when her cell phone rang.

"Always," she grumbled. "Why do those telemarketers always call at mealtime?" She slid back from the table and searched for her phone.

*They call at mealtime because they know we'll be home,* Ben thought, but wisely kept his mouth shut. He heard Deidre answer the call.

"Hello." There was a long pause, and he could tell Deidre was trying to place what the call was about. Then he heard her voice become sharper. "Oh. Oh, yes. This is she. . . . Oh, I'm sorry. I wasn't expecting a call so soon. . . . I put them up only two days ago. . . . Yes, yes, by all means. Do you want me to come into town, or would you like to drive out here? . . . I appreciate your concern so much. Do you know where we live? . . . Right, just go west out of town toward the airport. . . . Yes, that's the place. Right after you pass the large farm. We'll be waiting for you. Thank you so much."

Ben tried to make sense of the call from Deidre's reaction, but he couldn't guess to whom she spoke.

"What was that about?" he called from the table.

"Quick, get the table cleared off. He'll be here in less than twenty minutes."

Ben was moving, and he nodded his head at Jack and Steve that they better hop to or there might be trouble.

"Who's going to be here?"

Deidre looked at Ben with an air of exasperation. "Him. The guy who picked up the runner."

Within minutes, the dirty dishes were in the dishwasher, the table was wiped clean, and Deidre was sliding the chairs into place.

"Deidre, slow down, and get me caught up. I'm not sure what you're talking about, and I'd like to know before 'he' gets here."

Deidre realized she was so flustered she didn't know quite what she was saying. Deidre took a deep breath. "I told you the boys and I put up posters the day before yesterday." She looked at Ben like she expected him to say he hadn't been listening. "I had on the poster that if anyone had information about a hitchhiker on the Drummond last May to call me. He just did, Ben. He just did! He's coming here to tell us what he knows." She thought a minute and asked, "Should I call Jeff and have him come out, too?"

Ben tried to soothe her. "Listen, dear, by the time Jeff got here, if he's even around, we'd have had to entertain this guy. Let's just have some soft drinks for him, hear what he has to say, get his name and phone number. If we think what he has to say is important, then we call Jeff. Okay?"

Without answering him, Deidre said to the boys, "Somebody important will be here soon. I want you to go to your room and play video games or something. Just do me a favor and stay out of the way for a while. If it gets late, you know the drill. And be sure to brush your teeth before getting in bed. I'll change sheets tomorrow, so don't worry about taking a shower tonight."

Steve looked at Jack and they smiled at each other, not knowing what was so important but thankful for the carte blanche they had just been handed. Though Ben and Deidre had decided the boys had a right to know what was going on, they would wait to share the information until they knew whether it had any bearing on Maren's disappearance.

Deidre tried to calm herself, but her hands were shaking. She filled an ice bucket with cubes and set out a couple cans of soda. After sticking her head out the door to test the weather, she decided they would be comfortable on the deck, and she and Ben sat on the swing. As they slowly moved back and forth, she thought of all the meetings that had taken place there the past summer. None of them had made any difference.

She watched as a pickup truck slowed and then pulled into their driveway. It was a club-cab, probably a three-quarter-ton model. She could hear the clatter of its valves, a diesel. The driver climbed out and ambled across the lawn to where they sat, and Ben invited him to come up on the deck. He accepted a glass of ice and poured himself a diet drink.

Deidre wanted to yell, "Well, what do you know?" but she restrained herself. "Hi, Mr. Samuelsen?" she asked as she extended her hand, which he shook with a firm but not uncomfortable grip. Deidre liked that kind of handshake. "You saw my poster. Which one?"

"My boy and I were fishing on Stewart Lake. We go there probably once a week. Fishing wasn't good today so we came in early. Saw your notice on the board by the boat landing, and thought I'd better give you a call."

Before Deidre could rush in, Ben took over the questioning. "We'd sure like to know what you remember. How is it that you remember that far back? It was months ago."

"I remember the day perfectly. It was one of the first evenings my boy had free. He's in track, and they always had practice or a meet. He made it to state this year," he added proudly. "Anyway, it was three weeks before the section meet. I know that for sure, and the perch were almost jumping into the boat."

Deidre was getting jumpy, and she nearly blurted out, "Get to the damn point," but she held her tongue. Mr. Samuelsen continued.

"Anyway, we were late getting off the lake, dark, and we could barely see to tie the boat down on the trailer. Mosquitoes. I tell you, they about carried us away. Eventually, we got the boat strapped down. By the time we got rolling it must have been almost ten o'clock. Anyway, when we got just past the Spooner Road, we saw this guy jogging on the side of the road. He was trotting along at a fairly good pace. Now, I know most people don't just go jogging for fun that time of night. Figured he must have had car trouble and was trying to get back to town. I rolled down my window as we came up on him, but he just kept jogging. Never missed a stride. I asked if he needed a lift, and finally he stopped. Wasn't breathing hard. He said his car had broken down, just as I suspected, and that he'd take a lift out to the highway, where he could thumb a ride to his house."

Ben glanced at Deidre, and with his look tried to convey the idea that they should let Mr. Samuelson keep talking.

"Anyway," the man continued, "he climbed in the back of the cab. Didn't say anything the whole way. We let him out when we hit the blacktop, where the road Ts. He went left. We went right. That's the last we saw of him."

Deidre could stay still no longer. "Can you describe the man for us?" She hardly got the question out when he shook his head.

"It was really dark that night, and the interior light is burned out in my truck, so I couldn't get a good look at him. He had on a baseball cap pulled down low over his eyes. I remember that. Anyway, I know I couldn't pick him out in a lineup, if that's what you're thinking."

Deidre wasn't, but before she could say anything, Ben asked a question. "What was he built like? Could you tell?"

Mr. Samuelson thought for a moment. "When I stopped, he was silhouetted in the headlights. I'd say he wasn't huge, but not small, either. You know, kinda tall, athletic, like a runner who was in good shape."

"That's good," Ben reinforced the observation. "Do you remember anything about his cap that might be different?"

Again, Mr. Samuelson took his time answering. He said. "Well, now that you mention it, there was an emblem on the front, above the bill. The thread that had been used was almost florescent, you know, like blaze orange, but this wasn't orange, it was yellow. The emblem might have been crossed hockey sticks. . . . No, on second thought, it might have been crossed golf clubs . . . or even crossed baseball bats. I don't know. Anyway, I know it was a shiny yellow something."

"Is there anything else you can remember about that night? It's very important to us," Deidre added.

"Only that the guy made a mess in my pickup. His shoes must have been covered with mud, because gobs of the stuff dropped off while we rode. I think his pants were coated, too, because there are mud smears on the seat."

Deidre jumped at what he said. "You said 'are.' 'There *are*.'"

"Did I? I don't know."

"Mr. Samuelsen, is the mud still in your pickup?"

He looked a little sheepish. "Yeah, I guess it is. It's in the back seat, and, well, I'm not a clean freak." He chuckled. "I've got a lot of fishing junk back there and never took time to unload it all and sweep out the mess."

Deidre could have hugged the messy fisherman. "Mr. Samuelson, would it be okay if we looked in your pickup? If we find some mud, we'd like to take a sample of it."

Samuelson was taken aback by Deidre's enthusiastic entreaty. "Well . . . sure. Take all the mud you want." Then he added, "You can even take out the floor mats and clean them for me." He laughed.

Deidre rushed into the house and came back with a handful of unused Zip-Lock bags. It was difficult for Ben to keep up with her, and he caught her hand just before she opened the club-cab door.

"Hey, wait up," he said, a little more sharply than intended. "At least put on a pair of rubber gloves before you start rummaging around."

"Right," Deidre said, and raced back to the house. All she could find was a pair of gloves designed for cleaning toilet bowls. She quickly tore open the package and was back at the pickup in no time.

The seat was piled high with waders, bait buckets, and an assortment of other fishing paraphernalia, which she stacked as neatly as she could on the ground. Eventually, she worked her way down to the floor mats. Samuelson stood nearby, not quite sure what was going on. He watched as Deidre gently placed chunks of dried clay into bags, then took a roll of scotch tape from her pocket. She pulled off a strip, patted it on the seat, and bagged the strip. She repeated the process several times. When she was done and she and Ben had replaced the fishing gear, she turned to Samuelson.

"I need to ask one more favor of you. The sheriff will be contacting you tomorrow. Would you be willing to tell him everything you've told us?"

"Yeah, that'd be okay," he answered. "I get off work at four. Anytime after that would be all right." Deidre thanked him profusely and told him how grateful she was for his cooperation. Ben shook his hand.

"Well, anyway," Mr. Samuelson said, "I better get going. My boy was cleaning up the boat when I left, and he's going to think I was stalling until he finished."

Deidre and Ben watched as he drove away. "I'm going to call Jeff. Then let's go get a sample of the mud where we found Maren's car so we can make a comparison."

Ben laughed, and it registered in Deidre's mind how seldom he did that anymore. "Easy, there, Sherlock. I'm as anxious as you to get moving on this, but it would be dark by the time we got there. Let Jeff take it from here. You've done your part." As they stood in the driveway, he wrapped his arms around her. "Thank you."

Deidre felt the warmth of his chest but forced herself to push away. "Come on. I'm calling Jeff."

She rushed to the house, Ben trailing at a slower pace. It took only a few minutes to tell the sheriff what had transpired, and she could tell by his tone that he thought this was a significant break. After asking for Samuelson's phone number, he said he'd be out early the next day to pick up the samples and take them to the forensics lab. As soon as she hung up, she dialed another number. By this time, Ben was standing beside her.

"Dave. I had to call you right away. We've located the person who picked up the guy who left Maren's car in the woods." She realized she wasn't being totally coherent, but was so excited her words couldn't keep up with her thoughts. "Yeah, that's right.... Sure, come right out. I'm so wound up I'm not going to be able to sleep tonight, anyway." In her giddiness she realized she had used the "anyway" like Samuelson did. *Anyway,* she thought and giggled under her breath. *Who cares?*

Dave must have gotten into his car immediately after hanging up and must have broken the speed limit all the way. It seemed only minutes passed before Deidre saw the headlights of his car turn into their drive. He burst into the kitchen, out of breath.

Before either Deidre or Ben could say anything, Dave blurted, "Tell me what you found out."

They went into the living room, and Dave perched expectantly on the edge of a lounger. Ben let Deidre relay the news.

"But he couldn't ID the guy he picked up?" Dave asked, a hint of impatience in his voice.

"He said it was a dark night and that the dome light in his cab was burned out. All he could give us was the general build of the guy. That's about all he had, but those mud samples in his truck might confirm that he was the guy."

She saw Dave's shoulders sag and he sat back his chair, which she took to be a sign of dejection.

"I'm sorry if I got your hopes up, Dave," she said. "But this is something. If I learned anything in law enforcement, it's that one small thing adds to another and soon it snowballs. Sooner or later, we'll find out what happened."

Dave stuck around longer than usual, and Deidre could tell he was becoming more relaxed the longer they talked. She felt sorry for him, thinking of how lonely he must be. For an instant, she remembered the panic she felt for months after her fiancé had been killed when she was young and still the county sheriff. *I got over it; so will he,* she thought.

# Chapter Twenty-Five

JEFF STOPPED BY AT NINE the next morning to pick up the samples Deidre had collected. "You want to ride with? I'm heading out to gather more mud samples from where Maren's car was abandoned. I know the lab's already analyzed the samples we took before, but we want to be absolutely sure."

Deidre slipped into a pair of hiking boots and got in his SUV. It wasn't long before they were bumping over the rocks on the Spooner Road.

"There!" She pointed to the spot where she had discovered the footprints in the mud and where Jeff had made the casts. Jeff stopped and they got out. What had been mud was now completely dry. Deidre picked her way over the cracked surface.

"I can still see where the tracks were," she said excitedly. "This clay holds an imprint for a long time. Once it dries like this, it's almost as hard as brick."

Jeff followed her and agreed with her assessment. Even though the sharp outline of the tracks was deteriorated, the impressions were still visible. It would be no problem taking samples from where he had made the casts of the original evidence, but when he was securing samples of the clay, he wondered aloud if it was much use.

"Deidre, I hate to put a damper on your enthusiasm, but I hope you understand that even if the samples from Samuelson's truck match the clay from this spot, it won't prove much. Without him being able to identify the person he picked up that night, we won't have much to go on."

Deidre reflected on what Jeff said. "Yes, but isn't it better to have some evidence rather than none? Sooner or later the pieces will come together, and this might be one of those pieces."

On the way back to her house, Deidre was silent for some time.

"Dave came over last night," she said to Jeff.

"Did you tell him about Samuelson?

"I called him right after I called you. He was so excited to hear the news he asked to come out. He made it in record time. I'm surprised one of your deputies didn't pick him up for speeding."

"How did he take the news about Samuelson picking up a jogger?" Jeff asked rather matter-of-factly.

"I felt sorry for him," Deidre said. "He seemed so concerned, anxious, I'd say, to find out if this was the key that would unlock the mystery. When I told him that Samuelson didn't get a good look at the man, his whole demeanor changed. It was almost as if the tension left his body. I think he anticipated hearing that Samuelson could provide information to a sketch artist or something. You know how it is these days. Everybody watches murder mysteries on TV and think what they see is reality." She gave a short laugh. "Seriously, I think he was expecting a whole lot more. Maybe I sounded too excited on the phone, and that got his hopes up. He's a good kid who's gone through a lot. But I suppose he'll make it, like the rest of us will."

Jeff dropped her off at home, and before pulling away, rolled down his window to say a few words.

"I didn't mean to sound so negative back there. These dirt samples might be important. We don't know, and that's why I'm taking this seriously. I'll be in touch as soon as the lab reports come back. By the way, I'm meeting Samuelson after work tonight. We want to get his statement on record. He seems like a pretty good guy, at least from our conversation on the phone this morning. Take care." He drove away, leaving her standing by the mailbox.

*****

TWO DAYS WENT BY and still no message came from Jeff. Deidre knew that lab tests took time. Because Maren's apparent abduction was becoming at best a lukewarm case, she also knew that the tests would be moved to the bottom of the lab's work list. Still, it was difficult for her to be patient. That's why when her phone rang and the caller ID showed the call was from Jeff, she was in such a hurry to answer she fumbled the phone. She picked it up and answered.

"Jeff, what do you have?" she asked without even saying hello.

"Deidre, can you come into town right away? I've got something to tell you. We might be driving to Duluth, and if we do, is there any chance Ben could meet us at the St. Louis County Jail?"

Deidre's heart jumped. "Of course! Can you tell me what's up? Dang, the boys are at the river, fishing, and I'll have to round them up. Can this wait that long? Oh, and I'll have to get them to their grandparents before I can leave town?"

"Deidre. Slow down. What I have to tell you will wait. I've got some stuff to get done in the office. Be here in an hour or so, and I'll fill you in on what's happened."

Deidre ran to the river, glad that she knew the boy's favorite fishing hole. They turned in fear as she came crashing through the brush. They thought it had to be a pretty big animal coming after them.

"Gather up your stuff," she urged. "I've got to get into town. Jeff called and said he wants to see me. Hurry, now. We don't have a lot of time."

On the way into town, the boys wanted to know if Jeff had found out what happened to Maren. Deidre said she didn't know, but she suspected that was what he called about. She dropped the boys off at their grandparents' and was in Jeff's office less than an hour after his call.

Deidre stood at the locked door of the sheriff's office, waiting to be buzzed in. When she was finally granted entrance, she rushed through the door. Jeff was waiting for her.

"Let's head to Duluth, and along the way, I'll fill you in on what I know so far," he said in greeting. It took only seconds for them to reach his vehicle, and in minutes they were out of town, heading to Duluth on Highway 61.

"Here's what we have. A Two Harbors man was arrested by the Duluth police after raping a young woman. That happened two days ago. She was parked at Brighten Beach, watching the moon rise over the lake. Not a smart thing to do alone," he added. "But that doesn't excuse what he did to her. The suspect, Jamie Storder, sneaked up behind her car, crept around to the passenger side and forced his way in. He raped her and choked her, then dumped her body out of the car. He thought she was dead. Then he drove her car out of town and up the Homestead Road, where he ditched it on a logging road. Storder then tried hitchhiking back to Duluth. That's where he lives now. A St. Louis County deputy stopped him to see if he needed help, but he acted so suspicious that the deputy took a closer look. Storder had scratches all over his face and hands."

Deidre cut in. "There had to be more than that. You can't pick somebody up for walking beside the road, or because he has scratches on his face."

"True, but you can bring someone in if they match the description of a suspect. The girl he thought he killed? She lived. She was found by a couple of teens who had come to Brighten Beach to watch the submarine races in the moonlight. They called 911. She was able to give a pretty good description of her attacker. She also had a lot of her attacker's skin under her fingernails. When the deputy saw all the deep scratches on his face, that was enough reason to stop Storder and search him. Seems he also had a small packet of meth on him. We're going to question him about Maren."

Deidre was pensive. In a way, she wanted this man to be Maren's abductor. On the other hand, she didn't. The way things stood, there was always a chance her daughter would be found, alive.

"One thing doesn't fit," she voiced her opinion. "This girl was left for dead in a spot where she would surely be found. And it seems to me to be a crime of opportunity. Maren's abduction seems to have been planned out, more deliberate, don't you think?"

"I know what you're saying, but I've checked around. Storder comes back to Two Harbors quite regularly. I showed his picture to the waitresses at the restaurant where Maren worked. He frequented the place often enough that they recognized him. I think this is the best lead we've had yet."

By that time, Jeff and Deidre had reached the St. Louis County jail, and she recognized Ben's SUV sitting in the parking lot. He was waiting in the lobby.

"Ben, good to see you," Jeff said as he clapped him on the shoulder. "Let's go in. I've made arrangements for the two of you to watch as I interview this guy. This is a pretty modern place, and they have a comfortable viewing area on the other side of the glass."

Everyone was ushered to their places by jail personnel. Ben and Deidre sat near a one-way window. They could see in, but those on the other side couldn't see out. Through an intercom, they heard Jeff's chair scrape on the floor as he pulled it back from a table and sat down. In minutes, a guard entered with the prisoner. He was shackled. Deidre immediately noted that he looked athletic, perhaps six-two and slim. She could picture him being a runner.

Both she and Ben had expected him to look like a burned-out meth addict, but that wasn't the case. He was clean-shaven and his hair was neatly cut. The guard attached his handcuffs to a ring anchored in the tabletop. Storder was defiant, staring directly at Jeff.

"My name is Jeff DeAngelo, sheriff of Lake County. I'd like to ask you a couple of questions." Storder smirked and held out his hands palms up, a motion Deidre took to mean "Go ahead." Jeff continued. "The beginning of May, a young lady disappeared in Two Harbors."

Before he could continue, Storder asked, "So, what's that got to do with me?"

"I've checked. You grew up in Two Harbors."

"So did a lot of guys."

"You get back there quite a bit. Maybe once every two weeks or so."

"Yeah, well, even I know it's not a crime to visit your hometown."

Deidre thought Jeff was doing a remarkable job of not losing his cool. "I've checked at the restaurant and bar where this young woman was a waitress." Deidre cringed when he said "was." Jeff continued. "Employees say you spend quite a bit of time there when you're in town."

"It's a great place to sit and have a few. Great view of the lake, not too crowded. Peaceful, if you know what I mean." He grinned at Jeff, and Deidre felt Ben squirm in his chair beside her.

"This young lady disappeared the second week of May."

Storder interrupted Jeff. "You're wasting your time, Sheriff. I don't think you're going to charge me with anything right now. You're just on a fishing expedition, because if you had anything against me but a guess, you'd be reading me my rights by now."

"We've got the testimony of the guy who picked you up the night you got rid of her car," Jeff bluffed, watching for a reaction.

Storder didn't flinch. "Oh, yeah. And he identified me?"

Jeff didn't answer.

"Now how about you quit wasting your time and mine? I got other problems right now." Storder smirked, and Deidre saw Jeff's shoulders tense. He called for the guard to take the prisoner away.

In the parking lot, Jeff said to Deidre and Ben, "I'm sorry to have drug you down here for that. Damn, I was hoping he'd give some kind of reaction, but he's a tough nut to crack. He seemed pretty cocksure of himself. If he's bluffing, he's better at it than I am. Did either of you get a read on anything that I missed?"

Deidre laid her hand on his arm. "Hey, nothing to be sorry about. Thank you for what you're doing. We know you haven't given up on Maren's case. If this had worked out, it would have put a lot of ghosts to rest. I appreciate your keeping us in the loop. Thank you." She gave her friend and former colleague a hug. Ben put his arm around Jeff's shoulders and mumbled, "Yeah, thanks."

Ben decided to call it a day and go home, and Deidre rode with him. She opened the sunroof and let the August air blow through her hair. She closed her eyes and became lost in her thoughts.

"I don't know what to think anymore, Deidre. Secretly, I was hoping he'd deny any involvement with Maren. Then I wished he'd have confessed and the whole thing would be over. Now I'm back to hoping it's proven that Storder had nothing to do with it. That way I can go on believing Maren is still alive somewhere and that she's going to be rescued any day. Sometimes, in the evening, when I'm sitting alone outside, I think I see her walking up the driveway to me. That must sound insane to you."

Deidre sat more upright, and the wind from the open sunroof caused her blonde hair to whip around her face.

"Right now, nothing you think is insane. Everything about Maren's disappearance is insane, but you aren't. None of us are. Believe me, I know," she thought of Ben's first wife, "and so do you. There's a fine line between grief and insanity. After John was killed, my world fell apart. I'm sure yours did too, after Jenny died. What's different for me this time, is that I have you, and I hope you feel the same way about me." She paused. "Awhile ago, I talked to Pastor Ike."

Before she could continue, Ben took his eyes off the road and looked at her for an instant. "You did?" he asked, surprised. "What did you talk about?"

"I wanted to know where I would get the strength to make it through this time. Know what he said?" She continued before Ben could respond. "He quoted something from the Bible. I don't remember his exact words, but they were something like this. 'A single cord might be strong, but a three-strand rope is almost impossible to break.' Then he said you and I are two strands. He urged me to let God be the third. Honestly, I don't know how to do that, but I know you and I are a two-strand rope. Throw in the boys and Megan, we add a few more cords. We've got Jeff and Danielle, other friends, and Pastor Ike. We'll make it through. We have no other choice."

Deidre reached over and rubbed Ben's arm, and she saw he was silently weeping for his lost daughter.

# Chapter Twenty-Six

IT WAS A RESTLESS NIGHT for Deidre. Ben quickly drifted off to sleep, but she lay awake, listening to his regular breathing. Once in awhile he would mutter, and she figured he was having a bad dream. Deidre first turned to lie on her right side and curled her knees into a fetal position. Minutes later she flopped to her left side and stretched her legs out. That wasn't comfortable, either. Eventually she ended up on her back, her head propped up on the folded pillow, staring at the ceiling, which reflected the dim illumination of their night light. Deidre tried, but couldn't stop the thoughts that streamed through her mind.

Jamie Storder certainly fit the profile of a person who could have abducted and done away with Maren. She visualized his callousness and the sneer on his face when Jeff was interviewing him, and she found herself becoming agitated when she recalled his words. She wondered why, if he wasn't guilty, he hadn't denied any involvement. Then she thought he might be just the kind of person who would try to cause as much distress to as many people as he could, like making her and Ben think they might be looking at their daughter's assailant.

Her mind wandered to their decision the past evening not to call Dave and tell him about Storder. She and Ben had decided there was no use getting him worked up over a lead that seemed to be a dead end.

Deidre thought of something Megan had told her about the women's shelter and Maren, and then her mind flitted to Dave's jacket still hanging in the back of the downstairs coat closet. She'd try to remember to give it to him the next time he came to see them.

She looked at the clock, which read 2:51 a.m. She still hadn't fallen asleep, so she slipped out of bed, careful not to disturb Ben, and quietly made her way to the kitchen. She was preparing a cup of chamomile tea when she sensed someone looking at her, and she turned to see Ben standing in the doorway.

"Couldn't sleep, huh? he asked.

"Not a wink. Thought I'd better get up before I woke you. Didn't work, I guess."

Ben sat on one of the stools and rested his elbows on the breakfast bar. "I was awake when you got out of bed. Had a dream that Jamie Storder was ready to confess to Maren's murder, but at the last minute he laughed at everybody in the room and said, 'Sorry, folks. I was just foolin' with your heads.' I woke up just before you left and couldn't get back to sleep."

"Want a cup of tea?" Deidre offered. "It's chamomile. Supposed to help you sleep. Seems like all it ever does for me is make me need the bathroom, but I thought I'd give it a try tonight."

"Sure. Why not. Like they say, the family that runs together, stays together."

They sat up for the next hour, talking. Deidre had come to a conclusion she decided to share with Ben.

"I'm going about nuts waiting for something to break on Maren's disappearance, and I've decided I can't be passive any longer. I'm going to start looking into things on my own. I'll start by talking to the waitresses and waiters at the restaurant. Maybe I can get a better handle on this Storder guy. Also, I want to check with Megan about something she said a long time ago. She told me she thought Maren had an appointment scheduled with the women's shelter a while ago. When I checked with the shelter, the person answering the phone knew nothing about it, or couldn't tell me about it. I want to find out if Megan told me that or if I just imagined it. Then, too, I think we made a mistake not telling Dave about Storder. He deserves to know, and I'm going to invite him to dinner tonight so we can fill him in.

We haven't seen him for quite a few days, and I'd kind of like to make sure he's doing okay."

Ben and Deidre finally decided to go back to bed, and they managed a couple hours of sleep before the alarm went off.

*****

DEIDRE STUMBLED AROUND the kitchen thinking she must look like a zombie, if there was such a thing. Her eyes were puffy and her hair was a mess. Ben was no better. He sat at the table, a bowl of cold cereal in front of him, and stared at it for several seconds before picking up his spoon. Black coffee didn't help a bit. Both of them silently lamented the night of missed sleep. Somehow, Ben got out the door and headed to the FBI office in Duluth.

Deidre thought of going back to bed, but before she could act on that thought, Steve and Jack thundered down the stairs looking fit and ready to jumpstart the day.

"What's for breakfast?" one of them asked. Deidre didn't know which boy had spoken, and at the moment, she didn't care.

"How about cereal this morning?" she suggested, hoping to get off easy.

"Naw," Steve balked. "We've had that two days in a row, and I'd like something warm. How about omelets?"

"How about oatmeal?" Deidre bargained.

Jack laughed. "Meet us halfway with French toast?"

Deidre couldn't help but laugh at the exchange. "Okay, French toast. Bacon with that?"

"Fried lunchmeat," Steve finished the deal.

By the time the French toast was fried and the lunchmeat was in the skillet, Deidre was beginning to feel hungry, and when they began to eat, she had to admit the food tasted good. She finished her third cup of coffee, and checked with the boys.

"I'm going to be busy most of the day. What can we do to keep you two out of trouble?"

"You could drop us off at the pool hall," Steve suggested with a twinkle in his eye.

Deidre ruffed up his hair. "Oh, I could, could I? Maybe you'd better come up with another idea."

Jack suggested they get dropped off at Grandma and Grandpa's. Maybe he'd take them fishing or something. Deidre thought that sounded like a better idea.

It was midmorning when they finally got rolling, and going on eleven when she left her in-laws' house. She looked up the address of one of the waitresses Maren had worked with and called ahead. When she arrived at the small, rented house, the young lady was waiting for her.

"Hi, Jessica. Thanks so much for seeing me. Like I told you on the phone, I'm Maren's mom. Can I ask you some questions about her?" Jessica invited her in, and Deidre immediately felt at home in the cozy house.

"What can I tell you?" Jessica asked after offering Deidre a cup of coffee, which she refused.

"I'd like to know whatever you can tell me about one of the customers who frequents the bar at the restaurant where you work."

Before she could continue, Jessica cut her off. "I don't think I should talk about our customers. You know, what happens at the bar, stays at the bar. I could lose my job if management found out I've been talking."

"I understand. Believe me, I do." Deidre knew she was asking a lot from the waitress whose meager-paying job could be placed in jeopardy. "But this person I want to know about is a bad customer." She realized she had made an unintended pun. Thankfully, it either went over Jessica's head or she chose to ignore it. "He's in the St. Louis County jail, charged with rape and attempted murder. Some of us believe he might have been involved in Maren's disappearance. I'm asking for your help. I promise that anything you say will be kept between you and me. Please."

Jessica thought for a moment before nodding. Deidre took that to mean she'd talk.

"The person I'm interested in is Jamie Storder. I can't really give you a description of him. He's just an average-looking guy, about six-two, slim, athletic looking. He has neatly trimmed hair. He has quite an attitude, which made me feel creepy just looking at him."

She watched Jessica's face redden and saw a look of repulsion cross it.

"I know him. All of us girls who work at the restaurant do."

Deidre immediately picked up on the fact that Jessica wouldn't have much good to say about Jamie. "Just tell me your impression of him."

"He's a first-class jerk," Jessica blurted out. "He thinks he's a real ladies man, hits on anything that walks and has boobs. Gives me the creeps. He always has his hands going, on our shoulders, behind our backs, and if we don't move away from him they begin to wander, if you know what I mean."

Deidre didn't quite know where to go from there. She finally asked, "Do you think he could be dangerous?"

"He scares me and most of the other waitresses."

"Did you ever talk to management about him?"

Jessica gave a sarcastic snort. "She said there was nothing that could be done, because Jamie hadn't broken any law. She wasn't terribly supportive, just told us to serve him from behind the bar, and not give him a chance to touch us."

Deidre didn't tell her the manager was probably right, but she continued to ask questions. "Did Maren ever come in contact with him?"

"Oh, yeah. She seemed to be his favorite target. He was always throwing suggestive remarks her way. He would sit with his back leaning on the bar and watch her as she waited tables. You could see his stare following her wherever she went. We talked to her about it, and told her to be careful when she left work."

"Speaking of that, was Jamie at the bar the night Maren went missing?"

"I'm sorry. I don't really know the exact day of Maren's disappearance, and anyway, that was over two months ago. I can't tell you who was in the bar two weeks ago, let alone two months."

"Were you working the night Maren tripped on the stairs?" Deidre switched to another train of thought.

"Yeah, I was helping take down some of the decorations, heard a loud thump, and she let out a cry. Then I heard her hit the wall. We thought for sure she had broken a bone or something. But she got up and said she was getting clumsy in her old age. We all laughed, thankful she hadn't been badly hurt. The next day, when she showed up for work, her face was pretty swollen on one side. When we asked about it, she said she had gone face first into the wall, and her cheek had gotten puffy during the night. I remember she went to the ice bin behind the bar and made an icepack for herself. It was a slow night and she took a few minutes from time to time to place it on her face."

"Did Maren ever talk about anyone hitting her?" Deidre slipped the question into the conversation.

Jessica looked puzzled. "You mean hitting on her?"

"No. Hitting her, beating on her?"

Jessica shook her head. "Not that I know of. Course, we weren't as close as she and Andra were. Why do you ask?"

"Just wondering if she had ever mentioned anything." Deidre commented.

"Never. She was always upbeat and willing to pitch in. I know she was looking forward to starting back to school this fall."

Deidre asked for and got the full name and address for Andra, thanked Jessica, and hurried away to her next stop. She didn't take time to call ahead.

# Chapter Twenty-Seven

ANDRA STEVENS RENTED a duplex near the north side of town. When Deidre rang her doorbell, it took her several seconds to answer. She opened the door a crack and peered through the narrow slot.

"Yes?" she asked apprehensively.

"Hi. I assume you are Andra," Deidre began, not giving her time to confirm or deny her identity. "I'm Deidre Johnson, Maren VanGotten's mother. Can I come in for a few minutes and talk to you?"

Through the crack of the partially open door, Deidre could see Andra relax. She opened the door wider.

"Please, come in." She smiled a sad smile and motioned Deidre to enter.

The place was as neat as Jessica's had been. The only thing that bothered Deidre was that the drapes were closed and the only light was artificial.

"Thank you for taking time to speak with me," Deidre began, trying to gain Andra's confidence. She sensed the young woman was extremely ill at ease. Andra swept her hand at the closed drapes.

"Excuse the darkness, but since Maren's disappearance, I've been terrified of being here alone."

"Can you explain to me why you're so frightened?" Deidre asked, expecting that Andra may be the kind of person who tends to blow things out of proportion.

"Maren was my best friend at work. Sometimes we would have a drink together at the bar after working hours. She was always there for me, there to listen, there to encourage me. I was going through some tough times back then. I have to admit, the last couple months before she went missing we didn't do that much. She said she had to get home to Dave. That was understandable, I suppose. She really loved him."

Deidre tried to get Andra back on track. "I'm so glad to hear that you were good friends, but why are you so terrified now?"

"Oh, yeah. I guess I didn't answer your question. There was this guy who started to hang around the bar several evenings a week. He freaked all of us out, but he seemed more interested in Maren. He was always watching her or trying to get close enough so he could touch her. Nothing overt, I mean things like patting her shoulder or touching her hand. Or he'd brush against her backside when he walked past. Made it look inadvertent. We all knew better. A few days after Maren didn't show up for work, he came in and asked why she wasn't working. I told him she was missing. He leered at me and said, 'I suppose you're going to be next in line, then.' Ever since that night, I've been scared stiff."

Deidre looked at Andra through new eyes. "I don't blame you a bit. I'd be scared, too. But let me ask you, was this guy named Jamie Storder?"

Andra jolted. "Yes. How did you know?"

"I have some news you'll be relieved to hear. It hasn't hit the media yet, but Jamie Storder is in jail in Duluth, and I doubt if he's going to be getting out soon. He has been identified as the primary suspect in a rape and attempted murder case against a woman in Duluth. She lived and identified him."

Andra gave a sigh loud enough for Deidre to hear, and buried her face in her hands. When she looked up, she asked, "Do you think he's the one who got to Maren?"

"It's beginning to look like that might be the case. If it is, he'll get tagged with her murder as well." She caught herself, realizing that Andra had refrained from using words of death. Now Deidre had actually said it out loud. She added, "We'll have to wait and see."

For a few seconds both women sat in silence, staring at the floor. Finally, Deidre asked her last question. "Did Storder have anybody he hung out with, any friends?"

Andra thought before answering, her hand under her chin. "There was one person, a guy. I don't know his name, but he met Storder at the bar quite a few times. They seemed to talk about fishing most of the time. From the snippets of conversation I caught, I think they had taken some trips together. Trouble is, I don't know his name."

"Did he ever try anything funny with the waitresses."

"No. He ignored us, except for ordering drinks." Andra shrugged.

Deidre thanked her, and when she was leaving she said, "I think you can open your drapes now." Andra gave a half-hearted grin.

As she walked to her car, Deidre checked her watch and was surprised to see how late in the afternoon it was. Before pulling away from the curb to pick up the boys from their grandparents' home, she dialed Dave's number. He answered on the third ring.

"Dave, Deidre here. I've got some important news to tell you. Can you come for dinner tonight at our place?"

The pause on the line was so long, Deidre checked to see if the call had been dropped. Dave answered her question. "Sure . . . sure. What's up?" Deidre thought he sounded apprehensive, but she knew how he felt. There had been so many leads that went nowhere, and she knew what it was like to not want to get hopes up for a breakthrough.

"Too much to talk about on the phone. See you a six thirty?"

"Yeah, okay. See you then."

# Chapter
## Twenty-Eight

DAVE WAS EARLIER than Deidre expected, arriving before Ben came home from work. He gave a rap on the door and walked in, like the old days.

"Hey, good to see you," she said and gave him a strong hug. "How're you doin'?"

"Good. Good," he answered, and hurriedly asked, "What's the news you've got?"

Just then Steve and Jack spilled into the room. "Dave! Do you wanna play catch?" Steve had a football in his hands.

"Why don't you do that? I wanted to wait for Ben to get home so I didn't have to repeat myself. It won't be long, and the boys have missed being with you."

Dave looked let down, but he headed for the door. In seconds she heard one of the twins calling out, "Dave! Dave, over here. I'm open!" The boys' pleas for the ball went on for several minutes, and she looked out the window to see Dave sprinting across the lawn as he chased down an errant pass from Jack.

She turned back to the counter where she was beginning to fill the serving dishes when she heard the crunch of tires on the gravel drive. Ben was home.

Dave, Ben, and the boys came into the house together. She noticed that Dave was perspiring profusely.

"Sorry to put you through that, Dave, but the boys sure love it when you play ball with them. I saw you running across the lawn. Looks like you still have it, even in your old age." She laughed and playfully elbowed him in the ribs. For a moment he relaxed and laughed, too.

"I'm not sure how long that's going to last. After eight months behind and accountant's desk, I'm already out of shape."

Deidre had the table set and was putting the dishes of food on the table. "You guys get washed up for supper," she commanded, referring to Jack and Steve. "You too, Ben." She turned to Dave. "You remember where the bathroom is upstairs. You can use it to freshen up. You look like you could use some cold water on your face."

When Dave came down to the table, the others were seated. He was no longer sweating and had brushed his hair back. Deidre thought he looked as handsome as the day Maren brought him home to meet her family.

As they were passing the food around, each taking a serving, Dave asked, "So, what's the news?"

Deidre cocked her head toward the boys and rolled her eyes at them. Dave got the message that he would have to wait until after supper. Deidre thought he was particularly jumpy during the meal, and noticed that his hand had a slight tremor when he lifted his fork to his mouth.

"I'm worried about you, Dave," she said in a motherly way. "Are you getting enough rest?"

Dave finished swallowing the bite he had in his mouth. "Honestly, no. I have a hard time being in our apartment alone. Everything I touch and smell reminds me of Maren. I sit down to eat, and the pattern on the dishes remind me of her. I open the cupboard and the first thing I see is her favorite coffee mug. But I can't get myself to get rid of them. It's like a catch twenty-two. If I give them away, I'll miss them. If I keep them, they are a constant reminder of her. I have to admit I don't sleep well at night in our bed. Perhaps I should tell you, I've been thinking I should move to Duluth. It'd be closer to my job, and it might help me move on." He put his fork down and stared at his plate.

Deidre reached across and placed her hand on his. "We're all hurting. That's why we have to stay in contact, to support each other." She remembered Pastor Ike's story about the three-fold cord and how strong it becomes. They ate in silence until Jack spoke up.

"Grandpa took us to the rocks below the lighthouse today. He showed us pools of water and said a lot of small animals live in them. When we got down on our bellies and looked into one of them, we could see baby salamanders swimming around. We thought they were tadpoles, but he said they were efts."

Deidre thought, *Thank God for the innocence of children.*

*****

AFTER THE MEAL and after the kids were shooed outdoors, Deidre suggested they go into the living room where they would be comfortable, but Dave hardly looked comfortable as he perched on the edge of his chair.

"So what's the news?" he pressed, obviously anxious to hear what she had to say.

Ben didn't respond and seemed to be withdrawn from the conversation, so Deidre began her story.

"Jeff, Sheriff DeAngelo, called us yesterday and asked us to accompany him to Duluth. The St. Louis County deputies arrested a man for rape and attempted murder a couple of days ago. His victim identified him, and he's going to be placed on trial sometime in the future. The thing is, he has ties to Two Harbors, and some of the aspects of his crime in Duluth are similar to Maren's case."

Dave became animated. "Do they think he's the guy who took Maren? Have they found any evidence?"

Deidre could understand his agitation. "Everything is circumstantial right now, but something happened today that might make the case against him even more believable."

That statement pulled Ben from his thoughts. "What are you talking about? I haven't heard anything new." He looked at Deidre questioningly.

"I didn't have time to tell you because the boys were around, and I didn't want to bring it up during supper. I did some sleuthing today, talked to two of the waitresses from the restaurant."

Dave interrupted. "Who were they?" he asked, trying to disguise the urgency in his voice.

"The first was a young woman named Jessica. She said that the accused rapist hung out at the bar quite frequently. More than that, she said all the waitresses stayed as far from him as they could. According to her statement, this guy had his eyes on Maren, and I suppose we could say he harassed her. Nothing serious enough to bring charges, but he was always making lewd comments and trying to get close to her."

"Who is this suspect?" Dave demanded.

"I don't think that's for us to say right now," Ben interjected. "But you said you spoke to two women. What about the second?"

Deidre was glad to see that Ben had partially crawled out of his cave and was actively listening.

"The second woman is named Andra. Do you know her?" she asked Dave.

He pondered the question before answering. "No, I don't think I do. Should I?" He looked puzzled.

"Probably not," Deidre granted him. "Although she said she and Maren were very good friends. I just thought you may have gotten together at some time. They must have just had a workplace friendship. The thing that I found so damning was her fear of our suspect. Did Maren ever mention that a customer was giving her a bad time?" She again addressed her question to Dave.

He shook his head. "I don't remember her ever talking about any trouble. Could this Andra be a little overly jumpy about Maren's situation?"

"I don't think so. She told me that several days after it became apparent that Maren was missing, the suspect told her she would be the next on his list. I think she's legitimately frightened."

"Have you told Jeff all of this?" Ben wanted to know.

"No, I haven't had time. But I'm going to see him tomorrow to fill him in. Besides, there are a couple of people I want to check with tomorrow. In my gut, I'd like to think we can crack this guy and get to the bottom of it all."

Dave settled back in his chair. "Deidre, I'm so thankful you're going after Maren's abductor. Do you really think you can pin the crime on him?"

"That's the direction I'm leaning toward. I don't know why, but I want it to be him. Maybe I'm just tired of not knowing, but I want to get this over with."

"Me, too," Dave agreed. "Me, too."

Dave left soon after their conversation, saying he had an early morning appointment and needed his rest. Deidre and Ben were sitting on the couch together when the boys joined them. One sat on either side of their parents, and Deidre felt the togetherness of family for the first time in a long while.

"Do you miss Maren?" Jack asked after they had sat together for several seconds.

Deidre hugged him tight. "Of course we do. I think of her every day."

Steve, who was sitting next to Ben, looked up at his dad. "What about you, Dad? Do you miss her, too?"

The question took Ben by surprise. "More than anything." He paused. "Why do you ask?"

"I don't know," Steve said, and Deidre could see he was puckering up. "It just seems like you never say anything about her. I thought maybe you had forgotten about her. All you do is read the paper at night and watch TV. I miss you, Dad."

Ben looked shocked but recovered in time to pull Steve close to him. "I love you guys," was all he could say.

The four sat together for a long time, talking about how much they missed Maren. They took turns crying and being comforted. Deidre realized it had been some time since they really communicated with each, despite their daily check-ins. Although painful, it was a tremendous relief to her. She hoped the others felt the same.

She and Ben ushered the boys to bed, tucked them in, and assured them they'd be a family again. Afterward, as they sat on the deck in the faint light coming from inside through the window, they had a serious discussion.

"Have I really been that self-absorbed?" Ben asked as he stared across the neighbor's field at the rising moon.

Deidre gave his question some thought. "I'm afraid we both have," she said finally. "I don't know what to say, because I've never experienced this kind of emptiness in my life. It's as if there is a Maren-shaped hole in my chest that just won't be filled."

Ben nodded. "She's the first thing I think of in the morning and the last at night. I've tried to get my mind on other things, but I can't."

They sat in silence for a long time. Finally, he said. "We'd better try to get some sleep. Tomorrow's going to be another long day."

Their arms around each other's waist, they made their way up the stairs and to their bedroom. As they passed the twins' room, they could hear one of them crying.

# Chapter Twenty-Nine

AFTER BEN LEFT FOR WORK the next morning, Deidre checked in with Jeff at the Law Enforcement Center. She told him about speaking to Jessica and Andra and filled him in on what she had learned.

"I hope you don't care that I'm out talking to people," she half-heartedly apologized. "It's just that I can't sit home and think about things any longer. This makes me feel as if I'm at least doing something positive."

Jeff reached over and took her hand the way only a close friend would. "If it were anyone else, Deidre, I'd tell them to back off and let us do our job. But you, for you I have the utmost respect. I know you won't foul up any evidence or do anything crazy. Do what you have to do."

That afternoon she decided to visit the restaurant and bar where Megan had worked as a waitress. She wanted to find the identity of the man Storder sometimes sat with at the bar. She entered the bar area, intending to buy a Diet Coke, but before she could sit down, she recognized Andra. At the same time, Andra looked up and Deidre spotted a sense of recognition, not really a smile, but a slight upturn to Andra's lips. She came from around the bar and pulled Deidre into the dining room.

"Deidre, I'm so glad to see you. I wanted to give you a call, but I didn't have your cell number, and no one answered at your home." Before Deidre could respond, Andra continued. "Remember I told you that Jamie Storder sometimes talked fishing with another customer? He's in the bar right now, sitting alone at the table in the back corner. I haven't said anything to him, and he has no idea you might want to talk to him. Please, let me go back in and work for a few minutes. Then come in and go to him. I don't want him to know it was me who tipped you off."

Deidre agreed, but to herself she thought whoever the mystery man was, he surely must have seen Andra pull her out of the bar. She waited a good five minutes before going back in. As though she wasn't quite sure who she was looking for, Deidre looked the room over with a sweep of her eyes. Then she headed toward the table where the lone man was sitting. He looked up as she approached his table.

"Hello," she said as she extended her hand. "My name is Deidre Johnson. I'm wondering if I could speak with you a minute." Deidre observed a look of puzzlement cross his face, but he motioned for her to sit down.

"My daughter was a waitress here until a little over two months ago, and I'm wondering if you remember her. She was about five-five, blonde hair usually pulled back in a ponytail. She was quite nice looking, at least I thought so." Suddenly Deidre realized she was speaking of Maren in the past tense, and her stomach knotted. She was spared anymore discomfort when the man said, "Sure, I remember her, remember her well. One of the best waitresses they had. I read about her being missing, but from what you say, they must have found her body. I'm sorry for your loss."

Deidre's eyes misted. "No, we haven't found her yet. I guess I've just come to accept the fact that she's gone. Thanks for caring." She straightened her shoulders. "But that's why I want to talk with you. I'd like your help, if you're willing to talk a minute."

"My name's Dan, and sure, I'll try to help you if I can." Dan took a sip of the beer he'd been nursing.

"I was told that you know a Jamie Storder. Do you?"

Dan produced a sound midway between a snort and a guffaw. "Yeah, I knew him. He was always alone at the bar, and sometimes after work, when I stopped in for a beer or two, I'd sit next to him." He tilted his head toward the bar. "He talked a lot about fishing, and after meeting like that a few times, we started to swap lies about our favorite fishing holes. Seems we both were into brook trout." Dan more or less snickered to himself, and drained his glass. He held it up and motioned to a waitress for a refill. "We decided to take a trip up the Gunflint Trail for a weekend. I was going to take him to one of my favorite lakes. I've made a lot of mistakes in my life, and that was one of the worst. The guy was a total nutcase. He hit on every woman we met—at the bait shop, at the restaurant up there, even at the gas station. The further we got away from Two Harbors, the raunchier he got. It takes a lot to embarrass me, but after a while, I didn't even want to be around him." The waitress put another tap beer in front of him, and he took a drink before continuing.

"Then, up in the woods, all he talked about was women and what he wanted to do with them. I thought to myself, this is one sick asshole. I cut the trip short and headed for home. That's the last time I talked to him."

"Did you ever see him after that?"

"Yeah, I came in here the next week, and he was here, at the bar. He was hittin' on all the waitresses that night, especially your daughter. It got so bad that she left the room, and the bartender told him to get out or he was going to call the cops."

Deidre's shoulders sagged. "Did he leave?"

"Yeah, he picked up his change and swore at the bartender. He said something I couldn't hear, but the bartender sent a waitress to go find your daughter. He looked pretty mad about whatever it was that Jamie said."

Deidre thanked him, never having asked his last name. As she stood to leave, he said, "I hope you find your daughter. She was one of the friendly ones here," and he went back to his beer. Then he added, "Oh, tell the waitress that it's okay that she pointed me out to you." He hoisted his glass and smiled.

Deidre moved to the bar and waited for the other bartender to have a break in his serving. As he washed glasses, she edged over to where she could speak to him.

"How many male bartenders work here?" she asked.

He looked up, surprised at the abruptness of her question. He probably thought she was some equal rights advocate who was going to make a stink about only men being hired for the job he had. Rather defensively, he answered, "There are two of us," then quickly added, "There are four women bartenders."

Deidre was quick to apologize. "Hey, I'm sorry if I sounded demanding. I'm just looking for a guy who might have known my daughter, Maren."

The bartender's expression changed from one of distrust to one of sympathy. "Oh, man, I'm so sorry. I didn't know who you were. Your daughter was one of my friends, always smiling, always considerate to all of us. We really miss her." Then he asked, "Is there anything I can do to help?"

Deidre was waylaid by the sad look on his face, and she swallowed hard. "I'd like to talk to whichever one of you was working the night Maren disappeared. It must have been you or the other guy."

"It was me. Good thing, because Jim quit about a month ago and moved back to Wisconsin. If he'd been behind the bar that night, you'd have a tough time catching up with him. What do you want to talk about?"

"The customer over there," and she nodded toward the table in the back corner, "He said that Jaime Storder was giving Maren a tough time that night. Do you remember?"

The bartender's face clouded over. "Sure, I remember that night. He was really hassling Maren, and she left the bar area. I kicked him out and told him not to come back. On the way out, he made a pretty sick remark about Maren. You probably don't want to know what he said, but he said what he'd do to her if he ever had the chance. I had Andra go find Maren. She was in the women's washroom, and when she and Andra came back, I told her what Storder had said, told her to be careful when she left work that night. It's bothered me ever since that I didn't do more to help her."

Deidre reached out and touched his arm. "Don't be too hard on yourself. We haven't any evidence it was him. Thank you for sticking up for Maren. It means a lot to me that you did." She turned to leave and another idea hit her.

"Did Storder come back after that?"

"I don't know," he answered. "I went on two weeks' vacation the next day, but when I came back to work, he never came in again."

On the way down the stairs, Deidre reflected on the fact that Andra had said Storder came in after Maren's disappearance and switched his harassment to her, even threatening her in a way. She made a mental note to follow up on why Jamie Storder quit coming to that particular bar.

# Chapter Thirty

DURING SUPPER THE NIGHT after she spoke to Dan and the bartender, everyone was in good spirits. Ben joked with the boys and challenged them to a contest to see who could eat their peas with a knife. He told them about his great-grandfather, who had immigrated from Europe, using his knife as a shovel and his fork to load the knife. He recited a poem his great-grandfather had taught him when he was a child. "I eat my peas with honey. I've done it all my life. It makes the peas taste funny, but it keeps them on my knife."

Everybody laughed as they tried balancing the green pellets on the flat surface as they lifted their knives to their mouths. Ben waited a few seconds, chiding them when most of the peas rolled off. Then, using his fork, he mashed up the peas on his plate and scooped them up with the blade of his knife.

Jack hollered, "Cheater!"

"What?" Ben answered back with a mystified tone like so many teenagers use when caught red-handed.

"You mashed your peas up. That's cheating!" Jack declared, a hint of disdain in his voice.

"Hey, I didn't say how we were supposed to eat our peas. Only that we would use our knives." Ben laughed at the way the argument was going.

"But what about that poem?" Jack persisted.

"Oh, that. Great-Grandpa taught me that, all right. But he never ate his peas with honey." Ben continued to enjoy the moment.

"Would he be our great-great-grandpa?" Steve wanted to know. Ben said he would be.

Steve asked, "Did he trick you like you tricked us?"

"Only once," Ben answered and finished his peas.

Deidre relished what she was observing. She was sure Ben was making a concerted effort to interact with his sons, and she loved him for that. But she wondered how long he could keep up the façade, and if he did, whether his old, naturally happy self would eventually return. She worried about him, knowing that he was hurting as deeply as any human could hurt. Deidre had a pang of guilt for thinking about the negative when they were having such great fun.

Suddenly Jack burst into tears and put his face in his hands to cover his eyes. Simultaneously, Ben and Deidre asked, "Jack, what's wrong?"

He shrugged and tried to stop sobbing. The realization of what had happened hit Deidre.

"Is it Maren?" she gently asked. Jack nodded.

Both parents gathered around their son and put their arms around him. "Oh, Jack, Jack," Deidre crooned as she ran her fingers over his mussed hair. "I know it hurts . . . hurts so much. But we have each other to hold onto."

Finally, Jack could speak. "I know. But here we were laughing and having fun, and we don't even know where she is. It's just not right for us to be having fun when she might be suffering. What are we going to do?" he sobbed.

Ben said they should go into the living room where they could sit together on the couch. He suggested that they take turns talking about how they felt inside, and as they each opened up to the others, the same message was repeated over and over. They missed her. They wondered if she was suffering. They wondered if she was dead. All of them expressed the feeling of having a part of them ripped out, leaving damage they worried could never be repaired.

"Time will soften that feeling," Deidre reassured them. "It will always be there, but it will soften." She looked at the boys. "You remember that before we were married, your dad and I had other people in our lives. Jenny was Maren and Megan's mother before she died, and I was supposed to marry a man named John Erickson. We miss them, but now we have each other. That's one of the wonderful things about life. Something good is just waiting around the corner for us, and even when we are the saddest, we can believe that we will someday be happy again."

The boys looked a little shocked. "Who was John Erickson?" Steve wanted to know.

Deidre smiled wistfully. "He was a man who loved me and asked me to marry him."

"Did you say 'Yes?'" Jack asked, his attention now shifted away from Maren.

"I did," Deidre confessed.

"What happened?" Jack pressed.

"He was an FBI agent. One night some very bad men shot and killed him."

"Did Dad know about him?" Steve questioned.

"They were friends," was Deidre's answer. Then she continued, "But look what came of it. Dad and I fell in love and got married and along came you two. That's what I mean. We will be happy again."

She looked at Ben's face and hoped she spoke the truth.

*****

THE NEXT MORNING, after Ben left for work, Deidre took the boys for a walk along the river. It was late enough in the summer that only a trickle of water flowed between the exposed rocks and boulders in its bed, and to her surprise, they spotted a maple whose leaves had turned prematurely red.

"Not much longer," she said, "and school will be starting." Both boys groaned.

"Did you have to ruin our walk?" Steve complained, and Deidre realized that from a kid's point of view, he was probably right.

"Hey guys, let's forget about what I said and enjoy the day. Heck, we've got two weeks before we have to worry about school." Just then she spotted a grouse in the underbrush, and she hushed the boys. They stood like statues for several seconds, watching as the bird strutted nervously away, its neck feathers and topknot bristling. It suddenly burst into the air with an explosion of sound from its wingbeats. The three of them began to laugh, because the noise had startled them, even though they knew it was coming. Then another bird broke cover, and another, and another until eight grouse had flushed.

"Wow, that was quite a covey," Deidre exclaimed. From that moment on, all thoughts of the impending school year vanished.

By noon, everyone was getting a little tired and a lot hungry. They made their way back to the house, ate a quick lunch, and were wondering what to do next when Deidre realized she hadn't checked her cell phone all morning. When she did, she found a message from the sheriff. She quickly listened to her voicemail.

"Hi, Deidre. This is Jeff. If you get a chance, stop by my office today. I've got some news to share with you and Ben, and I'd like to talk to you in person."

Deidre's heart skipped a beat. She surmised that whatever it was that Jeff had to say must be important and confidential or he would have told her over the phone.

"Hey, kids," she called to the boys. "I've got to go to town and talk to Jeff. Do you mind if I drop you off at Grandpa's for a while?"

Steve came running. "Does he have word about Maren?" the boy wanted to know.

"He didn't say. Could be anything." She knew it had to be about Maren, but didn't want to get into a further explanation with her sons quite yet. To this point they knew nothing about Jamie Storder. Deidre hoped he had confessed or something had been found linking him to Maren.

*****

DEIDRE CLIMBED THE STAIRS to the sheriff's office, forcing herself to move. She really wasn't sure she wanted to hear his message. She was ushered into Jeff's office by his assistant.

"Deidre, I have some bad news," Jeff began. "Or good, whichever way we want to look at it." Deidre looked surprised. How could news about Maren be both good and bad? To her it had to be one way or the other. Jeff continued.

"Jamie Storder has an airtight alibi as to his whereabouts late the night of and for the three days after Maren was reported missing. He couldn't have been involved, because he was in jail in Cook County. Seems he got kicked out of the bar at The Shoals Tavern, got in his truck and headed up the Shore. He must have had an open bottle with him, because by the time he got to Little Marais, he was hammered, blew a .12 on the breathalyzer. The deputy hauled him in and he spent the next three days in the hoosegow. The good news is, we still have hope that Maren is alive. The bad news is you and Ben still don't have any kind of closure. I'm sorry."

Deidre didn't know how to react. She didn't even know what she felt at that moment. All she could wonder was if they would ever reach a conclusion.

"We do have a new lead, however." Jeff's words snapped her out of her daze. "Yesterday, a tip came in about a vagrant who wandered into town a day before Dave reported Maren missing. He was kind of an enigma. The reason we know about him is that a hotel worker called. Said a rough-looking guy registered at the hotel back in early May. I asked her why she hadn't reported that until now. We put out enough requests for information back then. She said she didn't want to get the hotel involved, but the memory of the guy has haunted her all summer. Guess she had a guilty conscience or something."

Deidre puffed out her cheeks and exhaled. "What do you know about him?"

# Chapter Thirty-One

JEFF GAVE DEIDRE the name of the hotel where the informant worked, and on the way there, Deidre wondered if the front desk clerk would be of any help. She entered the lobby, which was tiny. The place was a mom-and-pop operation with about ten units and looked like a leftover from the nineteen-fifties. No one was at the counter, but after Deidre rang a small bell placed in an obvious location, the door to a back room opened. A middle-aged woman emerged, peeling off a pair of rubber cleaning gloves as she asked, "Can I help you?"

Deidre gave her most disarming smile, or at least she hoped so. "Yes, I'd like to speak to Mary Lendo, please."

"That would be me," the cleaning lady answered. A look of apprehension crossed her face. "What do you want?" It was not a belligerent question, more wary than anything.

"Mary, my name is Deidre Johnson, Maren VanGotten's mother. Do you recognize that name?"

Worry lines wrinkled on Mary's forehead and her face flushed. Deidre thought she saw the woman's eyes tear up. "Yes, she's the young lady who disappeared last May. Oh, Lord, I'm so sorry I didn't say something earlier." Mary broke down and looked as though she were on the verge of an all-out crying jag. "Please, tell me what I can do to help."

Deidre suggested they sit down, and Mary directed her to one of the two threadbare sofa chairs in the corner. A wave of pity for the remorseful woman swept over Deidre.

"Please, don't beat up on yourself, Mary. We have no idea if your customer had anything to do with my daughter. In fact, we're grasping at straws right now, trying to follow any lead that presents itself." Mary calmed down somewhat.

"My husband and I had just become owners of this hotel, and we didn't want any negative publicity when we were only getting started," she explained. "But inside, I knew I should have called the sheriff. I just didn't, and now I'm worried sick that I could have helped. I'm so sorry."

Again Deidre reassured Mary that it was okay. She was only trying to get an idea of what the lodger had been like.

"Why does the memory of this man make you believe he might be involved with Maren's disappearance?" Deidre asked in as understanding a voice as she could.

"I wouldn't have thought anything of him under other circumstances. You can see this isn't exactly a five-star operation, and we get some customers who look to be pretty down on their luck. But after news broke about your daughter, I couldn't stop thinking about him. He was different, you know?"

Deidre asked her how he was different.

"Well, he was really dirty, muddy, as if he had been walking on a road and had splashed clay all over his pant legs. Then, too, he carried this pack that looked as though it was really heavy, had things hanging from it: a cup, a water bottle, stuff like that. Oh, and he had a large sheath knife attached to his belt. He hung around here for three days. After he cleaned up, he didn't look too bad. I saw him head to the laundromat with a few clothes, including his muddy pants. He was wearing them the next day with a clean, short-sleeved T-shirt on. I noticed that he had some really deep scratches on his arms, and when I asked him about them, he said they were really nothing. That's another thing, he hardly said a word to anyone the whole time he was here."

Deidre stopped Mary's monologue. "How would you describe the scratches?"

Mary thought a moment before answering. "Well, they were deep, I can tell you that. They were scabbed over and looked to be a little infected, all red and puffy. There were two on one arm and three on the other. I don't know which was which."

"Where on his arms were they?" Deidre wanted to know. She was sitting on the edge of her chair by this time. Mary pointed to the outside of her forearms, and Deidre's heart began to beat faster. *Defensive wounds,* she thought, *the type sustained by someone trying to protect themselves. Or the kind made by a person trying to ward off an attacker.*

"Is there anything else you can remember?" Deidre inquired.

"Only that after three days he checked out. The last time I saw him, he was walking toward the lake. I didn't think anything of it until I saw the notice asking for anyone with information that might be pertinent to call the sheriff." Mary put her hands to her face. "I wish I had called then. Perhaps it would have made a difference."

Deidre tried to convince her that it was okay, that she appreciated the information, and that the sheriff would be able to locate the vagabond. She knew he had gotten the name from the hotel's registry—that is, if the lodger had put down his actual name and address. They'd just have to let Jeff do his job.

*****

THAT EVENING AFTER SUPPER, Deidre told the boys that she had to talk to their dad in private and to go out and toss the football around or something.

Jack looked at her with pleading eyes. "We know this is about Maren, because you saw Sheriff Jeff today. We want to know what he said about our sister, and it's not fair that you always chase us outside when you and Dad talk about her case now. You used to tell us what was going on. I think you should let us stay." He folded his arms across his chest, not in defiance, but looking like he was proud that he had spoken his mind.

Deidre was a little shocked, but not angry. Before she could respond Ben cleared his throat, which made Jack slightly nervous.

"I think you're right," Ben said in a quiet voice. "It's not fair that we've kept you wondering." He looked at Deidre. "What do you think?"

"I think that anyone who has courage to speak up the way Jack did deserves to hear the truth. Let's sit down at the table, though."

When they were seated, everyone looked to Deidre, waiting to hear what she had learned from Jeff. First she explained to the boys about Jamie Storder and what he had done. Ben was exasperated when she got to the part about Storder having an irrefutable alibi for the time period corresponding to Maren's disappearance.

"Now Jeff has another lead," she informed the family. "About the same time as Storder was in jail, an apparent drifter was staying in a hotel in town. I talked to the owner of the place today, and she said the guy was a little different, a real loner. He would leave his room early in the morning and not return until after dark. She couldn't say where he spent his time. Then one day he packed up and left. The last time she saw him, he had his pack on his back and was walking toward the lake."

Ben got up and was pacing around the room. "Have you called Dave to let him know?"

"No, I wanted to talk to you first. I thought we should wait until we know more. Jeff told me he had gotten the person's name and address from the hotel registry, but I didn't ask for it. I knew he couldn't give it up yet. If you think we should tell Dave, I'll go along with it, but personally, I think it would be best to wait." Ben agreed it was best to not phone Dave. All the while the boys had been silent, listening to what was being discussed.

"What will they do to the person who took Maren when they find him?" Steve wanted to know.

"Well, first they will arrest him, and then they'll formally charge him with the crime. A judge will determine if he can be let out of jail until his trial. A jury will have to decide if he's guilty, and if he is, he'll either go to a prison or to an institution for a long time, maybe forever."

Steve blurted out, "I hate whoever did this. I hope somebody kills him."

Deidre was shocked by the honesty of that statement. "I know. Sometimes I think the same thing. But if he's killed, that won't bring Maren back to us. You know, boys, there is a fine line between vengeance and justice."

As she made that statement, a vivid image entered her mind. It was of the day she had held her service pistol against the side of the head of the man who had murdered her fiancé, John. When she thought of it, she could still feel the pressure of her finger on the gun's trigger as she began to squeeze it. She could hear her partner saying, "Deidre, don't do it." Now here she was talking to her sons about the difference between vengeance and justice, and she realized if she had pulled that trigger, her life would have been ruined. She would be in prison for murder, and the joy of having a family would have been nothing more than a dream.

"The law will take care of the person responsible. Let's trust the law."

The evening was pretty much ruined, and everyone turned in early, each mulling over the conversation in their mind.

# Chapter Thirty-Two

DEIDRE WONDERED WHO WOULD be calling at seven thirty in the morning and was surprised to see Jeff's name on her caller ID. Every time she saw his name come up, she felt a surge of anticipation. Today was no different.

"Hi, Jeff. What's up?"

She listened intently as he told her he had confirmed the identity of the wanderer who stayed at the hotel in Two Harbors, the place owned by the woman Deidre had spoken with the day before. She was surprised when he told her he was driving to the Cities to interview this person of interest and asked if she wanted to ride along. Her first impulse was to say yes, but then she had to consider her boys. Finally, she said no. After the conversation of the night before, Deidre knew that Steve and Jack were being affected by Maren's absence more than she realized. It was time to put their emotional security ahead her curiosity. Jeff said he'd be back in Two Harbors by about five in the afternoon, and he would stop out so they could talk about what he had learned.

After Steve and Jack ate breakfast, Deidre suggested they drive to Duluth and visit Park Point, a long sand spit that jutted into Lake Superior. Many days during the middle of August its shallow water was warm enough to swim in. Deidre called Ben on her cell before he had time to begin his workday and made arrangements to meet for lunch. It would be a day of R and R for the family. At noon, they met Ben at a soup and sandwich place on First Street.

"Jeff called this morning," she told him, before biting into her roast turkey deli sandwich.

Ben looked surprised. "What did he have to say?"

"He's driving down to the Cities to interview that guy I told you about, the one who wandered into town carrying a pack. The one I told you stayed in a hotel for a few days in May."

Ben stopped eating. "Did he say if he had any reason to think the guy is involved, or is it just a fishing trip?"

Deidre shook her head. "Just fishing, I think. He's going to stop over around five today. If you can get away a little early, you can be there when he comes. Any chance?"

Their conversation continued in a casual, almost detached manner, and it struck Deidre that the tension of the night before seemed to have eased. The boys were busy gobbling the dessert they had ordered, and she thought they hadn't been listening.

"Could this be the guy who took Maren?" Steve asked abruptly. The question took Deidre by surprise, but she answered.

"I think the chances are pretty slim, but we never know. That's why Jeff is going to see him. We'll know later today."

"Can we be there when Jeff tells us what he found out?"

"Yes, you boys can be there."

"Then I don't want to go swimming. Let's go home so we don't miss him."

Deidre reassured her son that they had plenty of time. It was a beautiful, warm sunny day, one of the rare times when the wind was from the west and not off the frigid lake. The sand would be soothing and the water comfortable, and she wanted some time to clear her mind. They finished their lunch in a half hour, Ben returned to his office, and she and the boys were on the beach by one. The sand felt better than she had expected as it worked its way between her toes.

*****

JEFF'S MIND WANDERED as he sped down I-35. The speed limit was seventy, but he was driving nearly eighty. Sometimes being sheriff had its perks. He found himself whistling to himself and thinking of his own children. Two were in college and the third would be a high school senior the coming fall. Retirement was only a year off and he imagined the things he and his wife, Danielle, would do with their free time. He gave little thought to the man he would meet in less than an hour. It was probably a wild goose chase, he surmised, but it was good to have an excuse to get out of town. His GPS led him to the address he had been given.

As he parked his vehicle in a lot across the street, he was surprised where the computer-generated voice had directed him. The address was an upscale office building, seven stories high, with polished glass doors. He rode the elevator to the top floor, where he found the office marked J.P. DAHLSTROM AND ASSOCIATES, P.A. SERVICES.

Jeff entered the waiting room of the business and introduced himself to the receptionist, who responded, "Is Mr. Dahlstrom expecting you?" Jeff said he was. "Why don't you pour yourself a cup of coffee while you wait? I'll tell Mr. Dahlstrom you're here."

Before Jeff could say "No, thank you," he heard her announce over the office intercom, "Sheriff Jeff DeAngelo is here to see you, J.P."

Jeff sat down and hadn't had time to select a magazine from the pile on the end table when a tall, well-groomed man strode across the room and extended his hand.

"Sheriff DeAngelo, why don't we go to my office where we can visit." As he led the way, he turned to his receptionist. "Tammy, please hold all calls until we're done." Then they continued down the hall to his office.

Jeff was surprised at J.P.'s demeanor. If the man had any worries, he was doing a good job of covering them up. He offered Jeff a seat and took one facing him. Jeff looked at the polished walnut desk that held a few papers and thought if J.P. had wanted to play the superiority card, he could have sat behind that expanse of wood.

"So, Sheriff, when we spoke over the phone, you said you wanted to talk to me about the days I spent in Two Harbors last spring. What exactly do you want to know?"

Jeff was a little taken aback by J.P.'s directness. "I have some questions I'd like to ask you, Mr. Dahlstrom. I'd really appreciate if you will consent to answer them."

"No problem," J.P. answered. "And please, call me J.P. All my friends do." He took a sip from the bottle of water in his hand. Jeff noticed it was steady, and J.P.'s eyes were looking straight at him.

"Were you in Two Harbors last May?"

"Yes, I was. What a great little town to visit." J.P. smiled a disarming grin.

"Did you stay at the Lake Inn while you were there?"

"Yes. I like to patronize places like that to give the owners some business."

"How long did you stay there?" Jeff was asking simple questions that were easily verifiable.

"Two nights and three days." J.P. wasn't wavering.

"Can I ask what you were doing in town? Frankly, I wasn't expecting you to look like this. Reports were that you looked like a drifter when you came into town."

J.P. laughed a relaxed laugh. "I suppose I did. Let me explain. My job here is extremely stressful and my company had worked for months to secure a very large contract. By the time the deal was sealed, I was on the verge of a breakdown, quite literally. After seeing a shrink a half-dozen times, we worked out a plan where I'd take time off from the job and let my partner and our employees carry the ball. We decided I'd do something I've always wanted to do that didn't involve being around people. I decided to hike the Superior Trail, the one that runs from just outside Duluth all the way to Grand Marais. Most people go in that direction. I decided to reverse the course, start in Grand Marais and head down the shore."

J.P. stopped to take another drink of water, and Jeff waited.

"That trail is well over two hundred miles long, and I planned on making ten miles a day for twenty days. At first my goal was difficult to reach, but as I got in shape, I found I could do fifteen miles a day without pushing too hard. I got ahead of schedule. I wish I could tell you what I experienced."

Jeff was genuinely interested in his story, but by now he was beginning to realize his trip to the Cities had been wasted. "I'd like to know what you discovered," he found himself saying.

"Well, naturally, there's the beauty beyond anything I had expected. But for me, being shut off from society was the most memorable part of the trip. I didn't even take a cell phone, just a map. The solitude of the trail was exactly what I needed. I think I must have experienced what Indian boys did when they went off alone in the woods to fast and meditate. I've read that they would have visions that determined what their adult name would be. I don't think I had a vision, but I discovered what is really important in my life: my family, my friends, my home. I realized my job is nothing more than a means of being able to enjoy all the things I love." He paused. "It changed me."

Jeff was silent for a bit. "Where did you go after you left town?"

"I started walking up Highway 2 to where the trail crosses, but a couple of guys stopped and asked if I needed a lift, and I took them up on their offer. They were good people."

"You don't happen to know their names, by any chance?" Jeff took out his notebook.

"I do. By that time I had hiked most of the trail and decided I was going to make some changes in my life. One change was to be interested in people I meet. So I asked them their names, what they did, about their families. Those kinds of things. One was Darin Thomas and the other called himself Sue-me Adolphson. I asked him what the heck kind of name that was, and he laughed. Said his dad was a lawyer, and all the kids had called him "Sue-me" because of it. I found out a lot of people in Two Harbors have crazy nicknames." J.P. smiled and shook his head.

"I know both of them, at least know their dads. You're right, they're good kids. What did you do those days you were in town?"

"Nothing much. Spent a lot of time by the breakwater, looking at the lake, thinking. I visited the museum, walked out to that pie place a couple of miles from town, just kicked around. Had a beer at the local brewery, a pizza at that place downtown. Just pretty much rested up."

"Did you ever get out to that fancy restaurant north out of town?"

J.P. thought a minute. "Oh, that place. No, I wasn't dressed for that kind of atmosphere." He laughed. "My clothes were clean by that time, but let's say not fit for fine dining."

"The owner of the motel said you had some pretty wicked scratches on your arms. Can you tell me how you got them?" Jeff waited for the answer, wondering if J.P. would stumble.

J.P. responded by pulling up his shirt sleeves, and Jeff could see the faint outline of scars.

"While I was on the trail a little north of Beaver Bay, I ran into a couple with a dog, a young black lab. I knelt to pet it, and like a lot of young dogs do, he rushed me in his exuberance. I put up my arms to fend him off, and he playfully pawed at me. God, he was strong. The owners were mortified, but I realized the dog was too full of energy to contain, and it was as much my fault as his for kneeling down without first letting him settle down. They gave me their card in case I needed medical treatment. Said they would pay for it. I think they were worried I was going to sue." He reached into his desk and took out a card folder, extracted a business card, and handed it to Jeff, who made a point of copying down the name and address on the card.

Jeff watched J.P.'s eyes for a reaction, but all he did was nod his approval. He asked if J.P. had any knowledge of what had happened during the days he was in town, and J.P. said he didn't.

"A very bright young lady disappeared and is presumed dead. She's been missing for almost three months with no trace. You can understand why I've had to check into your past. I must say, your résumé is impressive and your record is spotless. I wanted to touch base with you, hear what you had to say. I'll be checking with Sueme and Darin, but I'm confident they'll verify your statement." Jeff stood to leave and J.P. put out his hand.

"I hope you catch a break on this case, Sheriff. I have a real difficult time with the abuse too many women suffer."

As Jeff walked out of the building he was certain J.P. Dahlstrom had nothing to hide. But on the other hand, the man's mannerisms were almost too friendly and inviting. He would certainly be following up with the boys who had picked up J.P.

# Chapter Thirty-Three

DEIDRE WAS SETTING the table for supper when Jeff pulled into the driveway. She stepped out onto the deck to meet him.

"Jeff. Thanks so much for stopping. We've been anxious to hear about your interview." She stopped to yell for the boys.

"Steve, Jack, the sheriff is here." Then she opened the door and shouted upstairs for Ben. When they were all seated on deck chairs, Jeff began.

"Folks, here's the deal. Our happy wanderer turned out to be a very respectable and successful businessman who was up north for some R and R. He was hiking the Superior Trail and got ahead of schedule, so he decided to spend a couple of days in Two Harbors."

Ben interrupted. "But the trail crosses the highway eight or ten miles out of town. Do you mean to tell us that he hiked that far just to spend time here? There's not a heck of a lot to do in town. Sure, we love it, but wouldn't somebody from the city run out of things to do after a half day?"

Jeff could sense that Ben was frustrated and grasping for answers. "I did a thorough check on him, and I'm convinced that he's clean. One of my deputies found records of where he spent his time in Two Harbors. In addition to finding the hotel records, we were able to verify that he spent time at the historical museum and the lighthouse. Two people who gave him a ride remembered him. All his stories checked out. I know how badly you'd like closure, but I'm almost certain this is a dead end. By the way," Jeff added. "Have you talked to Dave recently? I thought you might have told him about Dahlstrom."

Deidre explained that Dave had recently moved to Duluth, and considering how upset he got every time there was news, she and Ben decided it would be best to not get his hopes up until they had something more concrete to report. "I don't blame him for moving," Deidre said. "He said the apartment held too many memories for him to be able to stay. I do feel bad, though. We've not had any contact with him for two weeks, and I'm sure when this is all over, we'll lose touch. I'll miss him." Jeff left the meeting with their thanks for all he was doing. Ben, Deidre, and the boys sat still for several minutes, listening to the late summer sounds of crickets chirping and the call of nighthawks that soared overhead.

"I miss Maren," Steve said, breaking the silence. "Is there any chance she is alive somewhere?"

Deidre knelt in front of him. "Until we know differently, there's always a chance, always hope. We'll just have to be patient and pray that we'll get some answers soon." She stroked her son's hair while she thought, *Our prayers have done nothing. Why did I even say that?*

After several more minutes, they went inside, the boys to their rooms to read, Ben to the TV to watch the Minnesota Twins play baseball, and Deidre to stare out the window as her flower garden disappeared in the dusk. Everyone harbored their own thoughts until Ben turned off the TV and announced he was going to bed. Deidre made plans to visit the women's shelter the next day.

******

THE BOYS HAD A SCHOOL orientation session, and Deidre dropped them off for the morning. She called ahead and made an appointment to speak with the director of the women's shelter in Two Harbors, and at nine o'clock she was sitting in the reception area, waiting to meet Joan Woodard. A few minutes later Joan appeared from the hallway and invited her to come to her office.

Deidre was delighted to find the room cheerful and bright, and as she settled into an upholstered chair, she felt at ease. Joan started the conversation.

"You told me what you wanted to discuss, but I'm not sure I can be of much help. It's been over two months, actually almost three, since Maren came to the shelter, and we only talked for a half hour or so. She impressed me with her questions and interest in women's issues. She said she was writing a paper about why battered women stay with their partners and how they could break free."

Deidre got right to the point. "That's what confuses me. You said she told you she was working on a project for school, but as far as her father and I know, she wasn't taking any classes. Do you remember where she said she was going to school?"

"As a matter of fact, I do," Joan answered. "She said she was taking a class at the College of St. Scholastica. I clearly remember that, because I graduated from there. I asked if she knew of one of my favorite professors, and she said she didn't. That confused me a little, because Dr. Green is the head of the department and is very involved with the program and its students."

"Do you remember any of the questions Maren asked?" Deidre inquired, her forehead wrinkled and a confused tone to her voice.

"I remember that day well for several reasons, one being that Maren seemed to have done a lot of research before coming to me. I had the feeling she had interviewed women who had been abused. Specifically, she wanted to know how secure our building is. She wanted to know if anyone had experienced a domestic partner coming to the shelter and accosting her. I assured her that this is a locked facility, and it would be improbable for that to happen. She also wanted to know about our confidentiality protocol. Again, I assured her that any woman coming here is safe and anonymous. The only way anyone finds out about our clients is if that client tells others where she is."

"This is a judgment call, Joan, but did she seem upset, as though she might have been talking about herself?" Deidre wasn't sure she wanted to hear the answer.

"No, on the contrary. Your daughter was poised and calm. I did get the feeling that she might have been here at the behest of a friend, but I didn't think it was my place to ask. I tried to answer her questions as straightforward as I could. Eventually, she got around to asking me why I thought women stayed in abusive relationships."

"That's the question, isn't it?" Deidre interjected. "What did you tell her?"

Joan thought for a time, and Deidre tried to discern if it was because she couldn't remember, or if the question had become too personal. After a period of silence, Joan realized her mind had drifted to another place, and she focused again on Deidre.

"There are so many reasons that women stay in abusive relationships. I'm sure I don't know them all, but most often it comes down to finances. Many women have nowhere to turn for financial support. They may have small children at home who need childcare they can't afford. Or they may not have an education that allows them to enter the job market. Some are afraid to leave for fear of what their partner will do to them. I suppose many don't have a clue about why they stay, they only know they do. Perhaps many are too embarrassed to admit they're being taken advantage of by a person who they thought loved them."

Deidre looked squarely at Joan. "Do you think Maren was searching for answers for herself? I mean, do you think she was in trouble and was using an interview to find answers?"

Joan didn't hesitate in answering. "If she was, she was an awfully good actor. I've had a lot of experience with sorting through the B.S. in people's lives, and I didn't get that sense at all. Like I mentioned, my own evaluation is that she was running interference for a friend."

Deidre looked at her watch and saw that she had been there an hour. "I'm sure you're very busy, and I've taken up a good chunk of your morning. Thanks so much, Joan. This has been a big help to me." Joan walked her to the door and waved as Deidre got into her car.

As she drove away from the curb, she thought, *Is it possible that Maren was helping a friend get ready to leave her partner, and he found out? What if a disgruntled abuser wanted Maren to stop interfering in his life?* She made a mental note to speak with Megan about that possibility, among other things.

*****

DEIDRE WAS SCHEDULED to pick up her sons from their school orientation in an hour, and she used that time to stop at the sheriff's office. She met Jeff as he was coming down the stairs.

"Deidre, glad you stopped by, but I'm on my way to a council meeting. Anything serious you wanted to see me about?"

"Nothing urgent," Deidre replied, hoping the disappointment of not being able to sit down and talk wasn't reflected in her voice. It seemed that as the days crept past, she had a need to continue talking to people about Maren. "I was hoping you could run a check on something for me." She and Jeff walked together toward the council chambers.

"Sure. Have you found something we've been missing?"

Deidre shrugged. "I just came from the women's shelter. Had a talk with Joan about Maren. Last spring she asked Joan for an interview about domestic violence issues. Maren said it was for a college class paper she was writing. The only thing, Jeff, is that I don't think Maren was taking any classes last spring. I won't be able to access her college records, so I thought perhaps, with the backing of your office, you could find out. Maren said she was taking a class at St. Scholastica."

Jeff let out a "hmmm" of acknowledgement. "Why do you think she'd say she was taking a class if she wasn't?"

Deidre felt a pang of guilt over the fact that she was doubting her daughter's word. "She told us she was taking a year off from school to work until Dave graduated. Then she was going back to school this fall to finish her degree. She hadn't said anything to anyone about changing her mind. Then, too, Joan said she picked up on subtle clues that Maren was using the interview to gain information for a third party, she thought maybe a friend who was in trouble and wanted a way out. I was thinking on the way over here, what if she did have a friend in trouble, and that friend's partner decided to get rid of Maren? Maybe she was becoming a thorn in his side. I know it's a weak argument, but will you check her story for me?"

By that time they had arrived at the council chambers, and Jeff promised he'd get on it as soon as the meeting ended. He gave Deidre a hug.

"Hang in there, friend. We'll get a break sometime. Believe me when I say we're not giving up on finding an answer for you and Ben. I mean it."

Two hours later, Deidre received a call from him. "I've checked five colleges in the area, including the two community colleges, and none of them have a record of Maren being enrolled in any classes this past year. I think you're right, Maren was on a fishing expedition for someone, or maybe even herself. It's something we have to seriously consider."

As she sat at her table, nursing a cup of tepid coffee, the thought came to mind that perhaps Maren was taking a correspondence course, but Deidre thought that highly improbable. With so many colleges within a twenty-mile radius, it made no sense for her to go out of the area. Besides, wouldn't she have told Joan if that were the case, rather than saying she went to St. Scholastica? Another alternative was that she was gathering information for herself, sort of the old "I have a friend" ploy, only this time saying, "I'm taking this class." Deidre quickly discarded that idea. Surely Maren would have come to her for help if she needed it.

The only plausible answer to the question of why Maren would have masqueraded as a student was that she was trying to help a friend, and Deidre knew how volatile domestic issues could become. She could easily envision Maren intervening in a dangerous situation to help someone who was in trouble.

# Chapter Thirty-Four

SEVERAL DAYS PASSED without any mention of Maren. For the Van-Gotten family, life had assumed a certain sense of normalcy, although Deidre suspected things could never return to what they had been before Maren's disappearance. It was as though a cloud hung over them, one that felt as if it would drop at any instant, bringing with it more trauma.

Megan's life had a hollowness to it that defied explanation. When she was out with friends, she might suddenly be engulfed by a surge of melancholy and loneliness and would simply shut down in front of them. They knew what the problem was but had no clue what to do to help.

Ben went to work, came home, and sometimes just sat on the porch, looking out over the neighbor's hayfield. Deidre could tell that he often forced himself to play with the boys, and sensed that his frequent periods of joviality were forced. As for herself, she most often busied herself by caring for her home: weeding the many flower gardens, touching up spots in need of paint, and trying to rearrange pictures to give the walls a fresh look. These inane activities left her feeling impotent and uncaring of the fact that her daughter was lost somewhere and might be needing her. But what else could she do?

Finally, more out of a need to feel she was trying than anything else, Deidre decided to talk to the employees of the restaurant one more time. If Maren was helping a fellow worker, one of them might talk. On the way to town, she decided to cross the male workers from her list.

Then a revelation hit her. She didn't like the idea and wished she hadn't thought it, but it occurred to her that perhaps it wasn't a man who had taken Maren. What if her daughter had become the third person in a love triangle and the other woman had retaliated? *No,* she thought. *I'm letting my imagination run a little too wild here. Stop the foolishness.*

It was late morning, and Deidre hoped that she wouldn't be interrupting the workers' sleep. She knew both Andra and Jessica worked the late shift at the restaurant. By the time they had an opportunity to unwind, drive home, and go to bed, it was often two in the morning. Deidre checked her watch, which read eleven thirty. She hesitated but rang Andra's doorbell.

It took a few seconds, but Deidre heard the sounds of movement inside and the door opened a crack. Andra's hair was still a rat's nest, and she was in her nightgown, but Deidre saw she held a cup of coffee. Andra had been awake, but not for long.

"Hi, Andra," Deidre began apologetically. "Do you have time to talk a bit? I've got some things I'd like to ask about Maren. Would you mind?"

Andra invited her in, and after they visited a couple of minutes she proposed that she call Jessica, and the three of them could think together.

"Jessica doesn't need as much sleep as I do," she said after hanging up the phone. "She was outside working in the yard and said she needed a break. She'll be here in five minutes."

Andra had just finished setting out two more coffee cups for her guests when Jessica rapped on the door and walked in without waiting to be invited. "Hey, Andi," she said, using Andra's nickname. "What's up? Do you have news about Maren, Deidre?"

Deidre cleared her throat. "No, unfortunately, nothing has surfaced. I may be grasping for straws, but I had a thought a couple of days ago." She went on to explain that Maren had posed as a student when she requested an interview from the director of the women's shelter. Then she postulated the idea that perhaps Maren was trying to intervene on behalf of a friend or colleague. Both young women looked pensive for a moment. Suddenly Jessica became animated.

"Andi, remember that waitress who was hired last winter? She only lasted a couple of months and then quit. What was her name?" Jessica groped for it. "Swerlee . . . Shonlee?"

"I remember," Andi spoke up excitedly. "She called herself Swania. She was from Germany and told me her real name was Svanja, but nobody ever pronounced it correctly. That was her name, Svanja, Svanja Birkebach. She met a U.S. military man who was stationed near her hometown. They married and she followed him to the States when his assignment was up."

Jessica broke in. "Shortly before she quit, she came to work pretty beat up. Her face was bruised, and she had marks on her arms. I asked her what had happened, but she said she didn't want to talk about it. I couldn't do anything. Just before closing time, I saw her and Maren having a deep discussion about something, and they left the restaurant together. A couple of days later, Swania quit. I didn't give it a second thought until now. That was at least three months before Maren disappeared. You don't think she had anything to do with it, do you?"

Deidre's heart jumped at this news, and for a moment, she was sure her made-up scenario was true.

"Do you have any idea what became of this Swania? Is she still in town?"

Neither Andra nor Jessica had any idea where she had gone after quitting her restaurant job. Deidre checked her watch and said she had to excuse herself. Before leaving, she thanked the two and told them how helpful they had been. Both young women hugged her and wished her the best in her search for answers.

Deidre called ahead to see if Jeff was in the sheriff's office and was relieved to find him there. In a few minutes she had bolted up the stairs to his office, was buzzed in, and was telling him about her theory and discovery.

"It shouldn't be too difficult to track her down," Jeff said reassuringly. "That's a pretty unusual name, even in Germany, I'd bet. Let's start with court records in our county and see if she has left a paper trail."

He turned his computer monitor so Deidre could eavesdrop on his search. In seconds he was logged into the district court records, and the instant he typed in the woman's unusual name, a match came up.

"We're in luck. According to this, she filed for divorce the sixth of May. Their final appearance before a judge is scheduled for September seventh, three weeks from now."

Deidre sat back in her chair and let a stream of air escape through her pursed lips. "I know this is asking a lot, Jeff, but will you give me her address? I'd really like to talk to her about Maren."

Jeff didn't hesitate. "This is public record, although I'd hate to have it get out that I was the one who gave you the info. Take a look." He turned the computer so she could get a better view without craning her neck. She wrote down the address on a notepad and tore off the top sheet of paper.

"Thanks, Jeff. You know this will remain between us. Take care."

On the way home, Deidre wondered if she and Ben would ever get an answer to Maren's disappearance. She had faith that the boys would bounce back. Their lives would unfold, they would probably marry and have families of their own, and Maren's memory would fade. It was her and Ben she worried about. Their lives would forever have a hole in it, and she wondered if, as they aged, the emptiness would grow rather than fade. She was home before she could ponder more. Supper had to be prepared for when Ben and the boys came home, he from work, they from ball practice and swimming lessons.

After supper, when the boys were settled in their room, Deidre and Ben sat on the deck, which had become their retreat at the end of most days. She made them each a gin and tonic, and they each took a first sip.

"I picked up another lead today," Deidre announced. "It's pretty flimsy, but it's something." Ben hardly reacted. They had been steered down so many roads that ended in dead ends that he had a difficult time allowing himself to believe any answer about his daughter's disappearance would ever be found. Her disappearance seemed to have happened a century ago, and to him, seemed more like a bad dream. He shifted in his chair so he was looking directly at Deidre. She took that to mean he was listening.

"I told you that I wondered if Maren went to the women's shelter to get information for a friend, so today I followed up on it. I spoke to her two best friends at the restaurant, Andra and Jessica. They said there had been a waitress who started work sometime in January. She quit after only about two months, but shortly before quitting, she came to work pretty beat up. They said they saw Maren talking to her at closing that night. I managed to track down her name and address, and I'm going to try to visit her tomorrow."

Ben had nearly drained his glass by that time, and he sat for an uncomfortably long time without saying a word. Deidre was beginning to think he had tuned her out.

"Deidre, I fear that you are going to continue to butt your head against this stone wall until you fall apart," Ben finally said. "How can you keep going when you meet one disappointment after another? I feel so worn down that I don't think I can face another round of getting my hopes up and then having them dashed. You go ahead with what you have to do, but I think I'm ready to admit to myself that too much time has passed without a clue as to Maren's whereabouts. I can live with that, I think. At least, I'm going to try." He hung his head in dejection.

Deidre's heart sank. She had hoped for some encouragement, but instead she felt as though she was more alone than ever. She wasn't angry at Ben. She felt sorry for him more than anything. Deidre slid her chair over and placed her hand on the top of his. Ben looked at her and smiled sadly. Then he raised her hand to his mouth and kissed it. Deidre felt a tear drip onto her skin, and at that instant, she loved her husband more deeply than ever.

# Chapter Thirty-Five

SWANIA HADN'T LEFT the area, and her phone number had the Two Harbors prefix, 834. At nine the next morning, Deidre punched in the number on her cell phone and anxiously waited for a number of rings, until she was about to disconnect. When Swania answered, Deidre hesitated, thinking a machine had picked up the call. After stammering the question, "Is this Swania Birkebach?" she composed herself, and before Swania could hang up, continued.

"Swania, this is Deidre Johnson. I'm Maren VanGotten's mother. May I speak to you for a minute?"

She was hopeful when Swania responded, and at the same time was surprised at the confident, heavily accented voice she heard.

"Of course I'll talk to you. I remember Maren well, even though I didn't work with her very long. She helped me through a most difficult time in my life. I must tell you that I was saddened when I heard she was missing. I hurt for you and your family. I assume you'd like to talk with me about Maren?"

Deidre affirmed that was indeed the case, and Swania agreed to have Deidre come to her home later in the day. Swania lived a way out of town, and Deidre thought it took courage, or perhaps foolishness, for her to be staying alone in the country.

After hanging up the phone, she called the church she and Ben attended and asked to speak to Pastor Ike. Fortunately he was in and said he had time that morning to meet with her. They set the meeting for ten o'clock.

Deidre puttered around the yard, cleaned up, and drove to town. At ten, she knocked on the pastor's office door. Pastor Ike was busy at his computer, and hearing Deidre's knock, he looked up.

"Deidre, I'm glad you called. For some reason, you and Ben were on my mind last night before I went to sleep, and I made a mental note to give you a call this morning. Just hadn't gotten around to it yet. Come in, come in." He stood and arranged two chairs so they were near each other at a table in the corner of his office. "How are things going for you and your family? We haven't talked for a few weeks."

Deidre looked at her hands and folded them. "Not good," she simply stated as she raised her eyes to meet his.

Pastor Ike paused a moment to gather his thoughts. "Can you share with me what's going on?" he asked. "I know sometimes it's terribly difficult to put into words, but I've found if we try, often thoughts come out that we didn't know we were harboring."

Deidre shifted uncomfortably in her chair, beginning to wonder why she had made this appointment. Then the words spilled from her mouth. "I'm so worried about Ben that I'm literally sick inside. He's pushed everything into the back of his mind, never saying Maren's name, never asking me how I'm doing. All he does when he comes home from work is sit and stare out over the fields. He plays with the boys, but even they can sense he's only going through the motions. He's pulled so far away from each of us that I'm afraid he's never going to come back, emotionally, I mean."

Without warning she began to sob, weeping more bitterly than she thought possible. She dug in her jeans for a tissue so she could blow her nose. Pastor Ike sat patiently, and several minutes went by before Deidre could calm herself.

"I know you're worried about Ben, but how are *you* doing, Deidre? You want to fix everything for everyone else, but what are you doing for yourself?"

Deidre had to think long and hard on that question. "I've been doing some investigative work on my own. I don't doubt that Jeff, Sheriff DeAngelo, is doing all he can, but I have my skills, too. I just think another set of eyes and ears on the case won't hurt." She stopped for a second or two, then added, "And I pray."

"So, how's that going for you? The prayer, I mean?"

Deidre drew in a deep breath. "Not so good. God, if he even exists, isn't listening to me." As soon as she had said those words, she regretted uttering them, and she waited for Pastor Ike's reprimand.

Instead, he spoke in a soft, reassuring voice. "Deidre, there are times when we all doubt. Sometimes I look at the condition of this world, and I wonder, where is God in all of this? I wonder, is God a being we have invented to help us explain the unexplainable? Then I stand outside at night, beneath the starry sky, and look at the vastness of the universe. The sight pulls me to the belief that God is so infinite that even though we can't understand, He is still present, just as the universe is, just as the stars are, just as our earth is." He paused for what seemed to her many minutes.

"Deidre, doubt is good. It causes us to think, to struggle, to find answers. I'm sure you have prayed that Maren will someday walk through the door and you'll be able to wrap your arms around her again. That may happen, or it may not. I know that you've probably heard people say that God knows everything, has a plan for everything, that he can do anything."

Deidre wiped away a trickle of snot that drained from her nose and nodded. Ike continued.

"I'm going to tell you something I'd probably never be able to confess to from the pulpit. If I did, I'd probably be run out of town on a rail." He snickered at the image. "I don't believe those things, and neither do many other clergy I know."

Deidre looked at him in disbelief. What she heard coming from his mouth would have sounded like blasphemy to her if she was more sure of her own belief.

"You see, Deidre, I just can't believe that a God who can do anything he chooses allows people to treat each other the way they do. Oh, I'm not talking about the day-to-day petty hurts we cause each other. I'm talking about genocide, about people starving when the world has enough to feed all, if we would only share. I'm talking about people using others and destroying their lives in the process, people who appear to have no feelings, no conscience."

Deidre interrupted. "But don't you think that God has a plan, and that everything fits into his plan? You're right that people keep telling me that." She was getting an uneasy feeling, as though she was listening to a confession she shouldn't be hearing.

"No, I don't," Pastor Ike stated emphatically. "Look, everyone has a free will. We can choose to steal or not to steal. We can choose to lie or not to lie. But it goes much deeper than that. A murderer chooses to kill. A wife beater chooses to beat his wife. We are responsible for our actions, not God and not the devil. Deidre, I've given this a lot of thought and study over my years, since childhood, really." He stopped and rubbed his eyes as if he were tired. Deidre had no response.

"I think we often pray prayers that are impossible for God to answer. Then, well meaning people say, 'God answered, and the answer was no.' Or they say, 'God's ways are not our ways.' I've even heard people say, 'Well, it was part of God's plan that this atrocity or that atrocity was perpetrated.' If that's true, then I want no part of that kind of God. Take Maren, for instance. I'm sure you have prayed that nothing evil has happened to her, but what's been done has been done, and God cannot change that. I know there are people in my congregation praying that she is safe. If she is, she is. If she isn't, she isn't. God can't roll back the calendar and give us a do over."

Deidre looked into his eyes and saw a profound sadness, and the thought went through her mind that he had lost his faith. She didn't quite know what to say, but finally she uttered, "If that's true, then why do we pray?" She saw a look of life spring up in his eyes.

"We pray for at least two reasons. I firmly believe God mourns for us during times such as what you are experiencing. Do you remember the account of Martha and Mary when their brother Lazarus died?"

Deidre shook her head and for a moment felt extremely inadequate. Pastor Ike laughed and his eyes twinkled, and he became more animated than he had been so far during their conversation.

"Lazarus was dying, so Martha and Mary sent word for Christ to come heal him. To make a long story short, Christ took his time, dallied, we would say, and Lazarus died. When Christ finally arrived, Martha and Mary were distraught, weeping and mourning, and we are told Christ wept. Then, according to scripture, he raised Lazarus from the dead." Ike went on to say that he never used that scripture during funerals, because he didn't think it appropriate.

"Deidre, one time when I experienced the death of a person I loved very much, I asked God if he cared that I was hurting so badly. Now, I didn't hear an audible voice, but I knew, I just *knew* the answer. It was a resounding 'yes.' And then the story of Lazarus made sense to me. Christ wasn't weeping for Lazarus. He was weeping for Martha and Mary. He was there for them."

After a long period of silence during which both he and Deidre pondered what he had said, Pastor Ike continued. "We pray that we feel God's presence with us when we walk through these frightening and confusing times. We pray that we see him through our human eyes, and know He is there to give us strength to make it through this day, and we do that tomorrow, and the next, and the next. Believe me, as the years have gone by, I've experienced the answer to this kind of prayer over and over, and I have seen this prayer answered in the lives of many, many people."

After Deidre had time to think about what he said, she asked, "You said there were at least two reasons to pray. What's the other?"

She could see that Pastor Ike was pleased that she was following him. "The other reason is to keep the lines of communication going between you and God. It's as simple as that."

Deidre wasn't quite sure she understood, but she wanted to discuss the issue more. Together, they kicked around the ideas Pastor Ike had put forth until finally she said, "I used to think I had to believe God was a magic God who could wave His wand and make everything better. You've given me an image of God without the magic. Pastor Ike, I think I like your God a whole lot better." They both laughed at her conclusion.

"Do you want me to pray with you?" Ike asked. Deidre said she would. She walked out of his office feeling more confused but more at peace than when their talk had begun.

# Chapter Thirty-Six

SWANIA LIVED TWELVE MILES from Two Harbors just off Old Highway 61, what was called the Scenic Drive by most locals. Deidre crossed the starting line for Grandma's Marathon and pictured the sight of ten thousand runners lined up, ready to attempt the run of twenty-six-plus miles to Duluth. The last race had occurred only a month or so after Maren disappeared, and she thought about how her life had been turned upside down. She remembered how they all planned to be at the starting line to watch the racers, and she couldn't help but think of how they had prepared for the event. Dave was scheduled to run, and he had hopes of finishing the marathon in under four hours. Actually, he had confided in the family that he was shooting for three hours and thirty minutes. Maren had planned to surprise him with a victory picnic at her parents' place after the race.

Naturally, Dave hadn't run the race, and for the first time in several days, she thought of him. She made a mental note to get in touch soon to find out how he was coping. Since he had moved to Duluth, they seldom communicated.

She passed through the village of Knife River, so deep in thought she realized she didn't remember doing so, and for an instant wasn't sure how far she had driven. Concentrating, she re-oriented herself and began paying attention to the driveway markers. A few minutes later, she slowed and turned off the highway onto a driveway that extended down to the lake. She was surprised by the small, neat cabin that sat at the end of the drive.

There was no doorbell, so Deidre gently rapped on the frame of the screen door. After no one answered, she tested the screen door and found it was unlocked, opened it and rapped louder on the wooden door. Again, she waited, but no one answered. Just as she was about to leave, she heard footsteps inside the building, and the door opened a crack.

"Hi," she said as disarmingly as she could. "I'm Deidre, Maren's mother. I called earlier this morning to ask if we could talk. Is this still an okay time? If not, I can return."

The door closed and Deidre heard a chain lock being unhooked, then the door swung inward. Standing in front of her was a diminutive young lady. Deidre thought she looked hardly twenty. The lady—girl, really—could have been a poster girl advertising the Austrian Alps. Her long, blonde hair was braided into a single rope, done off to the side so it looped over her shoulder to the front. Her blue eyes were the color of the sky on a clear summer day, and Deidre was struck by their clarity.

In a heavily accented voice, Swania invited Deidre in. The cabin had only four rooms that Deidre could see: a kitchen that was partially separated from a dining area, a small living room with a picture window looking out over the lake, and another room behind a closed door. She assumed it to be the bedroom. Swania asked her if she wanted a cup of tea, and when Deidre said that would be nice, her host hurried to take down two cups from the cupboard. In minutes she had brewed the tea, and Deidre noticed the water was already hot. From the refrigerator, Swania retrieved a plate of some kind of apple dessert. She escorted Deidre into the living room and asked if she wanted to sit so she could enjoy the lake view.

To Deidre, the situation appeared as though Swania was terribly lonely, and this was fulfilling her need to be with someone. Deidre began by thanking her for her time, and then sampled one of the apple squares. After complimenting the her, Deidre was relieved when Swania initiated the conversation.

"I'm so sorry about Maren. She was one of the nicest people I've met since coming to the United States of America." Deidre smiled at Swania's iterating the complete name of the nation. Swania didn't notice and continued. "She was one of my only friends, and I've missed her so much. She was always there for me when I needed someone to talk to about a very personal problem I was having."

Deidre didn't quite know what to say. Should she tell Swania that she was glad Maren was missed? Should she ask about what kind of personal problems Swania was having? Evidently she paused too long, because Swania quickly spoke.

"Oh, I'm sorry to have brought this up so suddenly. I know you must be grieving terribly. From Maren's and my conversations, I know the two of you were extremely close. I apologize for hurting you more with my abruptness."

Deidre smiled a forced smile. "No, don't be sorry. This is what I've come to find out, if Maren ever confided to you that she was afraid of someone, or if someone was harassing her. I'd dearly love to know what the two of you discussed. Is it possible she was trying to help someone from work escape an abusive relationship?"

Swania stared at the floor. "Yes, she was. It was me. I would guess this is what you want to talk to me about. Everyone at work knew I was being beaten by my husband, except they all avoided me, made me feel as if I was the one who was doing something wrong. Everyone but Maren, that is. The first time I came to work with a black eye, she stopped me in the hall and said I didn't have to tell her, but it looked as if someone had hit me. She said she would be there for me if I needed a friend. After that, we had many talks, sometimes after work, while sitting in her car."

"Did she give you advice, or did she just listen?" Deidre inquired as gently as she could.

Swania took a deep breath before answering. "Those were tough times for me. I was so confused I didn't know where to turn. Maren was always there to listen to my troubles, but then she said she was going to get me some information about what I could do to help myself. Everything in my life sort of settled for a while, but then one night my husband totally lost control and hit me in the face, hard. I came to work, but I couldn't tolerate the looks from the other waitresses or the whispers behind my back. I had a long talk with Maren that night, and she told me what she thought I should do. I quit the restaurant that night."

Deidre could sense there was more to Swania's story and she was interested in it, not only from Maren's perspective but out of concern for Swania.

"I may be asking too much from you personally, Swania, but would you mind telling me your story, from the beginning?"

Swania looked puzzled? "At the restaurant?" she questioned.

Deidre shook her head. "No, from Germany to now."

Swania gave a sad smile, but Deidre thought she detected a note of thankfulness that someone would care to hear her out.

"I suppose it's a story that has happened over and over. I was young."

Deidre almost chuckled and would have made a wisecrack if the situation hadn't been so troubling. Swania was hardly more than a girl now, and she was referring to when she was young.

"My father was a successful businessman in Landstuhl, where the United States Army has a facility. My husband, Jed Birkebach, was stationed at the military base. We met in a café and he asked for my telephone number. I thought he was good looking, and gave it to him. That night I told my mother I had met this nice-looking man from the base, and he even had a German name. She warned me not to get involved. How I wish I had listened to her," Swania sighed. "But I didn't."

She took a sip of her tea and nibbled a piece of the apple dessert. "To make a long story short, Jed treated me like a queen. Brought me flowers, took me to the best restaurants. We danced, traveled on his days off. He swept me off my feet with his ways." She looked wistfully out the window and across the lake. "He said he loved me more than life itself. I fell deeply in love with a man I really didn't know that well. He said his parents were doctors in the U.S., and that he intended to pursue a career in medicine when he got out of the service. I was so in love I never checked his story."

Swania's narrative held Deidre's attention, although she was sure she knew how it would end.

"Shortly before Jed's return to the States, we were married." Swania paused as she reflected on the day. "I've never seen my mother weep so bitterly in my life. Papa, always the stoic one in our family, clenched his jaw and said nothing, but I could tell he was hurt.

"Jed was discharged only a few weeks after we got here, and he said we were moving to Two Harbors, where he had been born. Everything changed from that day on. It was as though he had an iron fist that had been cloaked in velvet. We moved into this cabin and I loved it. A week later was the first time he hit me." Swania almost winced as she said the words. "He hit me so hard in the stomach with his fist that it knocked the wind out of me. As I gasped for air, he said, 'Don't ever forget who runs the show here. You ain't in Germany anymore.' I couldn't believe what had happened, but over the next few days, Jed was back to his caring self. In fact, the next day he sent me two dozen roses from the flower shop in town. I thought maybe I did something that night to trigger his anger. Jed was trying to find work at a nursing home. I found out that was to be his career in medicine."

Deidre saw that Swania was almost ready to burst into tears, and wondered if she should invent an excuse to leave her alone, but the narrative continued.

"I got a job at the restaurant to help support us, and that's where I met Maren. She immediately became my best friend, although I don't think I was hers. She was going to marry a guy she adored, and it seemed he reciprocated her feelings. Then the relationship between Jed and me became unbearable. One night he reached across the table and hit my shoulder so hard he knocked me off my chair. He didn't say anything, just got up and left. I heard him drive away, spraying gravel as he went.

"Another time, he got angry because I cooked the yolks of his eggs too firm. He threw the plate of food against the wall, grabbed me by the hair, and rubbed my face in the mess. He had a way of hurting me so he left bruises where they wouldn't show: my back, my chest, my legs. That's when I began to tell Maren about what was happening to me."

Deidre hesitated, and then said, "If this is too painful for you to talk about, you don't have to continue. We can sit and enjoy the lake and finish our tea. By the way, this apple dessert is delicious. What is it?" She wanted to give Swania an opportunity to stop her story if she wanted.

"It's just a strudel," Swania answered. "No, I want to finish my story. This is the first time I've had anyone be interested." She continued. "The final act was one day last winter. It snowed about an inch or so during the day, and I had finished sweeping off the steps when Jed drove in. He got out of his car in a rage. He said, 'You lazy German bitch, couldn't you have cleared the snow off the driveway?' I made the mistake of saying that it was only an inch and I didn't think it needed removing. He slapped my face and then kicked my thigh. When I fell down, he grabbed my head and smashed my face into the ground. Then, as he always did after he beat me, he drove away and left me lying there.

"I cleaned up and put an icepack on my face. That night I went to work for the last time. Maren and I sat in her car and talked long after our shift ended. She said I had to leave Jed or he was going to eventually kill me. I believed her. She had me follow her in my car to the women's shelter and offered to come in with me. I said she didn't have to, that I'd be okay."

Deidre interrupted. "Did you see her after that night?'

"Oh, yes," Swania said with a glimmer of remembrance in her eyes. "I think we saw each other at least a half dozen more times over the next few weeks. She accompanied me to my first meeting with an attorney. With Maren's help, I came to the conclusion that I would divorce Jed and go back to Germany, where I belonged. That was a difficult decision, because I was ashamed to ask my parents for help. When I told my mother what I was going to do and that I'd need financial help, she cried. But I think this time they were tears of happiness that I was safe and would be coming home."

"How did Jed react to all of this?" Deidre asked, sitting on the edge of her chair.

"Well, as you would expect, he was at first very contrite, making promises that he would change. He said we could go to counseling sessions, that he would seek help. He said he had PTSD. That made me laugh. The most danger he'd ever been in was trying to make it back to his base from a beer hall in Landstuhl. When his cajoling didn't work, he became verbally offensive. All this was over the phone, of course."

Deidre was on edge. "Did he know that Maren had advised you to call it quits?"

"He knew I was confiding with someone, but I don't think he knew it was Maren."

Deidre wondered.

"The legal process was proceeding well, and I thought I'd come here, to our cabin, to retrieve some of my things while Jed was at work. I didn't know that his schedule at the nursing home had changed, and now he worked nights. I let myself in and had just begun packing my things when Jed pulled up behind my car. I was trapped and he knew it. He grabbed the picture I had in my hands and threw it across the room. Then he began to beat and kick me until I was unconscious. That was the last I remember until I came to some time later."

"Is there any chance that Jed found out Maren advised you to seek a divorce? You see, I'm wondering if he could have had it in for Maren, and hated her so much he wanted to kill her."

Swania shook her head and snorted a sound of derision. "I wouldn't have put it past him, but he couldn't have done it. When I regained consciousness, Jed was gone, so I called 911 and a sheriff's deputy arrived in minutes. He put out a call to law enforcement and a half hour later Jed was stopped by a state trooper on I-35."

For a moment Deidre's mind spun with confusion. Why hadn't Jeff been on top of this? Then she realized Swania's cabin was two miles southwest of the county line. Swania would have been dealing with the St. Louis County Sheriff's Department. She breathed a sigh of relief.

"What happened after that?" she urged Swania to finish her story.

"Jed was arrested and indicted on several different charges. The most serious are assault with intent to commit great bodily harm and assault causing great bodily harm. He couldn't come up with bail and is sitting in the St. Louis County Jail."

"Those are serious charges. You must have been pretty beaten up," Deidre commented, her concern evident by the tone of her voice.

Swania twisted her mouth. "Yeah, I guess I was. He broke my nose, which needed to be set and packed. One of the major issues was a kick he administered when I was down. It left a six-inch hematoma on the back of my thigh. Those injuries, coupled with a black eye and numerous contusions and scratches, led to the charge."

Deidre shook her head in amazement. "I'm no lawyer, but I know the penalty for this is very severe, thirty years, I think."

Swania nodded. "I was able to return home after that. My parents have been sending me money so I can live here until Jed's trial is over. Then I'll be going home, with my tail between my legs, I'm afraid."

Deidre was about to reassure the woman that she need not be ashamed, but then it dawned on her that she hadn't asked Swania about the date Jed was arrested.

"Swania, what was the date you were beaten so badly?" Deidre asked. Inwardly, she hoped it was after Maren's disappearance.

"It was in April, April fifteenth to be exact. Your tax day. That's why I know Jed couldn't have been involved with Maren. He was where he should have been, in jail."

The day had been draining for Deidre. Another idea was shot down, with no new leads or theories on the horizon. She looked at Swania and wondered how any man could abuse such a lovely woman. Her scars had pretty well healed, although the faint remnant of a scar lingered under her left eye. On the one hand, Deidre was overjoyed that a greater tragedy had been averted and that Maren might have played a role in the outcome. On the other hand, she felt a tremendous letdown. She had been so sure she was on the right track.

In the end, she had to say goodbye to Swania, and after hugs and best wishes, Deidre got in her car and slowly drove home.

# Chapter Thirty-Seven

DEIDRE COULDN'T GET HERSELF to think of anything creative for supper, and as she scrounged in the refrigerator for something to cook, she drew a blank. They had leftovers last night, and the night before a scrambled egg-cabbage concoction that sounded terrible but was really quite tasty. The evening before that, she had fixed two frozen pizzas. A pang of guilt swept over her as she realized she had not been a very good wife and mother the last few weeks. Not that she ever considered herself a Suzie Homemaker, but because Ben worked all day and she supposedly had time, perhaps the least she could do was have a meal ready for him in the evening. Deidre thought maybe she had let her personal investigation into Maren's abduction become an obsession.

She closed the refrigerator door, poured herself a glass of ice water, and sat in her usual place on the deck. After holding the glass to her throbbing temple for a few seconds, she took a sip of water. It felt good washing down her throat, and for just a moment, she could feel the cold in her stomach. She closed her eyes and leaned back in the chair.

The next thing she was aware of was her glass being gently lifted from her hand and someone bending over her and kissing her forehead. She sat upright with a start.

"Hey, didn't mean to scare you." It was Ben home from work. Deidre didn't know how long she had slept, but she wondered how the glass could have remained upright in her hand. Ben sat down in a chair next to her.

"I picked up the boys at my folks. Don't know what we'd do without their help. You look like you had a rough day. Anything you want to talk about?"

Deidre shrugged, but started to tell him what had gone on. She omitted the part about seeing Pastor Ike.

"Visited with that waitress I told you about last night, Swania Birkebach. She's a lovely young lady who got suckered into a bad situation. It fries my behind how some men can be so duplicitous when it comes to selling themselves to women. She's from Germany . . . I think I told you that. Anyway, she met this U.S. soldier who wined and dined her, convinced her that he was her knight in shining armor. She married him, and as soon as they got to the States, he began to abuse her something awful." Deidre paused and shook her head. "It's beyond me why he would have married her if he wasn't going to care for her."

"That's an easy question to answer," Ben said as he met her gaze. "You know as well as I do that it's all about power. It's as though they have a need and a desire to dominate. What's going to happen to her?"

"She told me everything. As I suspected, Maren was trying to help her and had advised her to divorce her husband. When she said that, I was sure my hunch was right, and I was going to end up with a solid lead into Maren's disappearance. But no, her husband, Jed, was in jail for brutally beating her during the time that that Maren went missing. It couldn't have been him. Good news is he's facing a lot of prison time. Their divorce will be final soon, and after Jed's trial, Swania's returning home. Seems she has very supportive parents, but the girl has learned some hard lessons."

Steve and Jack came pounding down the stairs and as preteen boys are prone to do, almost tore the screen door off its hinges as they burst onto the deck.

"What's for supper?" Steve wanted to know. "I'm starving."

"Me, too," Jack added.

Deidre had been in such a daze that she forgot there was nothing prepared for their meal. She pushed her hair back from her forehead, and placed both hands on the sides of her head. Her headache was gone, but now she felt a pang of guilt.

"Guys, I'm so sorry. I got so wrapped up in my own business today that I totally blew off supper." Tears trickled down her cheeks, and before she could dry them, both boys were at her side. Steve had a dirty tissue out of his pocket and was dabbing her face. The scene was so out off context that she began to laugh through her tears.

"I'm okay, really. It's just that I was so tense all day, thinking I finally was onto something, that when it didn't pan out I felt like the bottom dropped out of everything I was trying to accomplish." She smiled and brushed away the remnant of a tear with the back of her hand. "Come inside. I'll fix us something."

"I don't think so." Ben stood up. "We haven't been out for a nice meal since I don't know when. You kids get cleaned up. Steve, put that snot-rag in the trash. Come to think of it, throw your clothes in the wash. They're a mess."

In spite of her protests, Ben dragged Deidre from her chair and hustled her upstairs. They each took a quick shower, and Ben was pleased to hear the shower on in the boys' bathroom. By the time they were on the road into town, it was long past their usual mealtime, but Ben ignored the boys' whining. He reached over and placed his hand on Deidre's knee. She looked at him and smiled.

Ben drove a few miles up the shore to a well-known restaurant. The place was made of huge pine logs, both stacked for walls and standing upright for support. Because it was getting late the parking lot was nearly empty, and a hostess escorted them to a table right away. Soon the four of them had their faces buried in their menus, trying to decide from the list of entrées.

"So, boys, what did you do today that was exciting?" Ben asked, trying to start a conversation.

"Nothin'," Steve answered and studied the menu further.

"Aw, come on, something good must have happened," Ben urged.

Jack put his menu down. "How could anything good happen? You're always at work, and when you're home all you do is sit and read or watch TV. And Mom's never home during the day. In the evening she just sits on the deck. We're always dumped at Grandma and Grandpa's during the day, and you know how exciting that is. I mean, we love them, but come on, how many picture albums do we have to look at? When are you and Mom going to start to do things with us again?"

Thinking he had gone too far and trying to hide his tears, Steve hid behind his raised menu. Deidre's face flushed, not from anger, but from the impact of what her son had said. Ben looked at his folded hands. Both parents sat in silence for a moment before Deidre could speak

"Jack William." She only used that name when she was about to give a lecture. "Jack William, put the menu down so I can see you. Now look at me, right in my eyes." Jack waited for the axe to fall. "Jack, you are absolutely right. Everything you said is exactly what's been happening." She reached over and placed her hand on his. "We've been through this before, but I guess Dad and I have slipped back into our own worlds again. I'm so sorry for the way I've been neglecting you boys. Can you forgive me?"

Ben placed his hands on both of theirs. "That goes for me, too, son. And Steve. We love you guys so much, and we would never do anything to hurt you. What about this, let's have a nice meal right now, and when we get home, I promise you we'll all have a good talk about this. I know we've done that before, but we probably should do it again. Okay?"

Deidre looked up and saw the waitress waiting on the other side of the room, and she realized they must have been the center of attention in the restaurant. Fortunately, there were only two other parties in other booths, and they at least seemed to be too interested in their food to have noticed the incident. Molly, their waitress, knew Ben and Deidre's situation well, and when she came to their table Deidre saw a hint of moistness in her eyes. "Hi, folks, what can we get for you?"

# Chapter
## Thirty-Eight

IT WAS AFTER NINE when they arrived home, and even though it was late, Ben held true to his promise to have a family talk. He spent a minute or two in the kitchen and came back with four glasses of soda and a few cookies on a plate. "We might as well be comfortable while we visit." He tried his best to make the situation at least seem normal.

After each of them had settled in, Ben began. "All the way home I thought about what you said, Jack, and I can't tell you how sorry I am that I've neglected you guys. I'm sure your mother is, too. Can you tell me what I've done that hurt you the most?" There was a long period of silence, and both Deidre and Ben let it hang. Jack spoke first.

"I think the thing I miss most is your laugh, Dad. I don't think you've laughed once since we lost track of Maren."

"Yeah, me too," Steve broke into the conversation. "But most of all, I miss your hugs. You never hug me anymore."

That comment cut Ben the deepest, because an eight-year-old boy's admission that he missed being hugged was telling. His boys were hurting as much as, or maybe more than, the rest of them. Perhaps they harbored a fear that if something so serious could happen to their older sister, they were also in danger.

"What about me?" Deidre queried. "What is the most hurt I've caused?"

Again, it was Jack who spoke first. "You're never here, and when you are, you still aren't. It's like you walk around the house, but your mind is always far away. You know what I mean?" Deidre knew.

"How about you, Steve?" she asked.

He thought for a second or two. "I miss the walks we used to take in the woods. They were so much fun, especially when we'd see animals and stop to watch them." He paused. "Will that ever happen again?"

"Yes, it will," Deidre said. "You boys are both one hundred percent right," she confessed. "But I give you my promise, I'm going to try to set things right, at least the best I can. Your dad and I have been so consumed with our own loss that we have almost deserted you. I'm so sorry." She moved to be closer to them.

"Starting right now, I'm giving up any idea I've had that I could catch whoever did this to Maren. That's Sheriff DeAngelo's job, and I should have just left it in his hands. Tomorrow, I promise you, we'll do something fun. What do you think?"

Before the boys could respond, Ben spoke up. "Tell you what, I've got a few vacation days built up, and I'll call my boss in the morning and take the day off. We don't have much on the table right now at work, so they won't miss me. You guys think about what you'd like to do, come up with a couple ideas. How's that sound?"

Both boys perked up at the thought of having a family day like they used to. They decided to go to their room and talk over what they'd want to do, and when they stood to leave the room, Ben gathered both of them in his arms. He whispered in their ears, "You're safe with us. Never forget that." He gave each a squeeze and playfully swatted their behinds as they moved toward the stairs.

Deidre called after them, "I'll be up in fifteen to tuck you in."

*****

OVER AN EARLY BREAKFAST, the family discussed what they would do for the day, and the boys elected to take the canoe up to Dunnigan Lake so they could fish for smallmouth bass. Deidre suggested they pick up some deli supplies for a picnic, and by nine o'clock they were headed north, up Highway Two. At ten thirty they passed the Happy Wanderer tavern and minutes later were unloading their supplies at the lake. Deidre couldn't remember the last time the boys had been so happy.

She watched Steve cast a line from shore, even before the canoe had been launched. His lure had hardly hit the water when he hooked a small bass.

"Well, that's one," he hollered to his brother, and the competition was on. Ben got everybody situated in the canoe with Deidre in the bow, the boys sitting on the floor, and him taking the stern. With a push-off from shore, they were underway, but Steve hollered, "Wait, backpaddle, Dad. Look at the sundews on that old log."

The water swirled around Ben's paddle as he put his muscle into the backstroke, and the canoe came to a halt near an ancient tree that had fallen in the water. It had a thick covering of moss, and growing in the moss were clusters of thumbnail-sized plants.

"Look at those," Steve gushed. "Aren't they beautiful?" Jack looked at them for a second.

"What's so great about them?" he scoffed at the sight of the red-green miniatures.

"Hey, take a closer look," Deidre reprimanded her son. "See all those hairs on the leaves?" Before she could continue, Steve took up the instruction.

"Look at the droplets on each hair. That's sticky stuff that traps insects, and then the leaf curls up and digests it. These plants are carnivorous, just like that one in *Little Shop of Horrors*. If you listen, you can hear them saying, 'feed me.' Be careful, or they're going to get you!" He giggled, and Deidre marveled at how different her sons were, even though they were so much alike.

"Come on," Jack urged. "Let's get fishing. I'm already one behind, and if I'm going to win the contest, I want to get around the point." He gestured toward a rocky peninsula that jutted out into the lake.

Dunnigan Lake was filled with bass, and the boys hooked one nearly every cast. Finally, Ben suggested that they pull up onto a large flat rock near shore and eat lunch.

Jack pretended to count on his fingers and toes. "Let's see, I think that makes nineteen fish for me. No, I take it back. It's twenty-one. How about you, Steve?"

"You know how many I caught. But mine were bigger than yours." He laughed, and Deidre enjoyed hearing the banter between her boys, knowing their teasing was a healthy sign.

The day was perfect. After lunch they laid on their backs on the rock and watched the fluffs of clouds drift across the sky. After a little more fishing, they headed for the landing. Each boy had caught thirty-nine fish. None of them were keepers, but it didn't matter. Ben made them put their rods away, figuring a tie was a good way to end the contest.

No one mentioned work, the approach of the school year, or Maren. It was the best day any of them had had the whole summer. Deidre figured they'd be home for a late dinner, and what they would eat consumed her thoughts.

*****

EVERYONE WAS IN GREAT spirits as they turned into their drive. The twins helped Ben untie the canoe and carry some of the gear to their storage shed. Deidre could hear them bantering, the boys still giving their dad a hard time for making them stop fishing before the tie had been broken. She heard him laugh for the first time in weeks, almost three months, actually, and it felt good. The day had been as close to normal as possible.

Deidre hummed a senseless tune to herself while she scrounged in the refrigerator for leftovers. By the time her family tromped into the kitchen, she had the table loaded with food: leftover roast beef from a couple of days ago, half a sandwich brought back from the restaurant the night before, lunchmeat, bread, cheese, veggies still in their tray, and an assortment of other edibles. Too, there was a half of a cherry pie that was only three or four days old. They dove into the food as if it was a gourmet feast.

She was cleaning up the dirty dishes and Ben was shooing Steve and Jack to bed when she remembered she hadn't checked her cell phone when she returned home. She had intentionally left it behind when they went fishing so their time wouldn't be disturbed by calls.

Ben had done the same. She powered it up and a message immediately flashed on the screen, alerting her to the fact that she had a voice message. She activated the phone's speaker setting, and instantly felt a spasm run through her body.

"Deidre, this is Jeff. Call me as soon as you can. We need to talk."

Deidre couldn't push the speed dial on her call list fast enough, and with shaking hands she held the phone to her ear while it rang. Jeff picked up on the third ring.

"Deidre," Jeff exclaimed. He had seen her name come up on his caller ID. "Is Ben there with you?"

From the tone of Jeff's voice Deidre knew something serious was coming next, and her heart began to hammer in her chest. "Yes, he is. Well, he's upstairs with the boys right now."

"I've news that you'll want to hear. I know it's late, but can I come out right now and talk to both of you? You might even want to include Megan and Dave in the conversation, if they are available."

"Can you share what it is now, or do you want to wait until we're together? I don't think Dave or Megan can make it. They live in Duluth, you know. By all means come right out. Is there anything you want?" Deidre paused, and then exclaimed, "Oh, God. I'm just babbling." She sat down at the kitchen table. "We'll be ready when you get here."

She rushed to the foot of the stairs and hollered to Ben. "You better get down here right away. Jeff called and said he's heading out to see us." She gasped for a breath. "He said he has important news."

Deidre tried to breathe deeply and calm herself but it didn't work. She put the rest of the dirty dishes in the dishwasher and threw out the leftovers that had outlasted their time. By then Ben was next to her side, and he wrapped his arms around her.

"Did he say what news he has?"

Deidre shook her head and wiped a developing tear from her eye. "No, he just said it was important. You better get the boys down. Remember, we promised them they'd be included in everything that we found out about Maren."

# Chapter Thirty-Nine

BEN WONDERED WHAT COULD be so important that Jeff would come to see them at nine thirty at night, but he went upstairs to rouse the boys. They were nearly asleep when he entered their room, but when he told them Jeff was coming out and they might want to hear what he had to say, both hurriedly got dressed and came downstairs. From an upstairs window, Ben saw a pair of headlights sweep across their yard as Jeff pulled up next to the deck. By the time Ben reached the bottom of the stairs, Deidre had let Jeff in and was attempting to make small talk.

"Jeff, it's so good to see you. Whatever news you have, it must be important."

From the other room, Ben heard Jeff's reply. "It is. I didn't want to break this news to you over the phone, because it's exciting and scary at the same time. Let's go into your living room where we can be more comfortable."

Ben sat down in an overstuffed chair before Deidre and Jeff entered the room. His legs suddenly lost their ability to support him, and his heart pounded against his ribs. Steve and Jeff sat side by side on the sofa, while Deidre eased herself into a rocking chair. She began to move back and forth mechanically while Jeff perched on the edge of a straight-backed chair he pulled in from the corner of the living room.

"This has been a long ride for all of you, I know. Frankly, I've been distraught over how little my department has been able to do in solving Maren's disappearance."

Deidre was fidgety, and thought, *Come on, Jeff, tell us what you've found*, but she kept her mouth shut. Her rocking lessened and she wondered if Jeff noticed. She tried to calm herself.

"I don't know if I told you, but right after we lost touch with Maren, I contacted the bank that carried her credit and debit cards," Jeff began. "I asked that they not put a hold on the cards, but that they flag any time one of the cards was used. This morning they called."

Deidre sat bolt upright, and from across the room, she saw Ben move to the edge of his seat.

"Someone's using Maren's card? Who is it?" Deidre blurted out.

"At the time, we had no idea. Her charge card was presented in a convenience store in St. Paul. It's not uncommon for a stolen card to pop up at one of those places."

Before Jeff could continue, Ben spoke up. "Don't they check IDs in those places? How could someone using Maren's card simply sign her name?"

Jeff sort of smiled. "They don't check often, especially if it's for a small amount. This was for cigarettes, a liter of Diet Coke, and a bag of chips."

"Well, we know it wasn't Maren," Deidre volunteered. "She never smoked, and she was always careful about what she ate."

The twins sat silently throughout the entire conversation, their eyes wide with questions they were too timid to ask.

Jeff nodded, then continued. "A few hours later, someone used her debit card to withdraw money from Maren's checking account at an ATM. Like with the cards, we had purposely not closed her account at the bank, and you had never asked about it. I didn't want to say anything until you questioned her accounts. Maren had two hundred dollars in checking, and the person who withdrew from the account took out eighty."

Suddenly the thought occurred to Deidre that ATMs, especially in banks, are usually guarded by security cameras. "Was a video taken when the ATM was used?" she asked, anticipation in her voice.

Jeff looked at the floor, then up at Ben and Deidre. "Yes, and I was sent isolated pictures of the individual who was using Maren's card. I'd like all of you to take a close look at them in good light. There are five separate frames showing the person at different angles. They're black and white and pretty grainy, but I think you'll be able to make out the person's features."

The group moved to the kitchen, where they could spread the photos out on the table, and Deidre removed the centerpiece so its surface was clear. She turned on the light above the table, and set it as bright as it would go. Jeff placed the first photo on the table and everyone peered at it intently. The angle was from behind and showed a woman who appeared to be about Maren's height at the machine. Her hair was tied up in a loose mass. Several stray locks escaped the clasp holding it, giving the person a disheveled appearance. She wore a loose shirt that hung out of her jeans.

Jeff said, "The next image is not the best quality, but perhaps it will ring a bell." He placed the next picture beside the first, and again everyone looked at it intently.

"From the back she reminds me of Maren," Steve volunteered. "But I don't think so. This lady is skinnier and kind of slumped over."

"Do you have a picture of her from the front?" Ben inquired.

"We do. It was taken as she turned from the machine. She was facing directly at the camera. She stopped for a moment to fold the money she had withdrawn and stuff it into her pocket." Jeff methodically placed the third picture next to the first two and stepped back from the table.

Deidre gasped, and Ben exclaimed, "My God, it's Maren!" Before he could say more, one of the boys let out a whoop, "Maren! It *is* her! Look at her eyes! That's her!"

"I thought so, too, when I first looked at the pictures," Jeff said. "Look again, and try to find reasons why it's not."

After minutes of staring at the photos, Jeff laid out the other two, and no one could do anything but believe it was Maren.

"I know you desperately want it to be her," Jeff cautioned, "So look at them as critically as you can. Did Maren have any identifying marks, a mole, a scar, anything that might help us? I know you told us that she didn't have any tattoos, but were there any other marks that might help us?"

No one spoke until Deidre answered. "Nothing significant enough to show on a photo. And I don't see anything on this girl that would make me believe it isn't Maren." The others murmured their assent.

"I just had a thought," Deidre offered. "If this was a person who had stolen Maren's ATM card, she wouldn't have the correct PIN. The person in the picture appears to be punching in the number. Jeff, have you seen the video, too?"

Jeff nodded. "I have, and it looks like this person steps up to the machine and correctly enters the PIN. In the video, she takes only a second, and a few seconds later she takes the money from the slot. That's one of the reasons I think this may be Maren."

Deidre felt as though her legs were giving out, and she suggested they return to the living room. After they were seated, Jeff continued.

"There are still too many questions that haven't been answered. Where has Maren been these past, what is it, three months? And why did she wait so long before she began to use her cards again? There are so many possibilities."

Ben agreed. "The pictures show only a small area. Was there any indication in the video that she wasn't alone? I wonder, was somebody with her, perhaps forcing her to use the ATM?"

"Or maybe she's been held by someone and has escaped. She would need money to get home," Deidre added.

"But that wouldn't explain the cigarettes she bought at the convenience store. I'd go with her being held by somebody and forced to cooperate," Ben postulated.

"I know what's happened. I saw it in a movie once," Jack said excitedly. "I bet she got hit on the head and lost her memory. She can remember some things, like her PIN, but she doesn't know where she's at or who she is." He looked at everyone's face and then in a subdued tone said, "Well, it could have happened."

Deidre took Jack in her arms. "Yes, it could have." He looked up at her, the look in his eyes pleading his case. "The important thing is that Maren is alive, and we're going to get her back."

Deidre abruptly stood up. "Oh, my gosh, we've totally forgotten about Megan and Dave. We've got to tell them the news right now. Jeff, can you wait?" He assured them he would. "Why don't you call Megan, and I'll call Dave," she suggested to Ben, and each went into separate rooms to make their calls.

Deidre's hands were shaking as she punched the number for Dave's cell phone into hers. She listened to it ring several times before he picked up.

"Dave here," she heard him say.

"Dave, this is Deidre. Are you sitting down?" She could hear music blaring in the background and thought she heard a woman's voice ask, "Who is it, Dave?" followed by a muffled rustling sound.

"Hey, Deidre. How's it going?" The music was no longer so loud, and Deidre assumed he had moved to a quieter spot. "I'm at a friend's party, and it's pretty loud in there. What's up?"

"I don't know where to begin," Deidre managed to get out. "Sheriff DeAngelo is here. He has pictures taken yesterday of Maren as she was withdrawing money from an ATM."

There was a stunned silence on the other end of the call, and Deidre wondered if she had been disconnected. "Dave. Dave, are you there?"

"That can't be," Dave stammered. Deidre could hear him breathing heavily. Then he recovered. "I mean, after all this time, I never expected her to show up. My God, she's alive! Do you know where she's at? Where was the picture taken? Is she all right? Is she coming home?" Dave's questions came like staccato notes, one after the other.

"Whoa, slow down, Dave. We don't know much yet. The ATM is in the Cities, Minneapolis. I've not seen the security video, but Jeff brought us some still pictures of her making a withdrawal. She looked okay, although her clothes were pretty ragged, and she looked awfully thin. We don't know how to find her, only that she's alive."

Deidre had just gotten the words out of her mouth when she heard an unfamiliar woman's voice in the background say, "Davy, when are you coming back inside?" Then she heard a sound she assumed was Dave covering the mouthpiece of his phone, but she could still hear his answer.

"In a minute, honey. This is important." He came back on the line. "I have to go, Deidre, but be sure to call me if anything comes up. I want to be the first to know."

Deidre said goodbye and disconnected. She had an uncomfortable feeling as she returned to the living room, but after thinking for a moment she realized that she would want Dave to continue living. *After all, he and Maren hadn't been married, and he needed someone in his life,* she thought.

Ben was waiting in the living room when Deidre returned. The boys were still sitting on the sofa, eyes filled with hope and confusion. It was as though they weren't sure how they should be acting.

"Megan is on her way here," Ben told the group when Deidre was settled. As he looked at his sons, he detected a glimmer of anticipation in their posture. "She couldn't believe what I was saying, and she wants to be with us. I told her not to speed, and she promised she wouldn't. She had some friends over for the evening, but said she'd shoo them out and leave immediately. She should be here in about a half hour. I told her if it's a minute less than that, I'll know she drove too fast. Megan was so giddy, I don't think she heard a word I said."

"I talked to Dave, but he's not going to come until we know more," Deidre said. "I told him I thought that was wise. Anyway, he was busy, and I didn't want to interrupt him." She thought it best not to tell the others what he was busy doing, because she figured they might not be as understanding. "He couldn't believe what I was saying, either. His first words were, 'That can't be possible.' He was so startled by what I told him that it took several seconds for him to comprehend what I said. I feel sorry for him, because I think he's trying to move on, and we keep bringing up these leads that get his hopes up, only to have them dashed. I don't blame him for not wanting that cycle to repeat. I promised him we'd call as soon as we know more."

Jeff filled them in on what was being done to locate Maren. "The Minneapolis Police Department is circulating the photos I showed you, and by now, all the beat cops are on the lookout for her. Her picture has gone out to all of the TV stations, and will be shown on their morning shows. Each station will also carry a short blurb on their evening news. We're working on getting an article in each of the daily papers. Honestly, I'm confident we'll find her in a couple of days."

The group waited restlessly for Megan to arrive, each of the family members trying to comprehend that Maren might still be alive. Before too long, there was a knock on the door and Megan burst into the kitchen. She hurried into the living room where everyone was still seated, and nearly jumped into Ben's arms. "Oh, Dad. Is it true, really true?"

Ben hugged her while the boys danced around, caught up in the excitement. Deidre experienced the urge to laugh and cry at the same time. In the end, she ended up doing both. After they quieted down, Megan began to ask questions.

"Does Dave know?"

Deidre related her earlier conversation with him, leaving out the part that she was sure he was at a party and didn't want to leave.

"Are you positive it was her at the ATM?"

Jeff handed her the photocopies the others had seen. He intently watched Megan's face as she paged through them, then went back to take another look.

"I don't know," she finally said, her brow furrowed in contemplation. "It sure looks like Maren, but she's so much thinner than the last time I saw her. And she seems so," Megan paused as she searched for the correct word, "dirty. I mean, she looks like a street person. Could she go downhill that rapidly?"

"It depends on what she's been doing. If, for instance, she got into meth, she'd go downhill pretty fast. I've seen dramatic changes in people over a period of time as short as four or five months, relative to how much they're using."

Megan broke in before Jeff could say more. "I know my sister, and she would never get involved with that crap! If this is her in the picture, and I'm not sure it is, something else is going on in her life. Have any of you considered that she may be suffering from some sort of mental illness?" She stopped short of saying "schizophrenia." "And anyway, why are you so sure it's her?"

Deidre tried to calm Megan. "For several reasons, including that this person used Maren's PIN at the ATM, we believe this is your sister."

"I warned her about this," Megan exclaimed. "She wrote her PIN inside the flap of the coin pouch of her purse. She wrote it backwards, and said it was in case she had a 'brain fart' and forgot the number. She should have known better, but she laughed off my warning."

Jeff shifted in his chair, and then stood up. "Well, folks, I've got work tomorrow and have to get home for some rest. You'll be the first to know if they find Maren, or whoever this woman is." He held up the pack of photos.

Deidre and Ben accompanied him to the door. "Jeff, thanks for all the time you've put into this and for your personal attention. We appreciate it," Ben said.

Once Jeff was outside, they returned to the living room and the family stayed up most of the night, talking over what they had learned.

# Chapter
Forty

THE NEXT SEVERAL DAYS passed with the family waiting expectantly, flinching each time the phone rang, not wanting to leave town for any reason. But after a week passed since Jeff had shown them the pictures from the ATM with still no word about Maren, they began to descend from their high. Everyone felt deflated and they were, again, thrust back into the abyss of the unknown.

On the first day of school, Deidre fixed a special breakfast and Ben paid special attention to his sons, wishing them a great first day. Deidre puttered in her garden after they left. Later in the morning, when the early September sun warmed the land, Deidre went inside for a glass of ice water and picked up the pack of photos Jeff had left. By this time they were getting a little tattered around the edges from being thumbed through so many times, but she wanted to look at them again.

The trail to the family's picnic spot by the river hadn't been used as much as usual, and in places the weeds had grown knee deep. Deidre paid little attention, plowed through them, and soon was slouched against her favorite cedar tree. She stared at the first photo, the one of a woman facing an ATM machine. She meticulously studied every detail of the picture. The way the woman stood wasn't exactly like the way Maren did, but on the other hand, she figured, a still picture represents only a point in time. Perhaps she was caught in an awkward pose. Deidre flipped to the next photo, and the next, which showed the woman turning so the camera caught her profile.

Deidre studied every millimeter of the photo, allowing her eyes to trace the outline of the woman's chin, her nose, the shape of her ear. The picture was grainy and slightly blurred, but Deidre continued to look for discrepancies between what she was seeing and what she remembered. A wave of sadness overwhelmed her, and she realized she had already begun to forget the details of Maren's features. A single tear rolled down her cheek, and in the warmth of the sun, she drifted off to sleep.

*"Mom, Dad," Deidre heard Maren call. Deidre saw a young woman standing in front of her. "It's me, Maren!" But the young lady had no face. Well, she had a face with no discernable characteristics, rather like her face was made from Silly Putty that had sagged until the features were totally blurred. "Mom, don't you recognize me? It's me, Maren, your daughter. Have you forgotten already?"*

*Try as hard as she might, she couldn't recognize her daughter's face. "Mom, say something." Deidre opened her mouth, but no sounds came out, and her guts tightened as her panic mounted. "Well, if you're not going to talk to me, I'm leaving." The blonde woman turned and walked away. Deidre tried to shout out, but it was as though she was in a vacuum. Her mouth moved, but nothing happened, and then the woman was gone in the haze of her vision.*

Deidre woke, confused and calling out, "Maren!" She looked around and realized she had been dreaming. The pile of pictures had slid off her lap onto the ground, her neck was kinked, and her head ached. She checked her watch. Almost an hour had passed since she sat down. Her heart beat rapidly, and she still felt vaguely panicked. Deidre sat, stunned, for several minutes, convincing herself that it was all a dream. Finally she picked up the pictures, forced herself to stand, and returned home, badly shaken.

*****

IN THE QUIET OF HER KITCHEN, Deidre worked to fix supper. She had absentmindedly picked four green peppers from her garden, thinking that a year ago the task would have been one of pleasure and not drudgery. She boiled rice, mixed it with pieces of chopped-up bratwurst, added onions and out-of-the-jar marinara sauce, simmered the concoction in a frying pan, and stuffed the hollowed-out peppers.

She placed them in a baking dish, sprinkled mozzarella cheese on top and slipped it into the oven. It was a mindless series of steps.

After a half hour, she checked to see how the peppers were cooking. The oven was cold. She had forgotten to turn it on. Deidre set the oven at three hundred seventy-five degrees, sat down on a chair, and wept while the oven went through its pre-heat cycle.

After it was cooked, Deidre set the evening meal in the refrigerator just in time to hear Ben's vehicle pull into the driveway. He didn't bother to get out, but waited for her to climb in the passenger's seat. Ben leaned over and gave her a quick kiss.

"How was your day?" he wanted to know.

"It was okay," Deidre answered. She didn't feel up to telling him about her dream. "Yours?" she asked.

"Okay, I guess."

They rode in silence until they came to the football field. Steve and Jack were preparing to play their first game of flag football, and when she saw them in their uniforms, Deidre was surprised at how grown up they were becoming. She waved at them, but both boys pretended to ignore her. With regret she thought, *So they've reached that age when they need their parents but don't want their friends to know they do.*

Deidre and Ben sat with the other parents and cheered for the home team. Well, actually both teams were the home teams, the Vikings and the Steelers. Jack and Steve played for the Steelers, and when the final whistle was blown, their team had won 63-56.

On the way home, both boys were jubilant, going over the game play by play. Deidre and Ben smiled at each other. It was as though they had been at a different game than the boys were remembering.

Supper was eaten two hours later than usual, and when they finished, Deidre steered the boys to the stairs. "I'll be up to tuck you guys in soon. Don't forget to floss and brush."

Amidst the grumbling and stomping on the stairs, Steve and Jack obeyed. Jack spoke over his shoulder, "You don't have to tuck us in anymore." Then he added, "But you can come in and say goodnight." Deidre thought that was all right. They still needed her.

# Chapter
## Forty-One

THE NEXT MORNING Deidre's routine was just that, routine. She fixed a simple breakfast for Ben and the boys: scrambled eggs, toast and jelly, a glass of juice, milk for the kids and coffee for Ben. While they ate, she made sandwiches, wrapped a couple of cookies for each of them, and added an apple to their lunch bags. Just in time for the boys to catch the school bus, she shooed them out the door, kissed Ben goodbye, and gave a sigh of relief. Mission accomplished.

She strolled to the mailbox by the road, looked at the clear, blue sky and inhaled the scent of early fall. As usual, the Duluth newspaper had been delivered in the early hours of morning, and she picked it out of the yellow plastic tube where it had been inserted by the delivery person. She made a mental note that when Christmas came she would give him a generous tip for his reliability.

Back in the kitchen, Deidre spread the paper out on the table, poured herself a cup of coffee, and waited for the toaster to give up the two slices of bread she had put in it. She sipped the steaming brew, and in two minutes that seemed like twelve, the toast sprung up from the guts of the appliance. She spread peanut butter on one slice and raspberry jam on the second, smiling as she did so. Jack called raspberry jam "seed jelly" because of the seeds that were so prevalent. Deidre plunked herself in a chair and nibbled at the peanut butter toast, then took a bite of the raspberry jam toast, trying to make up her mind which one to eat first. She thought maybe she'd alternate, a bite of this one, a bite of that.

The lead article on Section B was about domestic abuse, and she had her nose in the paper, concentrating on the article. She read, "one in three women will experience some form of abuse at some time in her life." That was a statistic of which she was aware, and she remembered sitting at a concert listening to an all-girls choir. She had actually counted the number of girls on the risers, and then numbered them off by threes. Every third girl would become a victim. Well, perhaps not the ones she called "three," but statistically, one-third of them. She was so involved in the article that when her phone rang, she continued reading while reaching for her phone.

"Hello," she answered, not bothering to look at the caller ID.

"Deidre." Jeff's voice sounded strange, and he didn't continue.

Deidre sat erect in her chair. "Jeff, what is it? Something's wrong, isn't it." Her first thought was of Ben, driving to work on the expressway. Her mind flitted to another scenario. One of the boys. Both of them? And Deidre's heart literally skipped several beats while her guts knotted.

"Jeff, are you there?"

Finally Jeff was able to speak. "Deidre, you'd better get a hold of Ben and the rest of the family as soon as you can. The police in Minneapolis have Maren in protective custody. They say she is so strung out on something that she isn't making sense, but she has her purse with her. Everything checks out: eye color, hair, height. But they say she's so wasted that they need us down there to make a positive ID. She's lost a lot of weight and appears to have been living on the streets for some time. Call Ben. You can pick him up on the way through town. I'll drive my sheriff's SUV and meet you down there, but I think you'd be more comfortable riding in your own vehicle. Call Dave and Megan. And if you think it's appropriate, bring the boys."

As soon as Jeff hung up, Deidre called Ben. Her hands were shaking so badly she had difficulty hitting the buttons on her phone.

"Ben, I hope there's a chair near you. Sit down."

"Deidre, what's happened? Is it one of the boys? Megan?"

"It's Maren. Ben, they've found her. She's alive!"

There was a stunned silence on the other end of the line. "What do you mean she's alive?"

"It's true, Ben. Jeff called just minutes ago. The Minneapolis police have her in protective custody and are waiting for us to come pick her up. I'll stop by your office in an hour or so. I've got to hang up so I can call Megan and Dave. Ben, she's alive!"

Deidre hurriedly dialed Megan's number, willing her to answer. "'Lo," the sleepy voice on the end of the line said.

"Megan, get dressed. They've found Maren, and she's alive!"

"Mom, what are you saying? Are you okay?" Then Megan snapped awake. "Are you serious? Oh, God, I never thought this would happen. Where is she? Is she okay? What do you want me to do?"

Deidre was able to settle her daughter down and explain she would pick her up in about an hour. "Be ready," was her final instruction before disconnecting.

She hit her speed dial for Dave's work number and anxiously counted the rings. One, two, three, four, and finally an answering machine picked up. "You've reached the voicemail of Dave Mason. Please leave a message, and I'll get back to you as soon as I can."

Deidre left a short message, and after disconnecting the call, waited impatiently for him to call back. She figured he was using his phone as a screening device. After five minutes, she could wait no longer and prepared herself for the trip south. Suddenly she remembered the boys, and a wave of guilt washed over her. How could she forget them? Deidre called the school and asked the secretary to have the boys meet her in the principal's office in twenty minutes. She gave no reason.

# Chapter Forty-Two

WITH THE BOYS SAFELY buckled in the backseat, Deidre had difficulty staying within the speed limit as she sped toward Duluth. The posted speed was sixty-five, and she figured she could push it to seventy without drawing attention. Halfway to the city she upped her speed to seventy-three, half expecting to hear a siren and see flashing lights behind her. Down London Road and through town she pushed the limits as far as she dared, looking at the digital readout of the dashboard clock every couple of minutes. Deidre was shocked when she reached the Federal Building in less than forty-five minutes from Two Harbors. Ben was pacing on the sidewalk when she pulled into a parking spot. Her vehicle had hardly stopped before he was in it, fastening his seat belt.

"Have you talked to Jeff since you left home?" he asked. Deidre admitted she hadn't, but said he was on his way to the Cities ahead of them.

Ben continued to pepper her with questions as she took Mesabi Avenue to Fourth Street, turned right onto the crowded route, and stopped for every red light along the way. What seemed like an hour later, she veered left onto Woodland Avenue and steered the SUV into an alley. Megan was waiting by a stand holding garbage cans and had the car door open before the vehicle's tires quit rolling.

"Let's go," she said excitedly as she buckled up, then unbuckled the seat belt to rearrange her crumpled sweatshirt. "How sure are you that it's her?"

Deidre answered, "All I can tell you is that Jeff called this morning to say the Minneapolis police had picked up a young woman off the street early this morning. She has Maren's purse with her driver's license in it, a credit card, a debit card, and a few bucks. They told him that this girl is on some kind of drug or drugs and is incoherent, but everything fits as far as eye color and stuff. She's lost a lot of weight, but they're pretty sure it's her."

The boys had been silent the whole time, their eyes large and questioning, their ears taking in everything. Finally, Steve had the temerity to ask, "But they're not sure it's really her, are they?"

"We have to trust that the officers who are taking care of her know what they're doing," Ben answered. "They don't usually call a family unless they're pretty sure they're right. This is about the best news we could expect to receive right now."

"Will she be okay?" Jack asked. "I mean, we learned in school that people who use drugs can catch some bad diseases, and even if they don't, sometimes the drugs kill them after a while. Will she ever be the same?"

Deidre's heart broke when she heard her son voice his concern. "Almost all diseases can be cured or controlled," she assured Jack. "As for being the same, no, she'll never be exactly the same. We all are changed by what happens to us, good and bad. I promise you this, our love for her will go a long way to helping her heal from whatever she's been through."

Jack didn't let the subject rest. "What do you think she's been through? Do you think she decided she was bored with us and wanted something different?"

Deidre thought she detected the beginning of guilt in Jack's comments. "I can say for sure that she didn't leave us by her own choice. Your sister loved you guys too much to have deserted you."

"Then what do you think happened?" Steve asked.

"I don't know, but I'm sure we're going to find out." Deidre didn't voice her next thought. *At least I hope we can find a reason for all this pain we've been through.*

Megan asked no more questions after they were out of Duluth. "Come on, boys, let's play a game," she said. "We can play alphabet license plates. We'll keep a list of the states we see on them, in alphabetical order. Whoever spots the most gets an ice cream cone before we start home. Aha, there's one from Texas up ahead. I've got one!"

Steve rolled his eyes at his sister. "You know that you're not going to buy a cone for just one of us." He smiled. "But I'll play anyway."

The game lasted for less than twenty miles before the conversation turned again to Maren, and Megan gave up trying to create a diversion. For once they sailed through Hinckley without stopping at their favorite bakery. From that point on everyone rode in silence, except for the nervous twitching and shifting they did in their seats.

*****

PARTS OF DOWNTOWN Minneapolis can be rather rough, and that certainly could describe sections of Hennepin Avenue. Jeff had said that Maren was being held at the First Precinct Station of the Minneapolis Police Department, located on that somewhat infamous thoroughfare. Deidre was thankful that the boys were engrossed in their video games and didn't notice the several strip joints that were just coming alive.

Ben pulled into a parking place across the street from a worn, brick-faced building. Deidre noticed a walk-up apartment house next to the station that had a sign in the window: FOR RENT BY THE WEEK. During the day, the neighborhood looked benign, but she knew that after dark it wasn't a place she wanted to walk through alone. Records showed that this precinct handled about a half-dozen violent crimes a week. They ranged from rape to homicide, from domestic assault to aggravated battery, with armed robberies thrown in for variety. She shuddered to think of her daughter being on the streets alone in this area.

Ben called Jeff on his cell phone and the others waited for him to finish his conversation, trying to piece together what Jeff was saying by Ben's side of the exchange.

"Jeff? . . . Yeah, we're here. . . . Right. . . . No it was a good trip. . . . Deidre, of course. The boys and Megan. . . . No, we couldn't get a hold of Dave. . . . He must be busy with something, because he hasn't called back. . . . Okay. What room was that again? . . . Right. First hallway to the left. See you in a minute or two." He disconnected and slipped the phone into his pocket.

"Well?" Megan demanded.

"Jeff's in the building, waiting for us. Maren is being held in an interrogation room on the sixth floor. He said we can take the elevator up." They moved into the lobby. "It's at the end of the hall." Ben pointed to the left.

The elevator was worn. Pieces of molding were missing from the frame as though someone had ripped them free, and the walls were scarred, abrasions that showed years of hard use. The cables rattled as it slowly ascended, and Deidre wondered when it had last been serviced. She absentmindedly looked for a certificate posted near the control panel. There was none, and she said a silent thank you when the elevator's door opened to the sixth floor. Jeff was waiting for them.

"Before you see Maren, we'd better talk." He motioned toward a room to the right. It appeared to be someone's office, and there weren't enough chairs for everyone. Jeff remained standing, as did Ben and the boys. It was awkward, because there was one empty chair. "Why don't you sit down," Jeff suggested. He moved the chair in Ben's direction, and Ben slowly lowered himself into it, not taking his eyes off Jeff's face.

"I know you understand that Maren has been through a great deal of trauma, and I want to prepare you for what you're going to see. So far we haven't been able to piece together what happened to her, but whatever it was, she isn't the same person she was the last time you saw her."

Deidre was aware of the boys anxiously shifting their weight from foot to foot. Megan's face was buried in her hands, and Ben was looking searchingly at Jeff, waiting for what he would say next.

"We haven't got a final tox screen back on Maren's blood, but the consensus is that she's strung out on meth. These officers have been around the block, and they know what they see. I agree with them. One of the only drugs that would have made her deteriorate so quickly is meth, and it's easily available on the street."

Ben came out of his stupor. "Is she physically okay, besides the effects of whatever she's been into? Infections? Cuts? Bruises?"

Jeff cleared his throat. "She's badly malnourished. Her driver's license shows her weight as one-hundred-twenty-two pounds. She was first taken to Hennepin County Medical Center to be examined before she was brought here. Now she weighs only ninety-one pounds. Other than being extremely unkempt and dirty, she has no lacerations or extreme bruising. She has gum disease, and a few of her teeth are very blackened." Jeff looked around the room before deciding whether to continue. Everyone, including the boys, were staring at him.

"She . . . she tested positive for two venereal diseases." He saw the boys look puzzlingly at Deidre. "They are gonorrhea and chlamydia." He hurried to add, "Now, those are only preliminary diagnoses, and the final cultures might come back negative." Deidre knew the chances of that occurring were slim to none.

"I wish I could be more positive, but I don't want you to be shocked by what you are going to see in the other room. Maren has been cleaned up, but she still looks like a war refugee. In a way, I guess she's been through a war."

Jeff moved toward the door. "Let's go see Maren."

# Chapter Forty-Three

AN UNIDENTIFIED OFFICER met the group as they stepped into the hall. He quietly asked them to follow him, explaining as they walked that they would be stopping by a window that looked into the interrogation room where their daughter was being held.

"Realize she isn't under arrest. The officers who discovered her passed out in an alley found no drugs on her person."

Deidre interrupted. "Where exactly was Maren found?"

"Two patrolmen were driving their beat, shining a spotlight up darkened alleys four blocks west of here," the officer explained. "One of them thought he saw a leg protruding from behind a dumpster, and when they investigated, they found your daughter. They suspected she was overdosed and called an ambulance. It turned out she was heavily under the influence of something, but not near death."

"What makes you so sure it's her?" Megan confronted the officer. Ben was taken aback by her pessimism, and had difficulty not saying so, but he managed to hold his tongue. He realized the entire family was under tremendous pressure.

"She was clutching her purse, and the paramedics allowed her to keep hold of it on the way to the hospital. Once there, the ER personnel took over, and were able to take the purse from her and search it. They made a tentative ID from its contents. Well, here we are," he announced, but he stood in front of the viewing window, blocking the family's view. "Maren was given some pretty potent drugs at the hospital to help her through withdrawal. She will have a difficult time relating to you, may not even recognize you," he warned them. "Are you ready?" Each gave a slight nod, and the officer stepped out of the way.

"Oh, Maren!" The words escaped Deidre's mouth, a combination of an exclamation and a moan. She turned to Ben and buried her face in his chest. He wrapped his arms around her, and Deidre felt hot tears dropping from his eyes onto her head. She felt his arms tighten around her, felt his chest convulsing.

The boys stood rooted in place until Megan knelt down beside them and pulled them to her. The family remained transfixed like that until Jeff, in his quiet, calming way said, "Let's go inside where we can be closer to Maren. She needs you right now."

Two other people were in the room with Maren, a female officer and a man who introduced himself as a representative of social services. The officer tapped the broken girl on her shoulder and said, "Maren, your family is here to see you."

The wasted girl sitting at the table raised her head and looked at them, but there was no sign of recognition in her eyes. The social worker said he'd wait outside so they could speak after their visit, and he and the officer left them alone with their daughter.

Deidre was in disbelief. If the girl hadn't had Maren's purse with her ID in it, she would never have recognized her as her daughter. This . . . stranger . . . was not the person she knew and loved. Her cheeks were sunken and her eyes were ringed with black circles, creating a face that resembled that of a raccoon. What shocked Ben the most were the lesions that covered her face, welts that verged on being festering, open sores. Her hair was a tangled mess, even though the hospital staff had tried their best to comb out the rat's nests. Deidre noticed that Maren's lips were dry and cracked, and for an instant, when she opened her mouth, Deidre saw that her gums were red and bleeding. Not only did Deidre think she saw massive decay along her daughter's gum line, but her breath was so putrid Deidre almost gagged. The girl laid her head on the table as if it was too much effort to hold it up.

"Maren, it's Dad. Maren, look at me." The girl struggled to lift her head, and it seemed to him her eyes somewhat focused.

"Daddy," she croaked through parched vocal cords. "Daddy, take me home."

Ben, ignoring the deplorable condition of her, engulfed her in his grasp and rocked her back and forth. "Oh, Maren, Maren," he kept repeating over and over.

Megan and the boys stood back from the table. She had a hand on each of their shoulders, and they moved closer to her, not knowing how they should react. Deidre placed her hand on Maren's back and recoiled when she felt how emaciated her daughter had become. No wonder it was so difficult to recognize this person, who had once been so full of life. Now she could feel every vertebra, her shoulder blades, every articulation of her shoulder bones.

The girl seemed to revive a little in their presence, and Ben and Deidre tried to communicate with her.

"We're here to take you home, honey," Deidre said reassuringly. "It's going to be okay. I promise you. It's going to be okay."

The blemished face contorted. "Okay?" It was more of a question than an assertion.

To be at her level, Ben knelt beside her, and thought he detected a sign of recognition. "We love you, dear one. We're going to step out in the hall for just a minute, but we're here. Remember that. We're here for you."

He knew they were being observed, and he motioned at the two-way mirror that they wanted to come out. The door opened and the woman officer entered the room while the social worker remained in the hallway.

"What do we do now?" Ben asked the social worker.

"Your daughter is out of danger as far as seizing, but she needs someone with her constantly for the next few days," he said gently. "Preliminarily, we're quite sure she has been using meth quite heavily, and that almost always causes severe depression, which causes a risk for suicide. I have the prescription that was given to her by the ER doctor, something to ease her discomfort until the drugs are mostly out of her system. However, the meds will not reduce her risk of suicide, so don't allow her to be alone for any length of time. Follow the directions on the bottle, one tablet under her tongue in the morning, one before bedtime. I'd suggest that you begin making arrangements to get her into a rehab program as soon as possible. She'll definitely need inpatient treatment. Here's a list of places that can help you."

Ben took the paper that was offered to him. As he glanced at it, he noticed that at the top of the list was Hazelden, a world-famous rehab facility located near the Twin Cities.

"Are we free to take her out of here, or does she have to remain in a cell?" Deidre wanted to know.

The social worker shook his head. "No, she's free to leave under your supervision. I'd recommend that you take her to a hotel for the night. Let her spend time in a warm shower. Put her to bed early. Right now, she needs sleep more than anything else. She should be more alert by tomorrow, and then you can take her home. But I can't emphasize strongly enough, she'll need intensive therapy to beat this monster that has hold of her."

He wished them all well and said he had to get back to his office before his day ended. Deidre and Ben looked to Jeff, who had stayed on the sidelines the whole time. "Can you help us?" Ben asked. "We're so frazzled, we don't really know where to turn." Jeff had never seen his friends so uncertain in all the time he had known them. He made arrangements for them to check into a hotel near I-35. That way they'd be on their way out of the city when they left the next morning. He volunteered to lead them to the hotel, but Ben told him their GPS would get them to the address. Amid their many thanks, Jeff left for Two Harbors, and Ben and Deidre made arrangements to take their daughter with them. Luckily, their SUV was a six-passenger vehicle.

By late afternoon, they had signed all the formal papers releasing Maren to their custody, and the six members of the VanGotten family crowded into the car to make the short trip to the hotel.

The boys stared at Maren in disbelief, neither of them uttering a word. They were seated in the backseat, and the one time Deidre looked back at them, she saw they were holding their noses and breathing through their mouths. The stench of Maren's breath was nauseating.

Megan tried to take her sister's hand, but Maren quickly drew hers away, as if she had an aversion to being touched. The short journey was made in silence. Once at the hotel, Ben checked them into two rooms connected by a shared door.

"Maren, why don't you take a warm shower?" Deidre suggested. "Maybe it will refresh you, and you'll sleep better tonight. Megan, I think it would be best if you helped her. She's so unsteady I'm afraid she'll take a fall. Do you mind?"

Maren mumbled some unintelligible words, and Megan nodded to her mother.

"Come on, Maren, I'll help you into the bathroom. Can we get you out of your clothes and into the shower? Or would you rather take a bath?"

It appeared that Maren was beginning to be aware of her situation. She nodded, which Megan took to mean she wanted a bath rather than a shower. In minutes, Deidre heard the tub being filled and Megan offering words of encouragement. There were a few minutes of silence, except for the muted sounds of clothing hitting the floor, followed by the gentle splashing of water as Maren submerged herself in the steamy tub. Deidre heard the bathroom door open, and Megan appeared in the doorway between the two rooms.

The family looked up, startled by the look on Megan's face. Deidre sprang from where she was sitting on the edge of the bed.

"Megan, what's wrong?" she wanted to know.

Tears of shock spilled from Megan's eyes. "She's not Maren."

"How can you be so sure?" Deidre blurted out, while Ben asked at the same time, "How do you know?"

Megan regained her composure. "I've seen her naked."

"Of course she looks different," Ben argued. "She's nothing but skin and bones. Give her some time to gain some weight back and she'll be her old self."

Megan gave him a cold stare. "I've seen her naked, I'm telling you!"

"We understand that, but your dad is right. Her body's bound to look different from what we remember. Is she safe in the tub by herself?" Deidre began to move to the other room to check on her, but Megan was blocking the doorway.

"She's okay. I left the door open and I can hear her from here. Look, Maren and I were identical twins. I knew from the time I saw her she wasn't my sister. In fact, I knew she wasn't even before we got here. Maren is gone. I sense it. I believe it. I know it."

"But, Megan, look at her face and think of what Maren would look like of she was thirty pounds lighter than when we last saw her. The eyes, the hair color, her height, her purse and driver's license, it all adds up."

Megan emphasized again. "Mom, we're twins. I've seen her naked."

Finally, Deidre was beginning to catch what Megan was saying. "What are you telling us?"

Megan looked at her father and her brothers, hesitated a moment, and then blurted out, "Her nipples are darker than mine, darker than Maren's." Megan blushed. "And her hair, you know, down there, is dark brown. Mine . . . I mean, Maren's was blonde. That's how I know." She buried her head in her hands not only to hide her tears, but also to cover her embarrassment.

# Chapter Forty-Four

DEIDRE PLOPPED DOWN onto a chair, and Ben moved to her side. Both of them were near shock and could only stare at Megan. The boys sat on one of the beds, confused at what this turn of events meant.

"What are we supposed to do now?" Megan asked almost rhetorically.

It took Deidre nearly a minute to respond. "Tonight we have to take care of this girl. Tomorrow we take her back to the police station. She's someone's daughter, someone who is as lost as we are, I'm sure."

Ben added, "And there are questions we need to have answered. How did she get Maren's purse? How did she know her PIN, and why didn't the police do a fingerprint check to spare us this roller-coaster ride?" He shook his head.

"I'll come help you, Megan," Deidre told her daughter. "That girl needs us for tonight, and we're going to be there for her." The two women retreated to the bathroom where the stranger in their midst was bathing. Ben heard them gently talking to her and listened as they struggled to get her to her feet and out of the tub.

Megan volunteered to stay in the same room with her, and in a few minutes they had her securely in bed. The girl's head hardly hit the pillow and she was wheezing in her sleep. Every so often one of her muscles would twitch involuntarily, causing an arm or a leg to thrash under the covers. Megan told her parents to go in the other room and try to get some rest.

"That isn't Maren?" Steve asked when his parents shut the door between the rooms.

"No, I'm afraid not." Ben's voice was filled with dejection, and he sat down next to his son.

"Then where's Maren?" Jack asked, his chin trembling as he fought back tears.

Deidre sat down with them. "I'm afraid we don't know the answer to that." She hugged Jack to her chest and began to convulse with wracking sobs. The four of them wept together.

After a bit, Deidre and Ben tucked the boys into bed, knowing sleep would not come easily for them.

"Mom and I are going downstairs for a little while," Ben said. "I'll leave my cell phone with you, and Mom will have hers." He showed the boys how to bring up his favorites list and click on the first entry, Deidre. "Call if you need anything, even if it's only that you need us by you. Otherwise, we'll be down the hall near the lobby. Okay, guys?"

Each of the twins nodded and pulled the covers up around their ears. Ben made sure a dimly lit light was left on, and he and Deidre quietly exited the room.

"Where are we going?" Deidre wanted to know

*****

BEN LED THE WAY to the front desk of the motel, and the front desk manager asked if he could help them.

"Do you have a conference room my wife and I can use? We need a place where we can talk privately."

The manager looked at them askance, and Ben could see the question in his eyes, *What's going on here?* But he said, "Yes, down the hall and to the right. But I'd need to unlock it for you."

Ben looked at the man for a moment, waiting for him to move. He didn't, and Deidre, who had her hand on Ben's arm, felt his muscles bunch. "Would you do that for us, please?" Deidre asked, trying not to bark out an order.

"I suppose so, but there's usually a seventy-five-dollar charge for the use of that room."

Ben lost control. "Look, you half-assed, self-important twerp, we've had a rough day. Get down the hall and open the room, and we're not going to pay for it, either. All we want to do is have a quiet place to talk. We aren't going to wear out your damn chairs, for God's sake. If it'll make you feel any better, we'll sit in the dark."

The manager's eyes opened wide. He started to say something, but then thought better of it. Deidre calmly said, "I think you'd better do as my husband said. We'll leave everything exactly as we find it." She looked the startled man directly in his eyes. "Please." He moved down the hall with a key in his hand, unlocked the door, and left without saying a word.

Ben slumped into a chair and covered his face with his hands while Deidre quietly closed the door.

"I'm sorry for acting that way, Deidre. I just lost it." Ben kept his face covered, but Deidre could tell by the convulsive heaving of his chest that he was silently crying. She stood behind him and wrapped her arms around his broad shoulders, and they wept together until they could weep no more.

Eventually, she left Ben to sit in her own chair across the table from him, and she sat silently, waiting for him to speak. Finally, after a deep sigh, he did.

"What do we do now?"

Deidre looked at her folded hands as though studying them for an answer. "We have no choice but to take the poor thing back to the police station in the morning. She's somebody's daughter, probably somebody who is as desperate to find her as we are to find Maren. We could call the police to come pick her up tonight, but I don't feel good about doing that. Let her rest tonight, and let her medication work. Tomorrow, she might be able to give us some answers."

Ben nodded his agreement. "I dearly want to know how she came to have Maren's purse. Do you think she even knows?"

"Maybe we'll get the answers we've been looking for. I don't know. Do we really want them?"

It was after two in the morning when Ben and Deidre finally turned out the lights in the conference room and quietly closed the door. They walked past the front desk, where the manager pretended he was doing paperwork so he didn't have to look at them.

# Chapter Forty-Five

THE TRIP BACK to the police station the next morning was strained, to say the least. Steve and Jack were terribly confused, and looked as though they wanted out of the car. Megan looked out her side window, watching a few street people who were beginning to rouse. Ben and Deidre were resolute in what had to be done, their faces stone-like, eyes unseeing. The nameless young woman was more alert this morning, and she seemed to be cognizant of her surroundings, at least more so than she had been the night before.

"What did the police say when you called this morning?" Deidre wondered.

"All they said was to bring her in. The desk sergeant said he'd set things up so we wouldn't have to stay long."

Deidre thought for a moment before responding. "I don't know about you, but I can't simply walk away without knowing who she is. Without knowing how she came into possession of Maren's purse." Deidre was talking as though the girl wasn't present until she heard a voice from the backseat.

"I don't want to go to jail."

Surprised, Deidre turned in her seat. "You can talk this morning. Last night you were pretty out of it. Listen, I don't think there are any plans for you to be arrested, unless, of course, you're somehow involved in the disappearance of the person who owned that purse." Deidre nodded at the purse the girl still clutched on her lap.

"We're here," Ben announced without emotion. He drove into a parking space and turned off the ignition. "Do you need help walking?" he asked their charge. She said she could make it on her own.

An officer and the social worker from the day before were waiting for them at the desk. "Come this way," the officer said as she led them down the hall to an interrogation room. A detective was seated at a table, on which was a coffee container and a cup, as well as an unopened bottle of diet soda.

"Have a seat," he said to the girl, motioning to a chair across the table from where he was sitting. He turned to Ben and Deidre. "I'd like you to step outside. Officer Holter will answer any questions you might have." They looked to the officer, and she motioned for them to go first.

"Good morning. My name is Ginny Holter," she told them. "Why don't you just call me Ginny. I know you've been through a miserable experience, but I want to thank you for the way you've reacted. If you want to leave, you may. But I suspect you want to know more about this girl and the circumstances surrounding her. You certainly can stay and listen in on the conversation between Detective Banks and the girl."

In unison, Ben and Deidre expressed a desire to stay. They wanted Megan to be present as well, but wondered about the boys. After a moment's discussion, the boys said they wanted to be in on what was unfolding.

Ginny parted a curtain covering a window, and the group could look into the interrogation room. She turned on a speaker, and the detective's voice sounded clear. He had a calm, disarming manner about him, non-threatening.

They heard him ask, "You've had a rough time, it looks like. Do you know where you are?"

"Am I under arrest?" she asked. The girl was far more with it today.

"Not yet. Although, you do have the purse and credit cards of a woman who has been missing for over three months. If you have an explanation for that, you're in the clear. However, if you don't, we might have to look at you as a suspect in the case. That would be for robbery, perhaps kidnapping, even murder if we find her body. I'll ask again, do you know where you are?"

"I'm in a police station," she answered.

"And do you know who I am?" the detective asked.

"You're a police officer."

"Well, not exactly. I'm a detective for the Minneapolis Police Department. Do you understand?"

"Yes," she answered.

"Will you give me your name and tell me where you're from?"

There was a long hesitation on the girl's part. Finally, she spoke. "My name is Sarah, Sarah James. I was raised in a small town in central Minnesota. You've probably never heard of it, Quamba."

"That's on Highway 23, isn't it?" the detective stated more than asked.

Deidre saw the girl's head snap up, and she showed more emotion than Deidre had seen from her yet. "Yes. Do you know anyone from there?"

The detective chuckled. "No, but I've driven through it. Do your parents live there?" Deidre saw Sarah's shoulders slump, and she hung her head. "Yeah, they do. Do you have to call them?" Her words were spoken so softly Deidre and the others could hardly hear them.

"How old are you, Sarah?"

She hesitated, and Deidre expected a lie. "Sixteen."

Deidre was amazed at how the detective gently led Sarah along, at times praising her for being so honest, at others showing sympathy as her story unfolded, until eventually he asked the question he had been leading up to.

"Sarah, how is it that you have this purse that belongs to someone else, to Maren VanGotten?" Deidre held her breath, thinking there was no way Sarah would give a straight answer.

Sarah hesitated, and Deidre thought her fears were being realized. Then Sarah's eyes seemed to brighten, as if she suddenly remembered what she was trying to recall. "Late last spring, a couple of weeks after

I had run away from home to be with my boyfriend, we traveled to the North Shore." Deidre's heart began to race, and Ben grabbed her hand. He squeezed so hard she thought she was going to have to pull it away. Sarah continued.

"My boyfriend and I stayed in a small motel in Two Harbors. It was cheap and he said we could afford it."

"Were you doing drugs then?" the detective asked in a conversational tone. By this time, Sarah was talking to him like a long-lost friend.

"Yeah, I guess we were. I met Jesse a year ago. I was working at a convenience store on Highway 23. He came in quite often, and we became friends. He was really nice to me. When he invited me to a party, I went. I didn't want to seem like a kid, and I did what everyone else at the party was doing. I had two beers, and got pretty drunk. The next morning I woke up in bed with him."

The detective looked at her sympathetically. "I'll bet you felt pretty lousy."

"Yes and no. Jesse told me he loved me, that nothing had happened, because I was safe with him. The funny thing was, nothing had happened to me, sexually, I mean. He took me home, and I had a big fight with my folks."

"Did you see Jesse again?"

"On the sly. I'd lie about where I was going, and then hang out with him. Two weeks later he said he had some powder that would make me feel really good. I found out later it was crack, but he was right. It made me feel like I had never felt before. We saw more and more of each other, and one night I took what I thought was crack, but this time I was hit by such a rush I couldn't believe it. Every night that week, we met and did drugs together. The stuff hit me harder than it did him. By the end of the week Jesse convinced me to run away with him. I did, and that's how I ended up in Two Harbors."

"Have your parents tried to contact you?" the detective asked.

"They have no idea where I'm at. We partied for a week in Two Harbors. One time we were at a gravel pit someplace in the woods, and Jesse had to go to the bathroom. When he came back to the car, he was carrying this purse. We looked through it, took the few bucks we found and looked at the ID. Jesse said, 'Look at this. The chick looks just like you.' He said she was my dopple something or other."

"Doppelganger?" the detective offered.

"Yeah, that's it. He said we could take it back to the Cities, and after a few months try to use the cards. Then I noticed some upside-down numbers inside one of the tabs. Jesse turned the purse over and said he thought it must be the PIN to her debit card. About two weeks ago we started to use the cards."

Sarah slumped back into her chair as though the story had sapped all of her strength. The detective let her sit for a few moments.

"Let me ask you something, Sarah. Did Jesse continue to supply you with drugs, and if so, did you ever find out what he was giving you?"

Sarah clenched her hands together. "He gave me as much as I wanted. One day I found out it was meth, and it scared the crap out of me."

"Did you try to stop using?"

"I did, but then he'd offer me more, and I couldn't stop wanting the stuff, needing it."

The detective reached across the table and put his hand on Sarah's. She looked at him like a beaten puppy, and Deidre wanted to rush into the room and wrap her arms around the waif.

"Sarah, did Jesse ask you to have sex with other men?"

A tear ran down Sarah's face, and she hung her head. She nodded.

"Lots of men?"

Sarah nodded again. "Sometimes three or four a day. If I said I didn't want to, he'd wait until I was really hurting, and then tell me I wouldn't get anymore meth until I did what he wanted. I couldn't stop," she wailed.

"I want to help you, Sarah, but first, I need answers to some questions. Will you help me?" She nodded and looked at the detective with a twisted half smile.

"Did you ever see the girl on this driver's license, Maren VanGotten?" He looked at her directly as if waiting for a clue as to her truthfulness.

"No. Like I told you, Jesse found her purse in the woods."

"Is it possible that Jesse might have done something to this girl?"

Sarah looked at him strangely for a second, and then the meaning of the question hit her. "Oh, no, No! Jesse couldn't have done anything like that."

"But look what he did to you," the detective tried to use logic, but Sarah's response wasn't what he expected.

"I know what he is, and I know he was capable of such a thing, but, you see, he never left me alone the whole time we were in Two Harbors. I think he worried that if I had the chance, I'd go back home. You don't know how I wish I could have." Sarah slumped in her chair, spent.

"One more question, Sarah. Do you know where Jesse is now?"

"All I can tell you is where he kept me, and where he used to hang out. Are you going to try to find him?"

The detective smiled at her in a fatherly way. "We're going to find him. When we do, will you help us convict him? Testify against him for what he did to you?"

Sarah nodded.

# Chapter Forty-Six

THE RIDE BACK TO Two Harbors was long. For the first hundred miles no one said a word, each member of the family wallowing in their own thoughts. Steve and Jack lost themselves in their video games, Megan looked out the window and watched the trees whiz by, and Ben and Deidre stared straight ahead. Deidre reached across the center console and placed her hand on Ben's thigh.

"Anybody have to stop?" Ben asked as he passed a sign saying there was a rest area a mile ahead.

Megan said she could use a break, and each boy said he had to go. Ben pulled off at the exit and stopped in front of the wayside rest station. After taking care of business, they met out front.

"There's a nice nature trail that goes down to a small lake," Megan said. "Let's walk down there for a little exercise. I could use a stretch." The group followed her to a spot overlooking a pond, and took a seat on one of the two park benches.

Megan couldn't choke back her tears, which triggered the others to begin sobbing. An older couple came down the trail, and, observing the grieving family, departed without saying a word.

"What now?" Megan asked, not really expecting an answer.

Ben wrapped his daughter in his arms. "Now we go home and try to pick up the pieces of our lives. Nothing we can do will bring Maren back, unless by some miracle she's still alive. But we can't ruin the rest of our lives by waiting for that miracle. It's time we got back to living." He let go of Megan and roughed the boys' hair. Then, taking Deidre's hand, he led them back to the car.

*****

THE NEXT TWO WEEKS went by without anything significant happening. Jack and Steve were busy with school. Megan was taking classes at college and working most evenings in the lab. Ben went back to work, and Deidre busied herself getting her flower gardens ready for winter. Even though it was at least a month off, the plants had been touched by an early frost, and the flowers were pretty well done blooming.

Dave never did call back to answer the message Deidre left before they had gone to the Cities, and it dawned on her that he really didn't want to continue a relationship with the family. The thought stung, but if he didn't want to see them anymore, that was his call.

Deidre worried most about Megan. She hadn't heard from her daughter since they had gotten home, and she hoped it was because Megan had buried herself in her work at the college. She made a mental note to give her a call that evening.

# Chapter Forty-Seven

DEIDRE WAS CORRECT. Megan buried herself in her research and schoolwork after returning from the futile trip to Minneapolis. But most importantly to her, she continued work on a project she hadn't shared with her mother or father. Not long after her sister's disappearance, Megan's friends had told her that Dave frequented a local bar, usually accompanied by a woman. Megan had only mentioned it to Deidre once, then let the matter drop. However, not only did this raise her curiosity, it made her suspicious of Dave's concern for Maren's well being.

Megan enlisted some of her friends from school to keep an eye on this woman and Dave. Her friends took the request seriously, more seriously than Megan had ever intended, and they set up a network to cover the bar every night. Soon, one or another of the group would casually say hi to Dave and the woman, and it wasn't long before they were acting as acquaintances, and then friends. They discovered the girl was named Jackie, and that she lived near the college.

Jodi, one in the clandestine group, called Megan the day after her return from the upsetting trip where what little hope she had was dashed.

"Hi, Meg," Jodi said, using the nickname Megan had picked up in college. "How ya doin', kid?" Megan answered that she was coping but it was more difficult now than before. Jodi continued.

"This might not be the time, but I've got news for you." She paused. "It's about Dave and Jackie. Well, Jackie, really."

Megan perked up with those words and wanted to know what was going on.

"The group and I have gotten to know Jackie well enough to be able to sit down and have a beer with her. Most of the time Dave is with us, too. Jackie is acquainted with the four of us who have been keeping an eye on them, like you wanted, and I don't think that our being in the bar so often has raised any alarms. Each of us is only there two, three times a week at the most. Once in a while, we'll go as a group or as a threesome, but not very often. Anyway, Dave will be out of town on business most of this week, so we're planning to have a girls' night out. We invited Jackie to come with us. Do you want to tag along? Maybe you can pick up some vibes from her that we'd miss."

Megan wondered if that would be wise. After all, she and Maren looked exactly alike. What if Jackie had seen Maren, or what if Dave had shown her Maren's picture?

"I don't think you have to worry about that," Jodi reassured her. "All she knows about Maren is what Dave has told her, and it hasn't been complementary, believe me."

Against her better judgment, Megan agreed to join them for a night of bar hopping when Dave was out of town.

*****

"HEY, MEG. OVER HERE!" Jodi was standing near a booth, wildly waving to get Megan's attention. The bar was filled with young people, mostly college students, but quite a few in their mid-twenties. Megan picked her way through the crowd until she stood next to Jodi.

"Girls, I'd like you to meet my good friend, Meg. Meg, these are my friends I told you about." Jodi went around the table reciting names. "That's Sheila over there," she said as she pointed at a pert little brunette on the far side of the table. "And that's Jo over there, nursing her brandy Manhattan. One more and she'll be under the table." Everyone laughed. "This is Patty." Patty raised her beer glass. "Last but not least, our newest friend here is Jackie." Jackie just smiled and didn't really acknowledge the introduction, and Megan worried about her reaction.

A waitress came by and Megan ordered a tap beer. When it was delivered to her a few minutes later, Jodi proposed a toast. "Here's to a night out, a night with friends, and a night when we're going to enjoy ourselves." The six young women hoisted their glasses and clinked them together. "To a fun night out," they echoed.

Megan nursed her beer as long as she could, left the half-full glass on the table and went to the bathroom. By the time she returned, the others had finished their drinks, and Jodi announced they were going to move on to another bar a few blocks away. The new bar was less crowded than the last, and the six were able to pull up chairs around one table. A disinterested waitress came by and took their orders. She wanted to know if they would be starting a tab, but Jodi quickly said they'd just be having one drink.

"Oh, there's a friend of mine bartending." Jodi looked surprised to see him. "Just a sec, girls, I want to say hi." They watched as she went to the bar and carried on a lively conversation with the man. She returned with a smile on her face. "Peter and I go back a long way."

The drinks were delivered, beers for Megan and Patty, another brandy Manhattan for Jo, and a brandy Diet Coke for Sheila. Jodi had ordered a gin and tonic and a Tom Collins for Jackie.

"My gosh, they don't skimp on the drinks here, do they," Jackie said after her first sip.

Megan took a swallow from her glass and incredulously noted that Jo was half finished with her Manhattan. She took another swallow of her beer and excused herself to the washroom. She wasn't in the mood to get tipsy. Jodi followed her in.

"So, who's your friend working behind the bar?" Megan innocently asked.

"Oh, I don't know him." Jodi smiled a knowing grin. "I just told him how we liked our drinks. Jo likes hers really weak, just a taste of brandy and vermouth. I said the same with the gin in mine, but I told him that Jackie appreciated hers as strong as he would make it. Patty will leave most of her beer in the glass. You can do what you want, but I'd pace myself if I were you." She winked at Megan and left her standing alone in the ladies' room. Megan didn't know if she liked what was going on, but decided to play along.

Jodi led them to two other bars, and by that time everyone was giggling and having a really good time, especially Jackie. There were only a few patrons in the last bar on their run, and Jodi steered the group to a table in the back. The place seemed to be a hangout for an older crowd, couples mostly. The waiter took their orders, and while he was getting their drinks, Jodi asked Megan, "So, Meg, how's the love life these days?"

The question baffled Megan for a second. Jodi knew she didn't have much time for dating, but she caught a look in Jodi's eyes.

"Oh. Oh, you know. I've been out with a few guys, but nobody I'd like to hook up with. Not many guys are interested in research science." She smiled.

"Smart girl," Patty broke in. "Men. They're all a bunch of asses as far as I'm concerned."

"But what about Jim? You were in love with him the last time we talked." Jo took a drink from her glass.

"Him? He decided that he didn't want to be tied down to one woman. Told me that." Patty slurred her words and Megan wondered if the last beer had been over her limit.

They bantered back and forth for some time, each sharing a few tidbits of how their love lives were stacking up. Finally Jodi asked Jackie, "What about you? It seems almost every time I run into you, you're with Dave. Things must be going well between the two of you."

Jackie giggled, and Megan could see she was quite tipsy.

"Well," Jackie drew out the word, "I think I've found my Prince Charming. I've seen the way other women look at him. He's really handsome, don't you think?" They all agreed, egging her on to continue. "We've been seeing each other for almost a year now. At first we had to hide our get-togethers, because he had some bimbo in Two

Harbors he was with. He said he was trying to get out of the relationship, but she was creating a lot of static over it."

Megan felt her back go rigid, and she took a swallow from her glass to disguise her reaction.

"Anyway," Jackie continued. "We kept seeing each other on the sly. Dave was always so depressed, telling me he needed my support, and that he was going to ditch her as soon as he could."

The group looked to be anxious to hear more, and by this time Jackie was happy to be the focus of their interest. "Did you ever meet this other woman?" Patty asked.

"No, but I heard enough about her from Dave that I hope I never do. He said she was a real bitch, and not very good looking. He said that after they had moved in together, she really let herself go. You know, gained a lot of weight and quit taking care of herself. She had a real drinking problem, and slept most of the day away. The one thing that convinced him he wanted out was that she started to hound him about having a baby. Dave said no way was he going to father a child with that slob."

The others gave Jackie all the sympathy they could muster. "So when did Dave give her the boot?" Jo wanted to know.

"He and I had a heart-to-heart one night early last summer. Dave said he wanted to have our relationship out in the open, and that he had moved out of his Two Harbors apartment. He asked if I was good with our going public. Well, I had been waiting months for that to happen, and almost jumped into his arms. A topic that came up that night was whether I wanted to have kids. I said hell no. I've got too much life to live to be tied down like that."

"Wow," Sheila blurted out. "That makes my life seem like vanilla ice cream. Are you living together?"

Jackie was all too eager to continue. She was on a roll. "That's the best part. Dave said he was leaving that woman that week, and he wanted to begin looking for an apartment we could share. The next day we leased a really nice place on Woodland Avenue. He said he had some things to clear up in Two Harbors before he could move in full time. About a month ago, maybe a little longer, he did. I'm happier than I've ever been. He's a really fun guy to be with."

"Do you have any idea what happened to the woman he dumped?" Megan managed to get out without sounding too strained.

"No. Dave just said he never wanted to hear about her again, which is perfectly fine with me. The longer he's away from her, the more relaxed he is. I guess all I can say is that I'm head over heels in love with the guy." Jackie giggled again and drained her glass.

"My God! It's almost closing time, and I have to go to work tomorrow morning. I'd better get you gals home." Everyone sobered up in what seemed an instant—everyone except Jackie, who needed a little assistance getting on her feet.

"I've never been with people who can drink the way you do. You must practice more than I do." Jackie's words were a little slurred, and the others helped her get to the car. They dropped her off at her apartment first.

# Chapter Forty-Eight

Absentmindedly, Deidre worked around home most of the morning, but in the back of her mind, she wondered how Megan was doing. She figured her daughter was busy in the lab or in classes, and she knew better than to call during the day. As Deidre was gathering together tools to work outside in her garden, her cell phone rang. She was a little surprised to see Megan's name come up on the caller ID.

"Hi. I've been thinking of you all day, and was going to call you tonight. This is really a nice surprise. What's up?" Deidre greeted her daughter. As soon as Megan spoke, she knew something was wrong.

"Mom, I've got to talk to you and Dad, soon. Tonight, if possible."

"Megan, what's wrong? Are you okay?" Deidre asked, a degree of panic in her voice.

"Sorry, Mom. I guess I could have been a little more tactful. No, I'm perfectly fine. It's just that I want to talk to both of you about Dave. I have news you'll want to hear, but I don't want to talk about it over the phone. Can I come home after school today?"

Megan's tone left Deidre wondering what could be so important. Perhaps she had found out that Dave was engaged to someone already, or perhaps he was moving out of state. Then again, the thought crossed her mind that Dave was in some kind of serious legal trouble.

"Sure, we're not planning anything. Will you be here for supper? I'm making one of your favorites, stroganoff."

Megan said she'd be home in time for supper, but she had to run. Before she hung up, though, she warned Deidre that perhaps the boys should do something else while they talked, but said it would be her call.

*****

THE CONVERSATION AROUND the table was stilted. Megan was anxious to begin telling what she knew, and yet she didn't want to discuss it over a family meal. Mealtimes had always been special at their home, a time to fill in the others on what had happened that day. Eventually, everyone was full, dessert had been served and devoured, and the dirty dishes were being cleared. Megan pitched in, and in minutes the kitchen was clean. Ben suggested they go into the living room, because in late September the temperature in Two Harbors gets quite chilly in the evening. Sitting on the deck might not be too comfortable.

"Would you like a glass of wine?" he asked Deidre and Megan. Both accepted the offer, and Ben poured three glasses of chardonnay. He brought two glasses of orange juice mixed with 7-Up for the boys. When everyone was settled, he looked at Megan and said, "Well?"

Megan looked at Steve and Jack and then, questioningly, back to her parents.

"Dad and I talked it over, and we decided it wouldn't be fair to leave the boys out of this conversation," Deidre said. "They deserve to know what you have to say."

Megan didn't quite know how to begin. She thought she'd better change her introduction because of her brothers' presence.

"Look, guys," she began, looking straight at the two of them. "I know you really like Dave, but sometimes things don't work out the way we think they should. People can fool us. You know, kind of like play acting. Know what I mean?"

Steve shrugged, and Jack said, "I think so." But there was a note of indecision in his tone.

"To be honest with you, Dave isn't the nice guy you thought he was." There, she had broken the ice and laid the groundwork for what was to come. She was still speaking mostly to her brothers.

"Dave didn't love Maren the way we thought he did. I think he was using her to help pay his way through school, and I don't think he treated her the way we thought he was."

"Are you saying he was mean to her?" Steve innocently asked.

"That's what I think. Let me tell you what has happened."

Megan went into detail about how several of her friends had told her of Dave hanging out with other women, especially Jackie. She filled them in on the fact that this had been going on even before Maren disappeared.

Deidre was getting uncomfortable with where this was going. "Are you just guessing or do you have evidence that Dave was messing around? We know you never cared much for him, but we thought it was because he was changing the relationship between you and your sister."

"I can't tell you why, but I never trusted him. Something in my gut told me that he wasn't who we believed he was. Here's how I know that he wasn't in love with Maren, that he was using her."

She went on to tell about her friends keeping an eye on Dave's comings and goings after Maren disappeared, and also filled them in on what had amounted to a sting operation they ran. When she finished relating Jackie's monologue from the night before, Megan said in a very quiet voice, "I think Dave killed Maren." Then she sat in silence, staring at her glass of wine, from which she hadn't so much as taken a sip.

The twins didn't know what to do. One of their friends, a person they admired and looked up to, had just been accused of murdering their sister. Ben shuffled his feet restlessly, and when Megan looked up, she saw a red flush creeping up his neck and inflaming his ears. She saw his knuckles go white as he clenched his fists, and when he set his glass down on an end table, his hand was shaking so badly the wine splashed over the rim of the glass. Deidre sat in shock.

"We welcomed him into our home," she finally muttered. "How could he betray us like that? If you hadn't gotten these words from, what's her name, Jackie? I'd never believe it. How could he do this to our precious Maren?"

It was a question that had no answer, and the group sat in silence. Suddenly Jack burst into tears and raced upstairs. Ben followed him, only a step or two behind, while Megan, Steve, and Deidre sat in silence. Deidre put her arms around her son and rocked him back and forth. Megan glowered at the floor, a look of embitterment on her face. Her intensity scared Deidre, and she hoped to God that Megan wasn't plotting to settle the score with Dave in her own way. About the time she was going to say something to that effect, Ben and Jack came down the stairs. Ben had his arm draped over Jack's shoulders, and Deidre could tell that both of them had been crying.

"This is so upsetting that we have to decide where to go from here," Ben iterated in a flat voice.

He started the conversation, expressing to the others his feelings—feelings about Maren, about Dave, about his loneliness, about the remaining part of his family. One by one the others opened up. The boys required some coaching, but eventually they were able to get out their sense of loss and betrayal. Deidre thought no child should have to face what her sons were experiencing.

"What do you think we should do?" Deidre directed her question to Megan. As her daughter began to slowly say the words Deidre was dreading to hear, her heart sank.

"My first thought is that we should hunt him down and do whatever we have to do to get him to tell the truth." She saw the look of dismay on Deidre's face.

"Don't worry, Mom," she quickly added, a wry smirk bordering on a smile crossing her lips. "That's just what I *want* to do, but I know that's not the answer. It'd just cause us more problems than we already have. What do you think, Dad?" Everyone looked to Ben.

He shrugged. "The first thing we have to do is tell Jeff, although we haven't much to tell him. Jackie's story is only hearsay. Maren's body hasn't been found, and there's no proof she's dead." He paused, reflecting on what he'd just said, knowing what the truth probably was. "Jeff's combed through Dave's story, and there just isn't anything but speculation to link him to Maren's disappearance. I do think we have to tell him what you've discovered about his character.

Somewhere down the line, this information might be a valuable piece of the puzzle."

It was midnight before everyone went to bed, and even then, they didn't fall asleep. Deidre noticed the digital clock, its green numerals glowing in the dark, read 3:17 a.m., and she and Ben were still mulling over what had transpired. They agreed that Dave was more likely than not responsible for Maren's death, but they felt helpless to do much about it. Finally, they were able to drift off to a restless sleep.

*****

BEN HAD TO GO to work the next morning, but he and Deidre agreed that she would pay a visit to Jeff as soon as the kids were off to school. Megan had stayed the night and was up early, although the stress of a sleepless night registered on her face. The boys stumbled out the door, and Deidre worried if they'd be able to function at all in class. She contemplated calling the school to give them a head's up, finally deciding she didn't want to go into the details of last night with anyone right then. She did call ahead to make an appointment with Jeff, declining to tell his assistant the nature of her visit.

At nine thirty, she climbed the stairs to his office, and her friend was waiting for her at the door to the squad room. One look at Deidre's face, and Jeff knew this wasn't a social call.

"Deidre, you look like hell," he said, half smiling. "Come into my office. Looks like we have to talk."

After a few words of greeting, Deidre got down to the reason for her visit. It took a half hour, but in the end she finished the narrative of what Megan had told them the night before. As she related the story, Jeff's forehead became more deeply furrowed, and he leaned further and further back in his chair, until Deidre began to fear he was going to tip over backward. She noticed his interwoven fingers become more tense and his eyes closed as she finished her story. For a moment, Deidre thought he had fallen asleep, and several seconds passed before he sat bolt upright, anger evident by the color of his face and his pursed lips.

"Damn! I knew it was him all along, but I couldn't say why. Everything about Dave's story was a little too pat, too contrived. Now we know it was, but with no way to prove a thing. Deidre, we combed their apartment, went over Maren's car with a magnifying glass, ran every forensic test we could think of, and still came up with a blank. We sprayed luminal in every crack and crevasse we could find, and nothing. It's like Maren vanished from the face of the earth. And all the time that smug S.O.B. has sat like a poor, innocent victim who lost his fiancée. If I could, I'd haul his lying ass in right now, but even an incompetent lawyer would have him out in twenty minutes." Jeff smashed his fist on his desk.

Deidre had no idea what to do. She hadn't any idea that Jeff would react so forcefully, but before she could act, she felt her phone vibrate in her pocket. Checking the number on the ID, she didn't recognize it, and didn't answer. The phone went to voicemail, and she decided to see who was calling.

The recorded message played back, "Mrs. VanGotten. Call the school as soon as you listen to this call. We've had an incident involving your sons, and it would be best if you came to discuss the matter immediately. Meanwhile, be informed that Steve and Jack will be in the principal's office until you arrive."

Deidre thanked Jeff for his time, and assured him that she and Ben appreciated all he was doing, and that she knew his hands were tied at the moment. Then she excused herself and rushed to the school. As she ran down the hall toward the principal's office, her mind was racing, wondering what had transpired.

# Chapter Forty-Nine

Jack rode shotgun, Deidre drove, and Steve sat in the back. Steve gently fingered his rapidly swelling eye. His brother wiped at the thin trickle of blood oozing from his nose. The trio didn't speak a word, and Deidre wondered where to go from here. She drove toward the lake, a place of refuge, it seemed, every time there was a crisis. After parking the car, she motioned for the boys to follow her, and they trudged across the park grass to a paved walking trail. Following it for a block or so, she veered to the left on a dirt footpath that led to a memorial bench set to expose a panoramic view of Lake Superior. Deidre sat in the middle of the granite slab and patted the cold rock on either side of her, a signal for the boys to sit. She put her arms around them, and they put their heads on her shoulders and sobbed. They sat there nearly a half hour, until Deidre thought it was time for her to talk.

"You don't have to tell me what happened. The principal did a pretty good job of filling me in on the details. I want to ask, do you know the meaning of displaced anger?"

Both boys shrugged and shook their heads.

"Displaced anger is when we take out our anger on something or someone who did nothing to us. For instance, a man might lose his job, come home and kick his dog."

Jack interrupted. "I'd never kick my dog."

Deidre sighed. "Yes, but you two picked a fight with a group of boys who weren't bothering you a bit. To make matters worse, they were older and bigger than you. You could have been seriously hurt. Do you have any idea why you did that?"

Neither boy answered.

"Well, I do," Deidre answered for them. "You're angry at Dave, more than angry. You probably want to hurt him right now. But you can't. So instead, you shifted your anger toward someone else. And do you know who I think you shifted it to?"

Again there was nothing but silence.

"You shifted it toward yourselves." Both boys pulled away from her at the same time.

"What do you mean?" Steve blurted out. "If that was true, we'd have gotten into a fight with each other." He paused. "Or jumped off a cliff or something."

"Listen, guys," Deidre tried to reason. "I think you see yourselves in each other, and you chose not to hurt yourself, but to let someone else do it for you. Thank God you have enough reasoning left that you didn't jump off a cliff. That would be too final. So you picked a fight with that bunch of older kids, knowing they'd hurt you, but not kill you."

Jack spoke up. "That doesn't make much sense. Steve and I never talked about any of this. It just happened. How can you think that we wanted to hurt ourselves? It's a stupid idea."

Deidre ignored his hostility. "I know it doesn't make sense, but our minds play tricks on us. Tricks we never see coming. Please, take time to think about this on the way home. After supper, we're going to sit down with Dad. We're all angry and confused. Not one of us knows what we should be doing, or even how we are supposed to be acting. This is the kind of thing that can tear a family apart, and I'm not going to let that happen to ours. Do you hear me?" She began to cry. The boys responded by coming close to her. This time it was they who hugged her.

*****

DAYS WENT BY WITHOUT another incident at school. Amid the routine of Ben going to work, Deidre putting her gardens to bed for the coming winter and the boys grumbling about too much homework, the last days of September passed without notice.

By the first week of October, most of the leaves had fallen from the trees, creating a mess in the yard. Lost in her thoughts, Deidre was raking furiously when her cell phone rang. She fumbled taking off her gloves, but managed to extricate it from her jeans' pocket on the fifth ring.

"Hello," she said, hoping she had hit the "receive" button soon enough. There was dead silence on the other end that lasted so long she thought it was a crank call or a butt dial.

"Deidre, it's Jeff," a voice said just as she was about to hang up. Deidre knew in that instant something was terribly wrong. She sat down on a large tree stump without saying anything. "Deidre, are you there?"

"Yes, I'm here," she heard herself say. "It's not good news, is it?"

Jeff cleared his throat, and there was a long pause. "No, it isn't. Can you get a hold of Ben and have him come home? I'm coming out to be with you guys in about an hour. Got important things to do before then. I'm sorry, Deidre. Do you want me to send someone out to be with you before I get there?"

Deidre sat in stunned silence.

"Deidre, are you there? Are you okay?" Jeff's voice brought her to her senses.

"Yeah. Yeah, I'm okay, I think. I'll call Ben right away." She hung up without saying goodbye, and mechanically hit number one on her speed dial. Ben answered.

"Honey," she paused. She never called him that and wondered from where it had come. "Jeff called just a minute ago." She got that much out and couldn't continue, because her throat was so constricted.

"He found Maren, didn't he?" It was more a statement than a question.

Deidre choked back a sob and said, "I'm not sure, but I think so. All Jeff said was that he wanted me to call you right away. He's going to be here in an hour."

The silence on the phone hung like a dark curtain between them. "Okay, I'm leaving right away. Be home soon. Deidre? I love you." Ben hung up without saying goodbye.

Deidre had enough of her wits about her that she remembered to call Megan, but ended up being connected to her daughter's voicemail. She left a terse message to come home as soon as she could, that there was news concerning Maren.

Deidre scrubbed the dirt off her hands and managed to clean under her nails with a brush. She acted as though this was a normal procedure, not shedding a tear, in fact, showing no emotion at all. After stripping off her work clothes and depositing them in the wicker laundry basket, she went upstairs, took a quick shower to wash off the sweat, and dressed in a clean sweatshirt and a pair of jeans. She combed out her hair in front of the mirror, pulled it back in a ponytail, and secured it with an elastic tie. Deidre examined herself in the mirror and thought, *I'm getting too old for this kind of hairdo. Closer to fifty than forty, and I'm still wearing it like a twenty-year-old.* She sat on the edge of her bed and thought how ridiculous that was. She was sure of the reason Jeff wanted to see them, and here she was wondering about what she looked like. With the back of her hand, she wiped away a lone tear that had trickled down her cheek. She wanted to fix something to have for Jeff when he arrived. Another inappropriate thought, she believed.

On the way downstairs, it dawned on her that the boys would be coming home from school on the bus, and she wasn't sure she wanted them to barge in while Jeff was divulging his news. She decided the news might be too gruesome to be sprung on them as soon as they came in the door. Deidre called her in-laws and asked them to pick up Jack and Steve from school. Then she called the school to inform them of the plan.

She scrounged up a few cookies and put on a pot of coffee and took a few minutes to process Jeff's call by retreating to her place of comfort, the stream that ran close to their backyard. She sat down on the grass under a maple tree whose leaves had turned crimson, pulled her knees up to her chest, and rested her face between them. She had no idea how long she sat that way, letting thoughts tumble through her mind, until she felt a warm hand on her shoulder. Looking up, she saw her husband's face, contorted in pain, staring down at her. She managed to stand up and he enveloped her in his arms. They stood that way, swaying back and forth in their misery, feeling the touch of each other's body.

Without speaking, Ben pulled away, took Deidre's hand, and led her back to the house. They had just walked in the back door when Jeff knocked on the front. Ben called out for him to come in, and Jeff opened the door. That was when Deidre lost it.

"Oh, Jeff," she blurted out as she rushed to him. He caught her in his arms and hugged her tightly, all the while looking over her shoulder into Ben's pained eyes.

After what seemed like a long, long time, Jeff said as gently as he could, "Let's go in and sit down. I've got some news to tell you." He walked over to Ben and placed his arm over his friend's shoulder. Still holding Deidre's hand, he led them into the other room.

# Chapter Fifty

DEIDRE FORGOT ABOUT the cookies and coffee she had ready. Instead, she sat on the edge of the couch beside Ben. He, on the other hand, leaned his lanky frame into the corner of the sofa, propped himself against a pillow, and closed his eyes. Deidre found herself unconsciously wringing her hands.

"Folks, I think you know why I'm here," Jeff began. Deidre felt the breath go out of her, and Ben's leg jerked involuntarily.

"We've found Maren's body," he continued. "There isn't any way I can soften the message. One of my deputies was called out early this morning to investigate a report, and he found her grave. I'm so sorry to have to tell you this." Jeff hung his head and tried to gather himself to say more.

"Where was she found?" Ben quietly asked, his eyes still closed.

"She's buried in a shallow grave near the Drummond Road. I think you know where the snowmobile trail crosses the road, by the Experimental Forest. There's a dirt road that goes back to a county gravel pit." He waited for a response from one of the two, but neither showed any sign of recognition. Jeff continued.

"A man from town was walking the trail with his dog, and it ran off into the woods. He tried to call it back, but it didn't return. He heard it barking repeatedly, something out of the ordinary, he said. When he got to where the dog was standing, he could see that something had been buried in a shallow depression. His dog had begun to dig at the loose soil."

Ben opened his eyes before speaking. "Was Maren's body . . ." He choked up and couldn't say the words. Deidre reached across and took his hand in hers. Ben swallowed hard and continued. "Was Maren's body intact?"

"She was wrapped in several layers of heavy plastic, the kind contractors use when doing cement work. It was duct-taped, sealed up pretty well. I don't know how the dog picked up the scent. It's not a trained cadaver dog, but it must have somehow sensed what was there. The man scraped away some of the dirt with his hands, and uncovered enough of the buried object to see that it was a body. He immediately left the area, because he said he didn't want to destroy any evidence. His cell phone was in his car, and he called as soon as he could. A deputy was in the area, and took only ten minutes to get to the scene. He immediately called it in and guarded the grave until I arrived."

Despite her shock, Deidre was able to voice a question. "Are you sure it's her?"

At that question, Jeff's face flushed. "Nothing has been confirmed by forensic tests. I've called in the BCA and they'll be here soon. I didn't want to take any chances of making a mistake, so I've requested they take charge of exhuming her body. Their forensics expert will be here quite soon. I gave them your address and they'll stop here so I can lead them to the site. In the meantime, I wanted to warn you in advance of what was found."

Pleadingly, Ben asked, "But how can you be so certain it's Maren? I know you wouldn't have told us this if you weren't sure yourself."

Jeff didn't want to present the grieving parents with graphic details, and he hesitated. "We did cut through some of the tape and plastic. The corpse is dressed in clothing similar to what Dave told us was missing from Maren's closet. We were able to see her hair, and it's the color of Maren's. It's very evident the body is that of a woman. But the reason we are so sure . . . she's wearing a necklace with a pendant inscribed, "To Maren with Love, Mom and Dad."

Deidre slid off the edge of the couch onto the floor. She wrapped her arms around Ben's leg and kept repeating "No . . . No . . . No," like a plea to God. Ben reached down and stroked her hair, trying to comfort her, even in his grief. Deidre looked up, her face screwed with anger.

"It has to be Dave. How are we going to get him?"

Jeff had an answer. "Now we have a body, proof a crime has been committed. We have the hearsay evidence of his girlfriend. That's a beginning. Few crimes are committed without the perpetrator leaving behind some kind of clue. Somehow he slipped up. Our job is to find out how. We'll get him. I promise."

Their conversation was interrupted by the crunch of gravel beneath tires as a car pulled into the driveway. A few seconds later, someone knocked on the door. Deidre answered it, abruptly throwing open the door. Her mouth dropped, but before she could speak, a woman rushed to her, threw her arms around Deidre, and murmured in her ear, "Oh, Deidre. How could this have happened? How could this ever have happened?"

It was Doctor Judy Coster, forensic pathologist and anthropologist with the Minnesota Bureau of Criminal Apprehension. Over the years, she and Deidre had worked two cases together, developing a strong mutual respect that turned into a lasting friendship. They had communicated infrequently the past two years, but theirs was a friendship that could withstand lapses of time.

"Judy! What a welcome sight your face is," Deidre exclaimed. Then it dawned on her the circumstances of her friend's visit. "Come in. Come in. Jeff is here, and I'm sure he'll want to get going on this as soon as possible." Deidre ushered Judy into the living room, still holding her hand. Jeff stood to greet Judy.

"You made good time. I didn't expect you for another half hour." Judy smiled sheepishly and shrugged. Before she could admit to driving well over the speed limit, Jeff turned his attention to Deidre and Ben.

"I've given this a lot of thought since Maren's body was discovered, and we're going to keep the information within the department as long as we can. Under no circumstances do I want you to contact Dave. Judy is going to supervise the exhumation, and my department will be there to assist her. When the autopsy on Maren's body is complete and any clues have been uncovered, that's when I want to spring the news on him. I'd like to see his reaction first hand. Is there anything we can do for you before we go?"

Deidre and Ben mumbled a "No" at the same time and began to usher Judy and Jeff to the door. Ben stopped.

"I want to go with," he blurted out between pursed lips.

Deidre grabbed her husband. "No. I don't want you to see Maren this way. Ben, there's nothing you can do out there. We'd just be in the way, and I want to remember Maren the way she was the last time we saw her, and I think you do, too. Whatever you'd see at the gravesite will be hideous, and that will be the image of her that will stick in your mind forever. I'm begging you, don't go."

Jeff took Ben by the arm. "She's right. We'll take care of Maren with the utmost respect, and as hard as it will be, we'll do everything we can to remain objective in our search."

"Ben," Deidre pleaded. "Let them do their jobs. They're skilled at what they do, and I have all the confidence in the world in them. Please." She searched to make eye contact with him.

Without saying a word, Ben allowed Deidre to lead him back to the couch, while Jeff and Judy closed the door. They heard them drive away before sitting down. Deidre curled up next to Ben and placed her hand on his shoulder before completely falling apart, and they held each other until Deidre had to get up to go to the bathroom.

When she returned, she asked, "Do you want me to call Pastor Ike?" She hoped Ben would say no, because she was in no mood to hear empty platitudes or words of hope. To her relief, he shook his head.

"But we'd better call Mom and Dad, because we can't just leave the boys there without a reason. What do we do? Do we tell the boys?"

Deidre mulled the question for a moment. "I think we have to. They can't be expected to stay with your folks for no reason. We should have your mom and dad bring them home, but tell them we need to speak with the boys in private. Do you think they'll understand?"

Ben and Deidre discussed the situation for several minutes, weighing the pros and cons, and eventually agreed the boys had to come home and be told the truth. They decided the solution would be to drive into town, pick up the boys, and bring them home before saying anything.

As they were about to pull onto the county road, Megan sped into the driveway. Breathlessly, she rushed to her parents' car, and as she opened the rear passenger door, said, "They've found Maren, haven't they?"

# Chapter
## Fifty-One

JEFF LED THE WAY to the Drummond Road. Judy followed, plowing through the cloud of dust that trailed his vehicle. Ten miles from Ben's and Deidre's, he turned off the graveled surface onto a single-track haul road that intersected the snowmobile trail. When Judy stepped out of her car, she couldn't help but notice the thick coating of dust on their cars. She wasn't accustomed to the silence of the forest that surrounded them. White pines as large as any she had ever seen towered above them, shading the forest floor and blocking any direct sunlight. The place felt almost sacred.

"The snowmobile trail is just ahead," Jeff instructed as he headed toward an opening in the trees. "I've had a deputy posted at the grave since it was discovered. He walked in from the other end, where the trail meets the Drummond Road. That's why his squad isn't parked here. Search and Rescue will be arriving in about twenty minutes to help with any digging and transporting we have to do. I'd like to be able to scour the area for clues before a crowd gets here."

"Will the press be here?" Judy wanted to know.

"I certainly hope not. I instructed the person who found the grave to tell no one. Told him it was important to give us some time. I know him and think he'll keep his mouth shut. The deputy used his cell phone to call me, so he couldn't have been picked up on a scanner." Judy nodded her approval and trudged along beside Jeff.

Any other day she would have been in her glory. The air was crisp and the sky perfectly clear. It was late enough in the afternoon that the sun was beginning to touch the tops of the trees in the west and the aspen leaves glowed yellow. The scent of drying bracken ferns filled the air, but it was the silence that was almost overwhelming. Neither person spoke.

Suddenly, something exploded from the underbrush beside the trail with the whir of beating wings, and a gray shadow dodged through the trees. Judy's heart leaped to her throat. It startled Jeff a little, but he laughed.

"Only a grouse," he casually said. "They can sure scare the heck out of you, though, especially when you don't expect them to get up like that." That would be the last pleasant experience they would have that day.

The deputy met them on the trail. "Heard you coming. We haven't met," he said, extending his hand to Judy. "I'm Deputy Berger, Al."

"Judy Coster. I'm with forensics. Good to meet you, Al." The introductions over, Judy was ready to get to work. "Can you show me the grave?"

Al led the way, Judy followed, and Jeff brought up the rear. She was relieved to see the ground was still pristine. It was obvious that the deputy and Jeff had been careful to follow the same steps going to and from. The grave was thirty yards off the trail in what should have been a beautiful spot under a huge red pine. The ground was covered with lycopodia, princess pine, and fallen pine needles. It was a spot Judy would have selected to sit and allow the world to pass by. Instead, it had been transformed into a place of death.

"Let's divide the area into quadrants," she instructed. "I'll take that one over there." She pointed at the northeast section. Al, you take that. Jeff, you search there. Hopefully, we can finish with them, and then look at the fourth before the squad arrives. We'll begin ten yards out from the center and move toward a focal point directly over the grave."

Each person got on hands and knees and began sweeping the assigned area, searching from left to right and back again. They inched their way toward the center, looking for anything that wasn't natural. It took almost fifteen minutes to reach the apex of each triangular-shaped area. Then they converged on the fourth. By the time they heard the Search and Rescue squad advancing up the trail, they had scoured an area twenty yards in diameter, the size of the floor plan of most houses.

"Let's hope we find more than that when we dig into the grave," Judy remarked, dejection evident in her tone.

Jeff hollered at the people coming up the trail. "Be careful when you come in. Stay single file and follow our tracks. We don't want to disturb things any more than we have to."

Scotty, the captain of the search team, was first to come into view. In one hand, he carried a wooden frame across which a coarse screen had been stretched, in the other a shovel. Another man followed him, carrying a stretcher. A woman was last, a body bag and a plastic tarp clutched under her arm. They stood in reverential silence before Judy started giving directions.

"We're going to go at this slowly. Spread out that tarp over there," she said, motioning toward an area away from where they had searched. "Shovelful by shovelful, we'll screen the dirt over there. I don't want the tiniest piece of evidence lost." The crew carefully removed layer after layer of soil until they could see the body quite clearly.

Through the clear plastic in which she had been wrapped, it was easy to see Maren had been placed on her side, slightly turned onto her belly. Her knees were drawn up as though she had been placed in a fetal position, and Jeff realized it hadn't been an act of thoughtfulness. Whoever had dumped her in the grave had positioned her so the burial hole didn't have to be any bigger than necessary. As it was, the killer had dug almost three feet deep. He had taken his time, not worrying too much about being interrupted.

The diggers tossed their shovels away from the hole and began to excavate around the body with their hands, sifting each scoop through the screen. By the time they exposed nearly all of the body, all they had garnered for their efforts was a pile of pebbles, none of which seemed unusual, and a rusted bottle cap. Jeff looked at it and remarked that a person couldn't go anywhere without finding evidence of civilization. Judy bagged the cap, not expecting that it would have anything to do with the crime. *But,* she thought, *you never know.*

"Okay, gang," she said, slipping into her casual way of addressing people. "Dump the sand off the tarp. Keep it in a pile in case we want to go through it again, and spread the tarp out next to the body. I want you to lift her onto it before we unwrap her." As the crew gently lifted the corpse, Judy instructed, "Careful not to turn her over. The hole where Jeff cut into the plastic to take a look is open. I don't want to lose anything." They gently laid Maren on the tarp, and Judy rolled the young woman over.

"Let's try to straighten her out. Careful now. Don't put too much pressure on her legs. That's right," she instructed.

Judy proceeded to cut the rest of the tape and pull back the plastic sheeting. When she was done, the body lay exposed. Jeff thought no life should end up like this. Maren's clothes were intact, but had deteriorated from the time spent under the soil. The ground where she was buried was a sandy gravel with plenty of drainage. The corpse was drier than he expected, and it looked desiccated. He thanked God Deidre and Ben hadn't insisted on coming along.

After a preliminary examination, which Judy recorded on both video and audio, she gently rewrapped Maren and stood up.

"I'd like you to take the body into town now. Strap it to the stretcher and be careful carrying it on the way out. I don't want you dropping it and causing postmortem damage. I'll meet you at the morgue."

Judy collected what few things she had bagged up and followed the squad out of the woods. It was dark by the time they reached the road, and the trail was illuminated only by the headlamps the team used.

She could hear Jeff following behind. Al had gone the opposite direction to where his county SUV was parked. She faced a long night.

# Chapter Fifty-Two

THE TENSION AT HOME that afternoon and evening was excruciating. Ben paced the floor, stopping every few laps to peer out the window, hoping to see Jeff's vehicle pull into the yard. He called his supervisor and made arrangements to be absent from work for the next several days. Deidre wasn't accountable to anyone, but she had called the school immediately after Jeff and Judy left, telling the office secretary that the boys would be out of school for at least the next week. When asked the reason she had simply stated, "Family emergency." The boys withdrew into their own worlds, something that deeply concerned Deidre, but she didn't know how to remedy it at the time. They retreated to their bedroom, where Deidre found them sleeping on top of the bedcovers. Megan found a magazine and buried her face in its pages. Each of them would deal with their grief in their own way and time.

It was late when Jeff called. His voice sounded haggard, and Deidre could picture the look on his face by his tone.

"Deidre, we've recovered Maren's body. Judy has begun the autopsy, and said she'll have the preliminary work done by tomorrow afternoon. How are you holding up?"

"We're fine," Deidre answered tersely, knowing full well she wasn't telling the truth. "Jeff?"

"Yeah, Deidre."

"How is it? I mean, can you tell if Maren suffered?"

Jeff was quick to answer. "If you're asking if she was beaten or somehow tortured, I would say no. I'm sure you understand that after this long . . ." Jeff paused, groping for words. "You know, it's been over four months." Again he paused. "There's quite a bit of decomposition, but as we moved her, it appeared all of her limbs were intact, as were her teeth, and I could see no damage to her facial bones or cranium." Deidre heard him inhale deeply as if he was stifling a sob.

"So what's next?" she wanted to know.

"Ever since we took Maren's body out of the woods, I've been thinking about that. If you and Ben are up to it, I'd like to stop out and discuss my plan. I hate to ask it, but I'm going to need you and Ben to play Dave for me. I think that's the only way we're going to get to him."

Although she was totally spent, and knew Ben must be too, she told Jeff to come right out. The boys were in bed, so they wouldn't have to hear the news. It was almost midnight when Deidre spotted the headlights from Jeff's vehicle swing up their drive.

She was shocked when she saw Jeff's face. Purple circles ringed his eyes, and worry lines crossed his brow. He looked beaten.

"Hi, folks," he said as he flopped into a chair without being invited. "Well, it's over. Like I think I told you over the phone, we have Maren's body in town, and Judy was beginning the autopsy when I left. She's going to do a preliminary examination tonight, and then will continue in the morning. She said she'd be done by early afternoon."

He stood up. "Deidre, would it be okay if I got myself a glass of water? And you don't happen to have a couple of aspirins, do you?"

Deidre walked ahead of Jeff, put some ice in a large glass and filled it with water. She heard Ben taking two steps at a time up the stairs, and then heard the medicine cabinet door close. He was coming down the stairs as she and Jeff entered the living room. Jeff dumped a couple of the tablets in his mouth and threw back his head to swallow them. He washed them down with a gulp of water.

"It must to have been a hellish day for you, but I'm glad you didn't come with us. Judy did a fantastic job of extricating Maren's body from the sand. She's a good person," he added. Jeff leaned back and closed his eyes and for a second Ben thought he had drifted off to sleep. Just as quickly his eyes popped open, and Jeff began to talk animatedly.

"Here's what we're going to do. I want you to call Dave early in the morning. If he doesn't answer, leave a message. Tell him that Maren's body has been found. Don't say where. In fact, tell him as little as possible, only that she's been found. Tell him that I'm coming here to see you at four o'clock tomorrow afternoon." Jeff looked at his watch. "I guess that would be *this* afternoon. You know what I mean. Don't tell him that Judy is working on the case or even that there is going to be an autopsy. Just tell him that you figured he would want to hear the details about what we know. Whatever you do, don't let him know he has become our one and only suspect. If we surprise him with what we know when he's with us, he may blurt out something to give himself away." Jeff drained his glass.

"I doubt if any of us will get much sleep tonight, but we better try. At least we can shut our eyes and try to rest. Is there anything I can do for you before we meet at four?"

Both Ben and Deidre said no, and escorted Jeff to the deck. He gave Deidre a hug and put his arm around Ben's shoulder. "I'm so sorry," was all he said. Megan was already on her way upstairs to the room she and her sister had shared for so many years.

*****

THROUGH THE BEDROOM BLINDS, Deidre could see the black of night turning gray, and knew it was about seven o'clock. She hadn't slept a wink since she went to bed. Ben had fallen asleep a few minutes after lying down, and she wished she could turn off the world the way he could. She wondered how much rest he had gotten, though, because he had thrashed around all night, muttering unintelligibly the whole time. She reached over and touched his arm, and saw his eyes were open.

"You're awake," he said.

"Yeah, still. I couldn't drift off at all. Too much spinning through my mind. You?"

"Every time I'd fall asleep, I'd dream. Sometimes I'd see Maren as a little girl, sometimes as a young woman. Then I saw her in the grave, looking like I imagine she would have looked, hideous."

Deidre stroked his arm. She decided words were meaningless. With a start, she remembered she had a phone call to make, and pulled the covers back so rapidly she jolted Ben.

"Is something wrong?" he asked, rolling out his side of the bed.

"I've got to call Dave. Maybe we can catch him before he goes to work."

Ben snorted. "More like, he can ignore our call before he leaves the house. But sooner or later his curiosity will get the best of him, and he'll listen to your message." They put on the same clothes they wore the day before and headed downstairs. "I think you'd better be the one to call. I'm so angry, I know it would show in my voice. You're a lot better at controlling your emotions than I am. That okay with you?"

Deidre was already unplugging her phone from its charger. Ben watched her type in her password and begin the search for Dave's number, then she placed the phone to her ear. He could hear it ring once, twice, three times, four.

"Uh, hello, Dave," Ben heard Deidre say. She was caught off guard by his picking up. "Uh, this is Deidre."

"Oh, hi, Deidre," Dave answered, plainly irritated by her imposition into his life. "What's up?"

Deidre stumbled over her words. "I . . . we . . . Ben and I . . . you should know Maren's body has been found." She couldn't go on.

The silence on Dave's end of the call was stifling. Finally, with a hint of panic, he answered. "Oh, my God. Somebody found her. When?"

Deidre remembered what Jeff had said about giving away any information. She answered noncommittally, "A short time ago."

"Tell me what you know," Dave almost demanded.

"We don't know anything right now, other than her body has been found."

"Who? How?" Dave stammered.

"We don't know."

"How can they be sure it's Maren?" Dave wanted to know. Deidre could sense that he was experiencing some confusion.

"They're not one hundred percent sure. I mean, there hasn't been time to perform DNA tests or even compare dental records, but we're positive it's her.

"When will you know?" Dave was getting more belligerent as the conversation progressed.

"Calm down, Dave. Jeff is coming to our place at four o'clock today to fill us in on the information he has gathered. He asked that we call you, because he was sure you'd want to know what he's discovered."

Dave answered immediately. "Why? What's he found?"

"I told you, I don't know," Deidre answered as calmly as she could. "I just know that as much as you loved her, you'll want to hear first-hand what Jeff has to say. I know this is a shock to you, and you must be terribly upset, having an old wound opened like this. But I think we have to stick together, now more than ever. Don't you?" she asked as gently as she could.

"Uh, yeah. We've got to stick together. What time did you say Jeff would be at your place? Four?"

"That's right," Deidre confirmed. "See you then."

"Yeah, see you then." As an afterthought, Dave added. "I can't get away from work until this afternoon, so I'll be there at the last minute, but I'll be there."

Deidre hung up and said to the phone, "I bet you will."

You were terrific," Ben assured her. "I'll bet he's shitting tacks right now. Suffer, you bastard," he said through clenched teeth. Deidre hugged him, and felt his muscles tense and bulging beneath his shirt. Then she felt them relax.

# Chapter Fifty-Three

DEIDRE NERVOUSLY LOOKED at the kitchen clock. It was three forty-five, and no one had arrived. She and Ben talked with the boys and told them that they would not be a part of the meeting. At first they resolutely voiced their objection, but eventually they came to understand that this was not just an informational meeting. It was part of a designed plan to get Dave to incriminate himself, and the fewer the participants, the better chance the plan had of succeeding. In the end, the boys were placated with promises that every detail would be revealed to them. In the meantime, they would stay at Grandma and Grandpa VanGotten's.

Megan opted out of being there when Dave arrived. She wasn't sure she could control herself, and didn't want to jeopardize his being trapped by his own actions and words. She walked along the river, found a familiar spot where she and Maren had once watched two fawns cavort in the new grass of spring, and sat with her back to a rock, listening to the rippling water with her eyes closed.

Deidre looked at the clock for the third time in five minutes, and had just walked out onto the deck when Jeff and Judy drove into the yard. Ben came out when he heard the crunch of the tires and the four exchanged hugs, recognizing the rising tension each was experiencing. They gathered in the living room, waiting for Dave, and a deathly quiet enveloped the group.

Deidre got up one more time to look at the clock. "He's ten minutes late. Do you think he'll show?" She barely got the words out of her mouth when Dave pulled up in a cloud of dust. Deidre noticed how harried he looked as he strode across the lawn and climbed the steps to the deck. She opened the door before Dave could knock.

"Come in," she invited. "You look like you could stand something to drink. Soda, coffee, even have wine if you'd like."

Dave didn't bother to hug or touch her. "No. No," he said to Deidre's offer. "Well, maybe a glass of ice water, if you have it." He went into the living room, while Deidre retrieved it for him. She steadied her hand as she filled the glass, and was able to accomplish the task without spilling.

This is Doctor Judith Coster," Deidre introduced Judy using her title. "She's a forensic pathologist from the Bureau of Criminal Investigation. You know Jeff." Dave mumbled his recognition as he took a chair across the room from Jeff.

Jeff looked at every person before he started, and let his gaze linger on Dave. He wanted to cause as much anxiety as he could before giving any information. Finally, he spoke.

"I want you to know how sorry I am for your loss, Dave. You must be devastated."

Dave murmured something unintelligible, and squirmed in his chair. Deidre thought he was trying to screw his face up, but to her it wasn't working.

Jeff continued. "When we exhumed Maren's body, we searched the area thoroughly for any clue as to who might have been involved in her murder. Unfortunately, we didn't turn up one bit of evidence, no foreign materials, no weapons, nothing."

Deidre had been watching Dave out of the corner of her eye, and she thought he breathed a sigh of relief when Jeff admitted that.

"Her body was taken to the morgue, where Dr. Coster performed an autopsy. I'll let her fill you in on what she learned."

Judy opened a folder that was sitting on her lap. "I know this is going to be painful for all of you, but I also think you want to know the truth about what happened to Maren. Please, if at any time you want me to stop, or want to be excused, say the word."

Judy remained silent for several seconds while she surveyed her audience. Like Jeff, she let her eyes focus on Dave, and held that gaze until he began to fidget with a hangnail on one of his fingers.

"My examination indicates that Maren was strangled by a very strong person. I base that opinion on several factors. First, there is a small, fragile bone in every person's throat. You've probably never seen it, even on a skeleton, because it doesn't articulate with any other bone. In examining Maren's throat, I discovered that bone was shattered. In itself, this would lead to a conclusion of strangulation. Second, there is evidence that two cervical vertebrae, those found in the neck, were misaligned, not enough to have caused her death, but enough to show evidence of a struggle. In my opinion, she was attacked from the rear, by someone with relatively large hands, and who was strong enough to have inflicted mortal damage to her system."

Deidre glanced at Dave, and was sure he had tried to cover one hand with the other, but then thought she might be reading more into his actions than really occurred.

"There are other factors that lead me to believe she was strangled," Judy continued. "There is no other evidence of her being assaulted. No other broken bones, no bullet holes or stab wounds, nothing that would lead me to believe she had experienced any other trauma than that inflicted to her neck and throat."

Through the whole monologue Deidre and Ben sat stoically silent. Dave tried to move nonchalantly as he took a handkerchief from his pocket and wiped his hands. His forehead had become shiny, and reflected the afternoon sun coming through the window.

"Is there any other possibility?" he questioned.

"Like what?" Judy asked.

"Some of the guys who came into the bar where she worked were pretty rough. Could they have drugged her?"

"That's possible," Judy agreed. "It takes a while to run a drug screen, and we're doing that. Did you ever know Maren to use drugs?" she asked, looking directly at Dave.

"No, nothing like that," he quickly answered.

"But, you see, Dave," Judy rejoined, still focusing on Dave, "Even if she was drugged, that still wouldn't explain the trauma to her neck. I'm sure you can see that."

Dave tried to be smooth with his answer, but it came out more as a squeak than his normal baritone. "I see that. Yes, I see what you mean." He took a deep breath and seemed to gather himself. He put his handkerchief back in his pocket.

"There is one more thing," Judy said, closing the folder for effect. "This may come as a shock to you. Well, probably not you, Dave." She kept shining the spotlight on him. "Did you know that Maren was four months pregnant?"

Dave let out a moan, slid off the chair to the floor and onto his knees. "My son. My son. I would have had a son," he sobbed while rubbing his eyes. When he looked up they were red-rimmed. "How could this happen to us," he asked, looking at Ben and Deidre as though expecting them to rush to his side. Neither moved.

"Then you knew she was pregnant?" Judy asked.

Sounding deeply offended, Dave snapped at her, "Of course I did. Don't you think she would have told me?"

Judy pushed more. "When did she tell you?"

"As soon as she found out," Dave was getting more bellicose.

"When was that?"

"I don't know, a while ago," Dave answered vaguely. Judy decided to back off directing her questions at him.

"Did the two of you know Maren was pregnant?" Jeff asked Deidre and Ben, acutely aware of the stress with which they were dealing.

Numbed by the news, all they could do was shake their heads. Dave withdrew into his own thoughts and stared at a corner of the room.

"Judy and I have to get back to town. She's got paperwork to finish, and I've got to close down the office for today. Do you have any questions we can answer before we leave?"

Ben looked at the investigators through tear-filled eyes. "When will Maren's body be released to the mortuary? We need to plan her funeral, and want to begin as soon as possible."

His words came as a shock to Deidre. In all the turmoil, all she had focused on was Dave's culpability, and hadn't given the matter of Maren's funeral any thought.

Judy answered immediately. "Her body will be released this afternoon, as soon as I sign off. You can begin making your plans now, if you'd like."

Deidre looked at Dave. "I assume you'll be attending," she said, more curtly than intended.

"Huh?" Dave came out of his world of thoughts, somewhat confused. It was plain to Deidre that his mind had been far away. "Oh, sure." He straightened up, and very pointedly asked. "Why wouldn't I be there? Maren was the one person in the world I loved. She was to be the mother of my child." Then he blurted out, "All of you think I killed her, don't you?" It was as though he had lost all composure. "Well, you're wrong. I'd never do something like that. Why would I? We were happy together, and Maren was there for me all the time." Dave jumped up. "Enough of this crap. I don't have to sit here and take your dirty looks or hear your veiled accusations. I know what you're thinking, and you can shove it."

His hands were shaking and his face was beet red. Dave's rage was obvious to everyone, and Deidre thought he was ready to crack.

"I'm done with this inquisition," he barked. "Call me when you know the time of the funeral. I'll be there." He slammed the door on his way out.

"Sorry you had to see that," Jeff said, comforting his friends, "But we got to him. He'll be sweating about this meeting, and who knows how he'll react. For now, let us know if we can do anything to help. Oh, and look, we're going to get that guy, bank on it.".

After Judy and Jeff left, Deidre sat down at the kitchen table. She was totally spent, and Ben stood behind her so he could rub her shoulders. She looked back at him and tried to smile, knowing that whenever her husband was stressed he rubbed her shoulders, as if the touch and action relieved him.

"Come on. Let's find Megan and fill her in on what happened. We've got a lot of things to do tomorrow," he said, seeming to just remember his other daughter. It was dark before they located Megan still sitting by the stream. She was cried out.

# Chapter
## Fifty-Four

THE DAY DAWNED DEVOID of cheer. Deidre went through the motions of putting a few things on the table for breakfast, but no one wanted to eat. Megan picked at a bagel and sipped from a glass of orange juice. Ben sat with a cup of coffee between his hands, rotating it slowly. Deidre busied herself at the sink, doing nothing. Everyone was startled when Ben's cell phone rang.

"Hello, Pastor," they heard him say, his voice lacking any expression. "We're holding it together as best we can. . . . No, I don't think we need meals brought out. None of us has much of an appetite. . . . Honestly, we have a lot of planning to do today, so no, I think not. We would like to see you this afternoon to plan her service, though. . . . Sure, one o'clock will be fine. In your office? . . . Okay, we'll see you then." He set the phone on the table.

"That was Pastor Ike," Ben explained to the others, before realizing it was a redundant comment. "He wanted to come out, but I said we'd be too busy. We're scheduled to meet him at one this afternoon." He sighed. "I suppose I might as well call the funeral home and schedule a meeting with them, too." No one objected, and he punched in the number.

*****

THE FUNERAL DIRECTOR was more than accommodating to the family's wishes, and said he'd be in his office at ten. After Deidre cleared the table with Ben and Megan's help, they drove to town, Ben driving so slowly without realizing he was doing it that several cars were backed up behind them as they followed the hilly road. Eventually, he looked in the rearview mirror and realized he was holding up traffic. Rather than speeding up, he pulled over to the side of the road and rested his head on the steering wheel. Deidre rubbed his back, and he raised his head.

"I don't want to go through with this, but we have to." He checked his side mirror and drove back on to the roadway. His first stop was to his parents, and they came out of the house to meet the trio at their car. They said nothing, but hugged everyone tightly, then led them into the house.

Steve and Jack were waiting at the table. The remains of eggs and toast were on plates in front of them, and Deidre hoped they had been able to get most of the meal down.

"Hi, guys," she said as cheerily as she could, but it didn't come out right. "We've got business to do today, and we'd like to have you come help us with some decisions. Will you?"

Steve ignored her offer. "Did Dave tell you what he did?" Deidre sat down next the boys.

"No, but that's not what we should be concerned about today. There'll be time for that later. We have to prepare for Maren's funeral today."

"Like where she's going to be buried?" Jack wanted to know.

"Yeah, like where she's going to be buried," Ben echoed.

*****

BY THE TIME ALL arrangements were made for Maren's funeral, the entire family was exhausted. Jack and Steve reacted as typical kids, wondering how they were supposed to act, alternating between being normal boys and grieving siblings. At the same time, they wanted to be active participants in the preparations. When they went to the flower shop, Deidre and Ben made sure the boys were able to express their wishes as far as the flower arrangements were concerned. They opted to have their own wreath beside the casket, with a banner that read, WE LOVE YOU, SIS. While they were at the florist, Megan had an idea the others bought into.

"I'd like to take a cross and some flowers to the place Maren was buried in the woods," she said. "I can do it alone, but I sure would like company. Does anyone want to come with me?"

Jack and Steve jumped at the opportunity, and Ben and Deidre, although they had reservations, said they'd come along. The florist had crosses on hand, and put together a bouquet for them. The drive to the Drummond Road was only twenty minutes, and they arrived as the sun was dipping behind the treetops. Ben figured they had time to walk in, leave the flowers, and make it back to the car before it got too dark.

The group talked among themselves as they trudged up the trail to a spot where it was obvious people had been going into the woods. As they got closer to where Jeff had said the burial site was, everyone became silent, and it was as though they were approaching a holy spot. They found an open area under the massive pine tree, but before they could move any further, there was a crash in the brush off to their left. Startled by the noise, everyone froze in their tracks, their hearts beating wildly. Ben expected to see the white tail of a deer disappear in the underbrush. Instead, he caught a flash of the back of a person, darting around trees and running deeper into the woods. Ben sat down so he could catch his breath. The others looked at him for some hint of what they should do.

"That was a man!" Jack exclaimed. "What was he doing here?"

"How do you know it was a man?" Ben asked, a little taken aback by his son's conclusion.

"He ran like a man," was Jack's reason.

Ben calmed his voice. "Let's not assume we know who it was. You can't always tell if a person is a man or woman by their gait. I think all we can say is that it was a person. Do any of you agree with Jack?"

Steve was hesitant to voice his opinion after hearing his brother rebuked. Megan said she couldn't tell, but figured the way the person had plowed through the brush, it was probably a man. Deidre remained silent, but only one name came to mind, Dave.

*****

As soon as they arrived home after placing flowers where Maren's body had been found, Ben phoned Jeff and reported that someone had been poking around the gravesite. There was little hope of isolating footprints, because so may people had been involved in the recovery of her body, and anyway, there was nothing illegal about curious onlookers. Jeff thanked him and said he'd check the site in the morning, just in case.

The boys, Megan, Deidre, and Ben spent the evening trying to think of things to do, but nothing seemed to matter. The day had been exhausting, everything that could be said had been said, and as a group they felt stranded in time. Deidre suggested they all go to bed early. The funeral would be in two days, and there were still loose ends to tie up before then. By ten, the lights were out, except in Megan's room. She looked through her and Maren's high school yearbook, bitterly remembering the joys she and her sister had shared, joys that would never be again.

*****

The news that Maren was pregnant when she was murdered troubled Jeff, and he couldn't understand why. He told himself it was natural to be upset by the circumstances, but there was something that kept eating at him. Finally, more to give himself some closure than anything else, he asked for and received a warrant to allow him access to Maren's medical records.

"Mornin,' Jude," he said as he leaned on the counter. "How's everything?" Judith Prig, Jude as everyone called her, knew this wasn't a social call, and ignoring Jeff's attempt to make small talk, smiled and asked, "What do you want, Jeff? I know you didn't come just to see me." She patted his hand. Jeff thought this was one of the perks of living in a small town, a lot less red tape.

"I've got a warrant to access the med records of Maren VanGotten. Can you get them for me?"

Jude briefly looked at the court document before saying, "I want to show this to our director before I get them, just to protect my behind. Be right back."

Jeff heard her talking to someone behind a partially open office door, but couldn't make out what was said. Then he heard someone walk down a hall, heard a printer hammering out copies, and in minutes Jude appeared, a folder in her hands.

"There's an empty office in here." She motioned to where she wanted him to go. "This doesn't leave the office. Okay?" Jude placed the folder on a table as Jeff nodded and took a seat. He opened the folder to the latest entry. His eyes skimmed over the introductory details:

Patient Name: Maren VanGotten
Sex: Female
Age: 21
Reason for Visit: Suspected Pregnacy

The patient was examined for signs of pregnancy and it was confirmed she is approximately four months pregnant. She informed me that she has not seen a doctor to this point, and needed confirmation. The patient was given information relating to sustaining a healthy pregnancy, and appeared to be relieved when told her condition seemed normal at the present time. The patient requested that an ultrasound be performed, and one was ordered. The results revealed that she was pregnant with a boy, and that everything was normal. Another appointment was scheduled for a month from this date.

The last three words of the report caused Jeff's eyes to move to the top of the page to where the date was stamped. It was May 3 at 8:45 in the morning, two days before Maren disappeared.

Jeff sucked in a deep breath of air. He decided he'd wait until after Maren's funeral to tell the family about this discovery.

*****

DEIDRE WOKE EARLY, long before the alarm went off, and slipped out of bed. In the dimly lit room she could see the outline of her dress, the one she had selected the night before to wear to Maren's funeral, hanging from a hook on the back of the closet door. Her first thought was that it looked too much like a ghost.

She tiptoed to the kitchen, and as quietly as she could, filled the coffeemaker with fresh water, poured grounds into the basket, and set it to brewing. In minutes she was sitting at the table, a steaming cup of her favorite drink between her fingers. She hoped she would make it through the day without falling apart.

She watched the eastern sky first turn gray, then become streaked with pink, and finally saw the red rim of the sun rise. At that time of the morning, against the perspective of the horizon, she could literally see the movement of the sun, and within minutes, it was a red ball in the sky. Wisps of fog rose like thin plumes of smoke from the frost-covered field as the ground warmed, and a profound sense of sadness swept over Deidre.

Her thoughts turned to the several conversations she had shared with Pastor Ike, and this morning she turned his words over in her mind. As she looked at the magnificent sunrise, she thought, *Is this all there is to God, sunrises and sunsets? If there really is a God, surely I should be able to sense Him, if He* is *a Him. Why can't I just believe like so many people do? But no! I've got to think and question. Shit, I'm so angry right now, if He . . . or She . . . or It was standing here, I'd ask right out, "what good are you? If you can do anything, why didn't you take care of my daughter? And if you couldn't do anything to save her, then what good are you?"*

Deidre looked at her hands and was surprised to see that her knuckles were white. She consciously forced herself to relax, and circulation returned to her fingers. Before she could come close to resolving her issues with God, she sensed, more than heard, Megan beside her.

"I love you, Mom," was all Megan said. She laid her hand on her mother's shoulder and gave a squeeze, then went to pour herself a cup of coffee.

In a few minutes, Ben joined them, and for a time they sat in each other's presence, not having anything they wanted to say. Suddenly, Ben burst into tears and left the house to go outside and stare at the woods. Megan started to get up to go be with him, but Deidre gabbed her arm.

"Give your father some time to be alone. He's where he should be right now, letting nature console him. The woods has always been his refuge. I think it speaks to him, and he hears its voice."

She and Megan climbed the stairs and gently woke the boys, Megan hugging one, Deidre the other.

"Time to wake up, guys. We've got to be to the church by nine thirty, and it's already eight. Get up and shower. Oh, and don't forget to brush this morning. Come on. Let's go."

Both boys grumbled and pulled their quilts up. The early morning chill made them shiver. Eventually, they were awake enough for the women to leave, confident the twins would make it out of bed.

As a parting shot, Deidre reminded them, "I set out the clothes I want you to wear today. No substitutions. Okay?" The boys mumbled something unintelligible, and Deidre took that to mean they had heard her.

*****

HARDLY ANYONE WAS at the church when they arrived, and for a fleeting moment Deidre felt a pang of fear. What if no one cared enough to show up for her daughter's funeral? She put that thought out of her mind. It was early.

The hearse was parked outside the main entrance, and for the first time that morning the reality of what was going to happen hit Deidre. She averted her eyes, slipped her arm inside Ben's, and together they entered the church, Megan ushering Jack and Steve behind them.

The smell of the sanctuary was familiar, the silence was not unexpected, and the sight of the altar was what she was used to, but nothing was the same. In the front of the altar, propped on a stand, was the wooden casket they had selected only three days ago. Flower arrangements, too many to fit, were placed in an ordered profusion, and the solemn-faced funeral director was standing beside them.

"Guests will begin to arrive soon." Deidre looked at him and thought, *Guests? What do you mean, guests? This isn't a party!. This is my daughter's funeral. I don't want any damn guests here.*

The director offered some advice. "The people who'll be gathering are here to grieve with you. They'll be coming because they love you, loved your daughter, and they want to help. Many will not know how, but let them hold you up today. That's why they will be here, to support you as only your friends can."

His words surprised Deidre, and she wondered if the others had been listening. His message didn't change anything, but they didn't hurt, either.

By ten o'clock, friends, relatives, and a few gawkers, Deidre thought, began to file in, each offering words of condolences. By ten thirty, Deidre was numb, hardly aware of who had passed by or who waited in line to say, "We're so sorry." She looked at Ben, who was greeting each person as though their words were the most precious gift he had been given. She wished she had his ability to accept their kindness.

# Chapter Fifty-Five

THE DAY AFTER MAREN'S funeral, Deidre sat alone, looking at the shriveled flowers hanging over the edge of a pot on the deck. *Life,* she thought. *So strong and at the same time so fleeting.* She sighed deeply, knowing that life would never be the same for any of her family.

She tried to remember Megan's funeral, and was shocked to discover she remembered hardly anything. Not what Pastor Ike's homily was about, not what was sung, not who had attended, not even what she had done. It was as though her mind had erased the service from her memory. She was both saddened and angered by that realization.

She remembered meeting with her family and Pastor Ike before the service, and he had said something about there being a time for something or other. That part was a blank. She remembered following him down the aisle in the church and the congregation rising. She remembered following Maren's casket out of the church, and congregants' eyes meeting hers, tears trickling down their cheeks. She remembered her knees sagging and catching herself before she fell when the pallbearers slid the casket into the hearse.

She didn't remember the drive to the cemetery, or the walk to the gravesite. She didn't remember plucking a rose from the casket spray or bringing it home. She didn't remember draping her body over the casket and sobbing "No, I won't leave her!" when the graveside service concluded. She didn't remember Ben gently lifting her away and leading her back to the car.

Today, all she remembered was that Maren would never be coming home again.

*****

A WEEK AFTER the funeral, Jeff stopped by in the middle of the day. He knew Ben had taken a leave from work and would probably be home with Deidre. After a few minutes of chit chat, inquiring about the boys and Megan, asking how they were doing, Jeff gave the real reason for his visit.

"I was able to get a court order to open Maren's medical file at the clinic. On the chance that she had visited a doctor concerning her pregnancy, I thought she might have gone to one of our local physicians. She had." Jeff took a sip of coffee from the cup Deidre had given him.

"It made for interesting reading," he added. "Maren saw Doctor Marjorie Phelp two days before she went missing. Until then, she hadn't sought medical attention. The doctor's notes indicated that she was four months along, just as Judy's autopsy revealed. Maren requested that an ultrasound be performed, and guess what? Like Dave said, she was carrying a baby boy." He let his words sink in.

"I wouldn't share news like this with just anyone, but we worked too long together and have been close friends too long for me to keep it from you. The doctor noted that Maren seemed upset with the news, and upon being questioned revealed that the baby's father was not going to be thrilled by the news."

Jeff stared at the tabletop, while Ben and Deidre sat silent, feeling stunned and betrayed.

"I know that S.O.B. did it, but I can't prove it." Jeff slammed his mug down on the table without realizing he did it. As he tried to rub out any mark he may have made in the wood, he said, "Sorry. I lost it for a moment. I'll be in touch as soon as we find out anything else."

In his embarrassment, Jeff caught the leg of his chair as he stood up and created more of a commotion. He apologized again and let himself out.

"Poor Jeff," Deidre commiserated. "He's taking this pretty personally. I hope he doesn't let it cloud his judgment."

*****

A COUPLE OF DAYS after Jeff's visit, and after Deidre and Ben had time to process his discovery in Maren's medical records, Deidre was basking in what would be one of the few warm days of autumn. It was the last week of October, and as she sat outside nursing a cup of hot cider in her hand, she recalled the frightful Halloween snowstorm that had hit the North Shore sometime in the mid-nineties. By the time it had subsided, almost four feet of snow buried the ground, and it didn't melt until April. With that thought, and considering the balminess of the day, she decided to visit the site of Maren's burial in the woods one more time. She left a message on Ben's voicemail, and drove to the Drummond Road.

She took her time walking to the tree under which her daughter's body had been buried, taking in the sights and smells of the forest. She discovered a downed tree near the grave, one she hadn't noticed before, and used it for a bench. The flowers she and her family had left were withered, browned by repeatedly freezing at night and thawing during the day. A red squirrel hopped erratically, stopping every few leaps to assess anything dangerous. Deidre sat motionless, and the furry animal came close enough that she could see its whiskers wiggle as it tested her scent. Suddenly it bolted up a nearby tree, perched on a limb, and aggressively scolded her for invading its territory. For a moment the little creature brightened her day, but a deep melancholy soon wiped out the pleasure it brought.

Deidre picked up a piece of hazelnut brush that had been broken off by the recovery team, and began to absentmindedly move dried leaves around, flipping them one at a time into the air. As she gradually cleared a small area of the detritus of fall, her mind became blank, and she was in a different place. She flipped one more leaf and started to stand, but froze. A glint of something caught her eye. She got down on her hands and knees to look more closely at it. Under that last leaf, and pressed into the ground by someone's foot, was a small brass button. As insignificant as it might be, Deidre's heart beat wildly as she fumbled in her coat pocket for her phone. The first thing she did was to take a series of pictures of her discovery, then she dialed Jeff.

She was relieved to hear his voice. "Jeff, get out here right away," she demanded without realizing it.

"Deidre? Is that you? Calm down a second. Where the heck are you?"

She took a deep breath so she could speak. "I'm sitting here by Maren's grave, and I've found something."

For a moment, Jeff thought Deidre was losing it. What could she possibly have found in the cemetery? Then it dawned on him. "You're out by the snowmobile trail?"

"Yes, yes," Deidre answered excitedly. "I've found what we've been looking for."

*****

JEFF ASSURED HER he'd be out right way, but it would take at least twenty minutes for him to get there. Deidre waited impatiently, and eventually heard the unmistakable swish of dried grass as he half walked, half jogged up the trail.

"I hope what you've found is as important as it sounded," he said, trying to regain his breath. "What is it?"

"There." Deidre pointed out the shiny button. It was somewhat tarnished, but still retained enough luster to reflect the mid-afternoon sun. Jeff looked closely at it before taking a series of pictures with his cell phone.

"Don't know what we did before these things," he said. He pulled a pair of rubber gloves from his jacket pocket and stretched them over his bony hands.

As Jeff dusted off the dirt that clung to the button, Deidre looked over his shoulder. "Damn, I've seen buttons like that before. Where?" She tried to conjure up the information stored somewhere in her memory, but to no avail. Still, it looked so familiar. Jeff bagged the evidence, and together they walked back to the road.

"I'll check with the rescue crew to see if any of them lost a button like this, but finding where it came from will be a long shot. It's something, though."

They said goodbye at their cars, Jeff telling Deidre to call anytime she or Ben needed to talk. She promised she would.

# Chapter
## Fifty-Six

By the time Ben and the boys came home from work and from school, Deidre had made supper, washed and folded a load of clothes, answered a few e-mails, and prepared a grocery list of things to pick up the next morning.

The men in her life were hungry and dinner was rushed. Everyone gobbled down the food she prepared, and too soon, she thought, they were ready to head into town for the last high school football game of the year. Deidre declined their invitation to go, making the excuse that she wanted time alone to think. Only after they left did she realize she hadn't told them about finding the button.

For the next hour she rambled inside the lonely house, first trying to read a magazine, then watching five minutes of a TV program, and finally deciding to put away the summer jackets still hanging in the hall closet. As she took them out and folded them, her mind wandered to the red squirrel that had chewed her out that afternoon. Without thinking, she reached into the back of the closet and took out a coat she didn't immediately recognize. Then she remembered it was Dave's, the one he had forgotten at their house the day Maren's car was found on the Spooner Road. She froze.

*****

"JEFF? THIS IS DEIDRE. I've got it!" she shouted into her phone.

"Got what?" Jeff asked, puzzled.

"I've got it, the proof we need!"

After a very brief explanation, Jeff told her to sit tight. He'd be to her place as fast as he could make it through town and out into the country. Less than fifteen minutes later, she heard his steps pounding up the stairs to the deck. Jeff knocked but didn't wait for a "Come in." He burst into the kitchen, where Deidre sat, still holding the forgotten jacket.

"Look," was all she said as she held out its sleeve. Two brass buttons on the coat's sleeve remained, but it didn't take a trained eye to see that one was missing, where ragged threads were still attached to the fabric. "This is where I saw buttons matching the one I found near Maren's grave," she exclaimed excitedly.

Jeff pulled up a chair and sat down, looking as though his legs couldn't support him. He fingered the buttons without saying a word, contemplated the find, then took a plastic evidence bag from his pocket. Inside was the button Deidre had found in the woods. It matched exactly.

"You know what a good lawyer would say about this?" Without waiting for an answer, he continued. "He'd say you planted the button. It wouldn't take too much digging to find someone who'd testify that your relationship with Dave wasn't, what should I say . . . cordial? And surely he could find a number of people who would say that Megan plain didn't like him. Do you see the problem we have with this?"

Deidre's heart sank. What could she have done differently? She knew the truth, but the truth could sometimes be hidden under layers of doubt.

"What are we going to do?" she asked dejectedly. "We can't just let him walk away from this and go on living his lie, can we?" Before she could begin to cry out of frustration, Jeff took her hand.

"He's not going to walk. I can guarantee that. But I'm going to need your help. Where's Ben?"

After Deidre explained that he and the boys were at the football game, Jeff said he would wait, if Deidre had something to go with a cup of coffee. He smiled at his attempt at levity, and she smiled back.

The game ended at nine thirty, and by ten, the trio of fans stomped into the kitchen, and the boys wondered if they could make hot chocolate. Ben looked quizzically at Jeff. Deidre helped Steve and

Jack make their drinks, and then hustled them off to bed while Ben filled Jeff in on the game. Two Harbors had won a nail biter.

Finally, the three adults could talk.

"Dave has played us like a pro. All his shock, his anxiety, his sorrow, it was all an act," Jeff began. "Some people are so skilled at lying, I think they actually believe they're telling the truth. My guess is that he'll never admit to what he did, even if he's confronted with all the evidence to the contrary. We once had a man in custody, awaiting trial, who killed his ex-wife's boyfriend and then held her hostage. She was set to testify against him, members of the SWAT team that rescued her were set to testify, and the SWAT team member who observed his behavior through a sniper scope gave his testimony to a grand jury. Still, he continued to adamantly declare his innocence. We need a plan to get Dave to incriminate himself on tape."

Neither Deidre nor Ben had given any thought to such a plot. For one thing, Ben's mind was still reeling from the recent knowledge about Dave's jacket with the missing button. Deidre was too busy wondering what she might have done differently when she found the button near Maren's makeshift grave. Jeff, however, had formulated a plan, which he laid out for them.

"Dave doesn't know you found a button that matches those on his jacket. In fact, I'm sure he has forgotten about the jacket being in your closet. Otherwise, he'd have collected it long ago. We have to get him to come get it. That's where you'll help, Deidre. Somehow, you've got to lure him out here and get him talking."

Ben held the jacket in his gloved hands. Ever since Deidre had made her discovery, she had worn rubber gloves when handling it in order to prevent contamination, but she thought it was probably too late for that. Ben and Jeff believed the same, but were taking no chances.

"Anything you think I can do?" Ben asked. To Jeff, he didn't seem too anxious to allow himself near Dave.

"I'd like you to stick close to me," Jeff said. Ben knew Jeff was afraid of his inability to control himself if he came face to face with his daughter's murderer.

Deidre wanted to know if she would work off a script.

"I don't think that would be possible, because we don't know how Dave's going to react. I'm afraid you'll have to play it as it goes," Jeff said a little apologetically. "Can you do that?"

Deidre thought hard on that question before answering. "Hopefully I can be a better actor than he's been." She hesitated. "It looks like this is our best bet."

Jeff's plan was to place a recorder on Ben's and Deidre's phone before she called. They doubted Dave would answer, but Deidre would leave a scripted message on his voicemail to make him wonder if he had left evidence on the jacket. Even if he picked up the call, Deidre would have a starting point and could go off-script as the conversation unfolded. Together, they composed the message, reading it aloud and rewording it to make the message concise yet intriguing.

They all agreed they would have only one chance at getting to Dave, and decided to not rush into the sting operation. Jeff suggested they give him two days to get everything set up. The house would be wired for sound, recording devices would be set up in the basement, where they would be monitored by deputies and Jeff, and tests could be run on the jacket and button before allowing Dave to handle it again.

After Jeff left, Deidre and Ben sat up until the early morning hours, mulling over their feelings, wondering about Dave's reaction and willingness to come for his jacket, and debating what the possible outcomes could be.

Even after going to bed, Deidre couldn't sleep. *I'll say this. He'll say that. Then I'll say . . . but if he says . . . then I can say . . .* She carried on hypothetical conversations until finally drifting off to sleep, but even then, her mind kept working, and she dreamed she was having a disjointed conversation with a stranger.

# Chapter Fifty-Seven

BEN DECIDED TO TAKE a few more days off from work, figuring he wouldn't be able to concentrate on anything but getting at Dave. Deidre worked on different scenarios for when she met Dave face to face, picturing in her mind how she would manage to not explode and ruin the entire operation. Jeff wanted access to their home, and by the next afternoon, a technical crew was busy installing microphones in any room of the house that Dave might enter.

Deidre was excited, but when Jeff called saying he had more news, she could hardly contain herself. Ben became so agitated at the possibility that more evidence had been found, he decided to go for a walk in the woods, something he always did when he was stressed and needed time to process. By the time he returned home, the wiring was pretty much completed, and a listening and recording station was ready to go in the basement. Jeff had already arrived and was sipping a cup of coffee. He stood when Ben entered the kitchen and patted his friend on the shoulder.

"We've found another piece of the puzzle," he said matter-of-factly, although the look on his face gave away his satisfaction.

"After you found the button from Dave's coat, I got to wondering if there was any chance we missed something when we searched Dave's and Maren's apartment. On a long shot, I went back to the building to talk to the manager. I knew any evidence in the apartment itself would be long gone, because new tenants moved in shortly after Dave left for Duluth. I was more interested in anything the manager might have forgotten to show us at the time of our search."

Jeff stopped and took another swig of coffee, then set the cup down before continuing.

"He was surprised to see me, and when I asked if there was anything he might have forgotten to tell us, his eyes widened. 'My God!" he exclaimed. 'I forgot all about what happened last spring. I was just getting ready to call Dave and ask if he wanted a box that was stuffed into a space above the rafters in the storage unit he had rented. Several of the units go un-rented in the summer, but when winter is on its way, people need a place to put their summer toys. The couple who live in the apartment that Dave and Maren rented paid for the storage space a couple of days ago, and when they were moving their stuff in, found a cardboard box. I figured it must be Dave's.'"

Jeff shook his head, and Ben and Deidre waited for him to continue. Jeff mumbled, almost to himself, "I sure don't know how we missed it when we searched the unit last spring." He went on to explain. "The box was wedged in the rafters above the automatic garage door. When it's open, of course it obscures the view of the rafters when you look from below. No one thought to close the door and then go back in through the side door. If we had, we'd have seen the box. At least, I think we would have."

Deidre couldn't take the suspense any longer. "Just tell us what you found, for God's sake!" she exploded. As soon as the expletive left her mouth, she regretted it. "Oh, damn, Jeff. I'm so sorry." She hung her head. "It just came out. I'm so sorry. Please, tell us what happened."

Jeff realized he had been taking too long. "No offense taken, friend. You're right. I got a warrant to open the box. Inside, among other items, was a pair of running shoes caked with dried red clay. I suspect they're Dave's, because the box contained some things with his name on them. I took the box and its contents as evidence. Remember when we collected soil samples from the road where Maren's car was found? The lab says the clay on Dave's shoes probably came from the same place. And, I know it's been a long time ago, but you put me onto the fisherman who had picked up a jogger on the Drummond Road. The mud left in his truck also closely matches the clay on Dave's shoes. There was also a cap in the box. It has an insignia above the visor that matches the description given to us by the guy."

Ben broke in. "That settles it, then! That S.O.B. killed my daughter. There's no doubt about it."

Jeff spoke softly to calm the situation. "You and I, all of us, know he did it, but everything is circumstantial to this point. A good lawyer will find reasons for all these coincidences. After all, there's no crime against jogging on a muddy road in the middle of the night, is there? That's why it's so important to get Dave to make some kind of incriminating statement."

Jeff set a timeline for when they would contact Dave and laid it out for the others to see and comment on. Deidre was to call him early the next day, trying to catch him before he left for work. She reminded everyone that Dave had consistently not answered or returned her calls for quite some time, and that she would in all likelihood be leaving a message. They talked again about what she should say.

"It has to be something that alarms him, but doesn't scare him off," Ben advised. "I don't think saying you have his coat will be enough. He'll just say it's old and to throw it in the garbage. Something has to be said about the missing button to pique his anxiety. But at the same time, not enough to cause him to run," Ben added. Turning to Jeff, he asked, "Do you think he might take off on us?"

Jeff shrugged. "He might, but if he does, we've got another marker against him. I've had him under surveillance since Deidre called me about the jacket, in case somehow he learned about the found button. If he runs, the airport will be closed to him and the routes out of Duluth will be shut off. We've got him by the short hair, and pretty soon we're going to begin pulling it."

# Chapter Fifty-Eight

DEIDRE LOOKED AT HER watch, took a bite of toast and tried to swallow, put her coffee cup to her lips and took a sip. She swallowed again, and the wad of dry toast went down. She glanced at the clock on the wall and shivered. Its hands seemed to be not moving, even though the second hand was sweeping around the clock's face. Across the table from her, Ben tried to concentrate on the morning paper, but nothing registered as his eyes skimmed the printed page.

"Couple more minutes," he said to Deidre as he reached across the table and placed his hand on hers. "Are you ready?"

"I guess," she answered, trying to modulate her voice to the tone she'd use with Dave. She looked at the clock again. "Close enough," she said, as much to herself as to Ben.

Deidre picked up her phone and punched in Dave's home number. She waited as it rang, and Ben shuffled his feet. Other than that, the kitchen was quiet. She and Ben hadn't said anything to the boys about what would be happening, and they were grateful it was a school day. The boys had gotten on the bus a half hour before. Deidre shook her head as Dave's answering machine picked up the call, and Ben heard her begin the planned speech.

"Dave, this is Deidre. Sorry I missed you, but I know you put in long hours at work. The last time you were here things got a little tense, and I want to say I'm sorry for that. We've been friends for quite a while, and I'd hate to see that end." Ben wondered how Deidre could muster such a sweet, unassuming tone. She continued.

"The reason I'm calling is that I was cleaning out our coat closet, and found one of your coats hanging in the back. I think you left it here last spring, the day Maren's car was found. I remember you were going to wear it, but forgot. You were awfully cold and miserable out there. Well, anyway, it's gray-and-red plaid wool, with a button missing on one sleeve."

Before she could go on, Dave came on the line, startling her.

"Deidre." He sounded out of breath. "Sorry it took me so long to get to the phone, I just came out of the shower and heard your voice on the answering machine. I didn't get all of your message. Something about a jacket or coat, I think you said?" Deidre could hear him breathing heavily, and she wondered if he really had run to get to the phone or if he had simply been screening his calls.

"Oh, it's good to hear your voice," she innocently greeted him. "How are you, Dave? We haven't talked since Maren's funeral. I know that was a difficult day for you, difficult for all of us."

"I'm fine, just fine," Dave answered too hurriedly. "What did you say about a coat?" he quickly interjected.

"Oh, yes," Deidre controlled her response. "I was cleaning out our hall closet—you know, the one off the living room entry—and I found your wool jacket hanging there. You know how it goes, something that's not worn everyday gets pushed further and further back until it's forgotten. I thought you might want to come get it tonight, if you have time."

There was a long pause on the line. "Oh, yeah. I remember it. It's just an old rag that I wouldn't wear anymore. Toss it in the garbage for me, will you?" Deidre had a rehearsed answer.

"This may not be the one you're thinking of. It's gray-and-red plaid, wool, I think, and it's in really good condition, except for a button that's missing on the right sleeve. It's the jacket you were going to wear the day we went with Sheriff DeAngelo when they found Maren's car abandoned in the woods. But, if you don't want it, would you care if I kept it? It's really good quality, and I could wear it around the yard."

Deidre waited out another long pause. "You say a button is missing off the cuff?"

"Yeah. There are three on one cuff and two on the other. The thread is still in the fabric. Looks like the button was torn off. Good buttons, though, brass, very distinctive. I doubt if I'll be able to find another to replace the missing one."

Deidre waited out another long pause. She thought she was causing Dave some consternation. Finally, he spoke. "Oh. Oh, now I remember the coat you mean. Man, I can't believe I haven't missed it. It's been one of my favorites, but you know how mixed up things have been all summer. Would you mind if I picked it up today? We could catch up on things and have a cup of coffee together." Deidre heard papers rattling before Dave continued. "It looks like I don't have much going on this afternoon. Would it be okay if I stopped out, say about twelve thirty?"

"That would be wonderful," Deidre heard herself saying. "Would you have lunch with me if I fix it? Ben's at work and the boys are in school. We can talk."

After hearing Dave say he'd like that, Deidre said her good-byes, put the phone down, and let the air gush from her lungs. Only then did she realize she had been so tense she wasn't breathing normally. As she sagged back in her chair, she asked Ben, "Did I sound natural to you?"

He smiled admiringly at her. "I don't know how you did it. I almost thought you had forgotten what you were trying to do. I'll call Jeff and fill him in on what's happening. It's the least I can do."

When Deidre picked up her coffee cup, it rattled against the saucer, and coffee sloshed over its rim. She tried again with the same results, and then held one hand with the other to stop its trembling.

*****

DEIDRE WAS READY when she heard the knock on the door. Dave was twenty minutes early, but from the tone of his voice over the pohone, she anticipated his being anxious to retrieve his jacket. Jeff had helped arrange the setting, and had conspicuously draped it over a chair in the corner of the kitchen. That way Dave could see it, but it would be obvious if he made a beeline for the corner. Deidre plastered a warm smile on her face as she swung the door open.

"Dave, it's so nice to see you again. I was hoping we could stay in touch." She hugged him closely, her eyes closed and lips pursed. Then the smile returned as she released her grasp of him.

"Come in, come in," she beckoned. "I wish Ben was here. He's wondered how you were holding up. He was worried that you had gotten the wrong impression the night we . . . well, we were all wound pretty tightly the last time you were here."

Dave had a strange look on his face, and he tentatively followed her into the kitchen. Deidre had the table set, and she checked the Crock-Pot on the counter.

"Go ahead, have a seat. I'll dish us up some of this concoction, and we can visit and eat before you have to get back to your job." She ladled out two bowlfuls of stew and carried them to the table. As he took the bowl from her, she noticed that Dave's hands were almost as shaky as hers had been when she called him that morning.

"So, how is work going?" Deidre asked as she buttered a piece of bread. She saw Dave's eyes repeatedly shift to the chair with his jacket draped over it.

"Uh . . . it's going pretty good." His answer was short and to the point, and he filled his mouth with the stew as an excuse not to elaborate. Deidre knew she had him on the defensive, and she kept up the chatter.

"I know it's none of my business, but I've wondered if you've found someone to be with. You're young, and we don't expect you to go through your life single. You know what I mean?"

Dave's face flushed. "No. No, I don't have anyone. Nobody could replace Maren," he managed to stammer, never making eye contact with Deidre.

After several minutes of chit chat, and noticing Dave's furtive glances at his jacket across the room, Deidre brought up the subject.

"I'm so sorry I didn't remember your jacket sooner. At least twice, maybe three times this summer, I ran across it when I was digging in the closet, and each time I thought, 'I've got to get that jacket to him,' but then I'd forget and it would work its way to the back again. Oh, well, we have it now. Maybe it was meant to be. This way I got to see you for a bit." Deidre prattled on, watching Dave get more uncomfortable by the minute. She could see he wanted to grab the coat and get out of there. Unhurriedly, she got up and retrieved the jacket, brought it to the table, but didn't hand it to Dave. Instead, she sat and continued talking in a conversational tone.

"I have to admit that I had a moment of grief when I took this off its hanger. There were several long, blonde hairs on its sleeve. I picked them off, and they looked like they were Maren's hair. It was a solemn kind of thing. Know what I mean?"

Dave began an explanation, but before he could get out more than two words, Deidre added. "But of course, that would be natural, wouldn't it? She probably wore this jacket at times, or she might have leaned her head on your arm."

Dave was quick to agree. Deidre fingered one of the brass buttons on the sleeve. "These are really unique buttons. Are they brass?"

Dave said he thought they were, but that he really wasn't sure. Deidre pressed on. "You don't happen to have the button at home? A seamstress could sew it back on in seconds. It would be a shame to have the looks of this jacket ruined by a mismatched button."

Dave said he didn't have the button. "I have no idea where it is," he admitted, then added, "It's been gone for so long, I'm sure it'll never turn up."

Deidre turned up the heat. "Gosh, I remember you wore this coat several times when we did things together. In fact, one time I do remember you giving it to Maren when she was cold. I don't remember the button being missing then." Before Dave could respond, she added, "Of course, it doesn't matter now, does it?" She looked at him, and her eyes drooped with sadness. He agreed, and began to reach for the jacket. Deidre pulled it down to her lap.

"I know where the missing button is, Dave."

The blood drained from his face, and Deidre thought for moment he was going to topple from his chair. Then Dave's expression turned livid and his eyes flashed with anger.

"What do you mean you know where the missing button is? I told you, I lost it a long time ago. I remember the day. I wore it to class when I was at the university. On the way out of the building, I snagged my sleeve on a handrail. When I got to my car, I noticed the button was missing, and I went back to look for it. A janitor was sweeping the floor, and I asked if he had found it, showed him the others on the sleeve. He said he hadn't seen it. I suppose somebody picked it up. Like you said, it's pretty unique."

Deidre was shocked at how quickly he fabricated his story, but she noticed a trace of perspiration forming on his top lip.

"I'm glad you cleared that up, Dave, because I was wondering where this button came from." She pulled a plastic bag from her pocket and set it on the table. Dave bent over to get a closer look, and sat bolt upright when he saw the button inside.

"Where did you find this?" he demanded.

"Where do you think I found it?" she countered.

"How the hell do I know where you found it? Are you going to tell me, or should I just take my jacket and leave now?" Dave's tone had turned belligerent and Deidre was alarmed, fearful he would bolt from the kitchen. Before he could rise from his chair, she quickly shot back.

"I found it a few feet from Maren's grave in the woods, the same place you buried her."

Dave's face contorted into a menace. "You didn't just find it there," he sneered at her. "You planted it, didn't you?"

Deidre kept her cool and in a decidedly collected way stated, "How could I have planted it, Dave? You just told me that you lost the button at UMD, when you were still in school, and there's only one button missing from the jacket. Your story of losing it occurred months before Maren was murdered. Really, Dave, do you think somebody found the button, saved it until she was strangled, and then months later gave me the button to plant near her grave? That seems a little far fetched, don't you think, Dave?"

So far, Deidre was ad libbing wonderfully, her law enforcement training and experience serving her well.

Dave gritted his teeth. He wasn't going to go down easily. "I don't care what lies you've rigged up against me, I didn't do it, and you'll have a tough time proving otherwise. I'll say that the buttons were all on the coat when I left it here. Your word against mine."

"Well, maybe you're right, Dave," Deidre seemed to acquiesce. "I suppose the button isn't enough, is it? But what about your running shoes? What about the cap that matches the description given by the fisherman who picked you up the night you killed Maren?"

"What running shoes? What cap?" he asked, a look of puzzlement in his eyes.

"The ones you left in the storage space you rented when Maren was living with you."

Suddenly, a look of remembrance came into his eyes and his face clouded. "I didn't have any running shoes."

"Don't lie to me, Dave. Do you mean to tell me that you ran marathons and didn't own a pair of running shoes? That's pure bull. Sheriff DeAngelo found them a couple of days ago. They're caked with mud, the same mud found in the pickup owned by the fisherman who picked you up on the Drummond Road the night you killed Maren, the same kind of mud found near Maren's abandoned car. You did it, Dave, didn't you?"

In a rage, Dave leaped from his chair, tipping it over in the process. It looked as though he was going to go after Deidre, then thought better of it. He stepped back, but before he could move to the door, the sound of footsteps pounding up the basement stairs froze him.

The basement door burst open and Ben leaped at Dave, grabbed him by the throat, and pinned him against the wall. Dave's face began turning blue as he struggled to pry Ben's fingers away from his throat, but the grip was like a vice. Deidre grabbed her husband's arm, but his muscles were bunched like steel cords, and she couldn't budge him.

Dave's eyes were beginning to bulge, and Deidre could tell his legs were weakening. The only reason he was still upright was because of Ben's hold. To Deidre, the time elapsed seemed like minutes. In reality, all this happened in seconds. Suddenly, Jeff was at Ben's side, shouting in his ear.

"Ben! Stop right now, or I'm going to have to knock you off him. Step back! I've got him." He grabbed Ben's arm and jerked his hand away from Dave's throat. Dave crumpled to the floor, gasping for breath between coughs.

"I want to file charges against him," Dave managed to get out. "You saw it, he tried to kill me."

As he struggled to his feet, Sheriff DeAngelo clamped one handcuff on Dave's wrist, spun him around and secured the other so both hands were shackled behind his back. Dave started to object, but Jeff cut him off.

"David Mason, you are under arrest for the murder of Maren VanGotten. Anything you say can and will be held against you in a court of law. "

# Chapter
## Fifty-Nine

IT WAS MAY, almost a year to the day from when Deidre had received the frantic call from her daughter's live-in boyfriend declaring that he was worried because he couldn't locate Maren. Today, she sat on a newly placed marble bench situated beside the walking trail in Two Harbors. Whoever sat on it was treated to a panoramic view of Lake Superior. It wasn't a place Maren had frequented, so Ben and Deidre put a similar bench in their woods on the bank of the Knife River. That was their private meditation spot. This was for the public to use, and they hoped would be a place for people to reflect on the ugliness of domestic abuse. As she sat on it, she wondered how many other men in Two Harbors were wearing a velvet glove over a steel fist.

As she stared over the water, Deidre was acutely aware that the family's pain wasn't over. Dave had demanded a lawyer before he said anything. Months later, he was still declaring his innocence, and in a few weeks his case would be heard by a jury. He had procured one of the most successful law firms in Duluth to represent him, and the county prosecutor had warned her and Ben that this wouldn't be a slam-dunk case. The admissibility of the recordings made when she pretended to be returning Dave's jacket was in question. The judge had yet to decide. Dave had posted bail, and was still living in Duluth.

His attorneys were claiming entrapment, and were questioning the validity of the button from Dave's jacket sleeve. After interviewing countless people, they were concocting an alternate scenario to what the prosecutor was presenting. Deidre only hoped that the truth would prevail.

Their side had the sworn testimony of Jackie, Dave's now ex-girlfriend. She was willing to testify against him. The state had ample evidence—much of it circumstantial, that was true, but it was a lot. The verdict would boil down to which side would be more convincing. Then there would be appeals.

Deidre thought of her family. The scabs covering the wounds caused by Maren's death were still festering. She imagined they would be torn off many times before healing took place, and the scabs were replaced by scars. Only then could the memories of Maren become sweet rather than bitter. She hoped the family would hold together until that happened.

Her mind flitted from one thought to another, finally settling on a topic she'd rather not dwell upon. But her mind wouldn't allow her to stop thinking. As she took in the sweep of the lake and felt a gentle breeze at her back, Deidre couldn't help but wonder if this wasn't what God intended for creation. The beauty of the day overwhelmed her for an instant, and then her gnawing doubts began eating away at her peace. How could all of what happened occur if God was real? Where was He in all of this? She remembered Pastor Ike's explanation, and somehow it didn't help. Damn it, she wanted answers, not platitudes. Is there, or is there not a God, she wanted to know, and if there is, why wasn't He there to protect Maren?

If life is just random, she thought, then why did this have to happen to her? The answer came back, Why not?

# Author's Note

In writing the Two Harbors mystery series, I selected societal issues and attempted to shine light on how they affect the lives of many people. *An Iron Fist, Two Harbors* has domestic violence, an expression of the need for power and control, as the basis for its plot. This is not a problem peculiar to Two Harbors—it is a nationwide, in fact, a worldwide problem.

According to the American Psychology Association, three or more women are murdered by their boyfriends or husbands each day in the United States. As shocking as that statistic is, according to the Centers for Disease Control and Prevention, twenty-four people are victims of intimate partner violence each minute. Putting that in more graphic terms, since 9/11, more women have been killed during domestic disputes than all of the people who died in the Twin Towers, soldiers in the war in Afghanistan, and soldiers in the Iraq War—combined.

*An Iron Fist* is fiction, and is not based on an actual incident. In molding my novels, I gather facts, select incidents from news articles, editorials, and other writings, and form composite characters. Then, using actual sites in the Two Harbors area, I put together a story that will, hopefully, raise the public's awareness to a problem that needs to be brought to the forefront.

A cardinal rule for any novelist is that the writer should determine why he is writing the book, what the central premise will be. In the case of *An Iron Fist*, my intent is to show that domestic violence stems from the need of one party in a relationship to control the actions of their partner. It also is written for the purpose of alerting people to the signs of a person being abused: denial, cover-ups, manipulation.

With the completion of this book, Deidre feels she is ready to retire to her home in the country, where she will find peace among the flowers, wild animals, flowing water, and the love of her family. You first met her in *Convergence at Two Harbors*, when she was a twenty-something-year-old deputy. You have followed her through life's ups and downs, and now, as she approaches fifty, she has run out of steam to face more adventures. Deidre sincerely hopes her experiences have alerted you to some of the problems found not only in Two Harbors but in every single community in our nation. She hopes her stories have motivated you to, in some way, make a difference in this world.

